# Winterton Blue

TREZZA AZZOPARDI was born in Cardiff and lives
in Norwich. She is the author of two previous novels:
*The Hiding Place*, shortlisted for the Booker Prize
in 2000, and *Remember Me*.

Also by Trezza Azzopardi

The Hiding Place

Remember Me

Trezza Azzopardi

# Winterton Blue

**A NOVEL**

**PICADOR**

First published 2007 by Grove Press, an imprint of Grove/Atlantic, Inc., New York,
and simultaneously in Canada

First published in Great Britain 2007 by Picador

This edition first published 2008 by Picador
an imprint of Pan Macmillan Ltd
Pan Macmillan, 20 New Wharf Road, London N1 9RR
Basingstoke and Oxford
Associated companies throughout the world
www.panmacmillan.com

ISBN 978-0-330-49348-2

3 5 7 9 8 6 4 2

A CIP catalogue record for this book is available from
the British Library.

Printed and bound in Great Britain by
Mackays of Chatham plc, Chatham, Kent

Visit **www.picador.com** to read more about all our books
and to buy them. You will also find features, author interviews and
news of any author events, and you can sign up for e-newsletters
so that you're always first to hear about our new releases.

*For Steve*

# Winterton Blue

# Cardiff

Lewis can see the world up here: balanced on the top rung of the ladder, his view is dazzling. It's not just the height he's at, or the clean cut of morning; it's the smell of being back home. He's breathing deeply, he's taking it in: the salt scent of foreshore, and wet tar, and Wales. Lewis grips the rattling frame of the window to steady himself; falling on his first day at work would not be clever. But everything is so different. Looking left, he can just make out the white spar of the Millennium Stadium with the thin brown smudge of the Taff running beneath, and beyond it, a mile away, a cluster of tall new buildings. There's a pure white dome, a silver arch, a thin spire pricking the skyline; there's even a building with wings. To his right is a tangle of railway lines and the dirty smoked back of the station. This at least is familiar.

Down in the real world, a cat is crying like a baby. Lewis follows the sound, and finds it, perched on the high wall which separates the property from everywhere else. Directly below him is an overgrown garden, more like a jungle, and a narrow path cutting between the outbuildings and the lake. There's a new-build complex in the adjacent field, sitting in a bowl of orange mud. The doors are freshly painted in leaf green, royal blue, letter-box red. Caught in a flare of early sun, it reminds him of a cardboard cut-out. Lewis looks again: it's not the sun, it's security lighting, shining over the entrance to the site. There are several heaps in the yard, savagely lit. He knows it's only gravel, but from the height he's at, they could be snow-capped mountains, giant cones of sugar. They could be moonrock.

He catches the ghost of his reflection in the window: he should get down to the job; a week's money will give him enough cash to buy the time to look for something better, something that won't involve working for Carl Finn. He casts his eye over rotten sashes and crumbling mortar. Picking at the paintwork, it comes away under his fingernails like an old scab. Carl said it was a job that would need a gang, and asked Lewis if he was up for it. Cash in hand. No papers. You takes your chances. It sounded like easy money, the way he said it. Up close, Lewis can see it'll be more than just a tosh job; the woodwork will need stripping, the rails replacing, the sashes re-hung. He sweeps his hand along the sill and feels gritty dew and the sharpness of the paint flakes on his palm. Turning his hand over, he inspects it with a kind of wonder: it feels tight and sore, there's a faint blue bruising, a jagged split across the knuckles. Under his nails there are dark brown cracks.

The tools are in a metal box in the back of his van. Lewis takes each rung of the ladder carefully; the dew has made them slippery. It's now he sees the mud caked on his boots, and scuffed on every rung, and with it comes the recollection of Carl's father Manny, early this morning. He was leaning against the sink in the kitchen, drinking tea and watching as Lewis rummaged through his kitbag. He nodded down at Lewis's feet.

Don't go treading that into my carpets, he'd said. But Lewis was paying scant attention; his mind was on the contents of his bag. It was important to check that everything was in order; more important than worrying about a few clods of mud on a stretch of worn shag-pile.

He moves quickly along the side of the house, trying not to notice the shimmer of water through the trees. He sees well enough the deep ruts of tyre tracks down to the lake, and he knows, but he doesn't know how, that it is a heart-shaped lake. It could be a scene on a Valentine's card: all you would need to complete the picture are two figure skaters circling each other. But Lewis can't know this, because he's sure he's never been to this lake before.

The sun comes up, shining on the water like a silver coin, so it's mostly surface, Lewis can't really see in. It isn't his job to see but he looks anyway. The change is sudden and irrevocable, as is the certainty that he can't take it back. He can feel the soft give of ground beneath his feet, he can smell the stagnant water; he can hear the anguished cry of the wood pigeons; but he can't unsee what's been seen. Pulling a rag from his pocket and holding it to his face, he tells himself that he's wrong.

At the edge of the lake, jutting out from a straggle of rushes and reeds, Lewis sees an arm. One finger of the right hand is proud of the rest, as if it's pointing at him. Further in, half-submerged in a sludge of weeds, he sees the back of a head, bobbing gently on the surface.

Lewis folds the rag over, wipes his eyes, and trying not to panic, wipes his hands of the greasy dew-dirt from the window and the body there in the water, wipes away any sign of what he's seen. He takes the path in a slithering, winded rush, not stopping until he's slam against the wide trunk of an oak, and still not stopping until he can feel the rough bark breaking the skin on his forehead, as if force alone will let him push right through the tree and out the other side. He takes a series of sharp breaths.

It's not him, he says, It's no one. Go back, have a proper look. You know it can't be him.

Lewis turns and raises his head. The sun has lifted up across the sky, cutting a pale yellow path through the clearing and turning the fallen leaves to gold. He tries to look again, but a black pain is flowering in his vision, blotting out the light. Covering his left eye with his hand, he focuses on the water's edge, seeing now only what is actually there: a tangle of bent branches caught in the weeds, a punctured football covered in slime. There's no one. There's nothing.

It was a mistake, he says, It was a mistake to come back. Lewis is fast now, running to the back of the house where he'd parked the van. He'll tell Carl where to stick his job. He'll tell him it was a mistake.

But the van is gone, and so is Carl. On the ground, under a dripping hedge, Lewis finds his kitbag. He takes one quick glance around, picks up the bag, and walks.

It's far too early for a phone call. Anna lies face down on the pillow, not quite awake, but aware of voices: she's left the radio on again, and the presenter is talking about the threat of London flooding. In her almost-dreaming state, the sound of ringing becomes wave after wave of muddy water as it sweeps through the back garden and into her flat. She gets to the telephone just before her answer message cuts in. Sitting in the kitchen with the receiver to her good ear, Anna looks for signs of damage: everything appears to be in order—dry, at least—but she still avoids putting her bare feet on the flagstones, just in case. The voice on the other end of the line is vaguely familiar. It's Vernon Savoy, her mother's lodger. Her mother had taken another fall, this time on the steps outside her house.

You've no need to panic, he says, She's going to be perfectly all right. No need to rush up here.

I understand, says Anna, So this is just a social call at—er—six a.m.?

Vernon's intake of breath is clearly audible.

Actually, it's nearly seven, he says, and assuming a more nonchalant tone, And if you must know, I haven't really slept. I merely assumed you would wish to be kept informed.

I do wish it, Mr Savoy, says Anna, You did the right thing. So, how is she?

Vernon plays his trump card.

You'll be relieved to hear that they'll discharge her later today, he finishes, All being well.

You didn't say she'd been taken to *hospital,* Anna cries, suddenly wide awake. She imagines Vernon, standing at the phone box in the hallway, in silk pyjamas and monogrammed slippers, waiting for what he considers the appropriate time to phone.

I took her last night, as a precaution. There was some swelling, you see. As a matter of fact, she didn't want to go. Made a terrible fuss. Now I'll be in her bad books.

I'll come as soon as I can, says Anna, Will someone be there to let me in?

Of course, says Vernon, his tone at once more ordinary and chivalrous, I shall await you here.

**jetsam**: *n.* discarded material washed ashore, esp. that thrown overboard to lighten a ship.

# ONE

Brendan hovers at the door of the lock-up, glancing back to the garden gate, which Anna has left swinging open. He hears the sound of a thump and immediate swearing.

Are you alright in there, Anna?

'Course, comes a voice out of the darkness, Never better! Now hand me that bloody torch before I brain myself.

Brendan takes two steps in, and finds the torch on the bonnet. There's the roll of wheels on concrete as Anna slides out from under the car. She raises her hand, grabs the torch, and slides back in. Brendan stares at the floor where Anna briefly was. He is full of admiration until he sees her toolbox, which is full of tubes of glitter and sticks of Pritt.

Didn't know you were good with engines, he says, picking a paintbrush out of the box.

I'm not, she says, I'm trying . . . to find . . . this . . . leak.

There's something familiar about the board she's using, but it's too dim to see. Brendan bends his head under the chassis, but all he can make out in the wavering torchlight is Anna's hair, spilling over the concrete like oil itself.

Quite a big leak, I'd imagine, he says, straightening up to better view the sticky patch under his feet, Not something you can fix with a bit of Blu-Tack.

Anna slides back out again. She's been using an old skateboard as a truckle. She stands up, flails a length of crepe bandage at the car.

No. Well, it was worth a try.

You were going to *bandage* it? asks Brendan.

I saw it in a film, says Anna.

And this is the crisis? he says, You know I'm hopeless with things that go.

Brendan shines the torch directly on Anna, then clicks it off. She has spatters of oil on her face and in her hair.

I've got to get to Yarmouth, says Anna, thumping the bonnet, But not in this old crock.

The sun outside is bright and warm, despite the early hour. Anna opens the lid of the wheelie bin and throws the bandage in, leaving a clear pattern of her hand on the lid.

Stand still, says Brendan, licking a finger, Just a *tiny* speck here.

He rubs at the tip of her nose.

Clean as a whistle, he says, starting to laugh. Anna looks down at her filthy clothes, and spreads her hands at him.

Think I'll just have to take the train.

Good plan. But get a wash before you go, says Brendan, Your mother will have a fit if she sees you in that state. And you don't want to go making things worse.

Brendan swings the gate behind him, lifting it up on the hinges so the catch slots into the housing. They stand and inspect Anna's garden. The path is littered with weeds and broken pegs. At the far end, caught on the brambles, a plastic carrier bag dances in the wind.

I'm going to have to bring her back this time, she says, She's not fit to be left. Don't suppose you could do me a favour, Brendan?

Now what could it be, I wonder? he says, following her gaze.

Anna goes to tuck her arm in his, stopping when she sees the oil on her hands.

My mother loves her garden, the birds especially, says Anna, Could you just tidy it up a bit? Maybe get a bird-table? Some pots? Make it look lived-in.

As opposed to died-in, he says, And how long have I got to effect this transformation?

Anna kicks at a clump of grass growing through the paving.

I'm hoping to bring her back in a day or two, she says, not daring to meet his eye.

I see. So I'm supposed to spend my weekend in the garden centre with a load of humbug-sucking geriatrics, while you go to the seaside. Can't see what's in it for me, he says.

Anna gives him a nudge.

They have geriatrics at the seaside too, Brendan, *And* you get to feed my squirrels.

His eyes flicker with distaste.

How tempting. I suppose your mother loves *them,* as well?

You're joking, cries Anna, She uses a pump-action water pistol in her own garden if she gets even a sniff of one. Her aim is brilliant. She calls it 'dispatch'.

Brendan considers for a moment. He stands in the centre of the path, squinting up at the trees and pale morning sky.

I like the sound of your mother, he says, But what if she won't budge?

Forgetting the state of her hands, Anna rubs her fingers against her brow, pressing them into her eyes and dragging them down her face.

I'm taking no prisoners, she says, She'll come back if I have to drag her by the hair.

Her face when she looks at him is fierce.

What's so funny? she says, seeing Brendan's grin, C'mon, share the joke.

Minnehaha wash off warpaint, he says, And then I'll walk you to the station.

~ ~ ~

Lewis puts his hand between the doors and forces them, just as the driver is about to pull off. He gives Lewis a look, but thinks better of saying anything, and presses the release button to let him on.

Do you want that stowed? he asks, pointing at Lewis's kitbag.

You're alright, says Lewis, snatching his ticket and moving along the rows of seats. There are more people than Lewis expects at this time of the morning, and he takes them in immediately: a pair of elderly women at the very front, sitting on opposite sides and exchanging weather talk across the aisle; a teenage boy fussily putting an ear-piece into his ear and looking out of the window, down at his iPod—looking anywhere but at Lewis. Directly behind the boy are two Chinese girls, both wearing brown uniforms and serious expressions. Mid-way along, two workmen in overalls have their eyes closed and their mouths open. At the back of the coach, where Lewis is headed, he sees something which makes his heart miss a beat: a bent figure in a red lumberjack shirt. The man straightens up, unfolds his newspaper, and Lewis breathes again. It's not Manny.

He puts his head against the window. The cold glass is welcome after the brisk walk to the bus station. Once they move onto the ring-road, Lewis takes off his jacket and throws it on the back ledge. He catches a glimpse of the stadium before the coach dips under the new fly-over. His return home to Cardiff has lasted only a week. He doesn't want to go through it, but he knows he can't not. As soon as he closes his eyes, he sees again the sun, shining like a searchlight through the trees, and the finger pointing at him, and the water lapping at his feet. He hears the cry of the wood pigeons; *Don't go, don't leave me. Don't go, don't leave me.*

He should have gone back to Manny's and told him about it. Manny would have helped him through. He hears Manny's voice, calm and low: You need to put this to bed, son. The dead can't hurt you, only the living can hurt you. There's no such thing as ghosts. Now, let's go through it again.

He could have stayed at the site and waited for Carl to turn up. But Carl wasn't going to turn up, was he? Not now he'd got himself a set of wheels. Thinking about the van, about the whole business of his return to Cardiff—that idiotic idea he had, of making his peace with his mother—Lewis is glad to be done with it. It wasn't as if it were his van, anyway. Not as if his mother had wanted to see him. Going back was just another mistake.

It was an error, Lewis says, precisely and out loud, as if saying it will make it true. The man in the lumberjack shirt twists his head round and looks at him.

The early morning sky has lost its fresh pink light; chasing the bus to London is a bank of dirty grey cloud blowing from the west. Lewis isn't noticing the weather: he's focusing only on the pattern of graffiti scored into the head-rest of the seat in front of him. He's putting his hand on the letters; he's thinking of nothing.

# TWO

From the end of the road, Anna sees her mother's house, the last in a row of identical villas cutting a pale crescent around the edge of the promenade. The whole terrace, with its façade bleached and flaking and its salt-crusted windows, has the appearance of withered grandeur. Most of the houses are B&Bs, each with a Vacancies sign in the window. Some of the proprietors had made an effort for the summer, putting out pot-plants and hanging baskets, which now twirl straggled and limp in the breeze. It's the dog-end of the season. The wind brings a fret off the ocean; not cold, but achingly damp. Despite being later than she'd planned, Anna walks slowly along the road, enveloped by the mist rolling in off the sea, and the fine, even light it brings. It makes the terrace look unreal, as if it's about to float up off the pavement. Closer, this fantasy is soon dispelled; Anna can see that the cream-coloured front of her mother's house is specked with grime, the railings need painting, and there's a scuttled nest of litter in the basement. Her mother never did get that netting done. Aware that she's being watched, Anna peers up into the bay window, shielding her eyes from the reflected sky, and sees a figure there. It takes a minute to recognize her mother: she looks like an old lady, one of the winter guests. Only the gesture she makes, that frantic, happy, child-like waving, gives her away. With her arm above her head, Anna mirrors the wave before negotiating the stone steps to her mother's home.

Those steps are very slippery, mum, she says, taking off her coat and throwing it over one of the many armchairs in the room, You had a lucky escape.

She's trying not to look at her mother's face, which is bathed in light from the window. It wouldn't surprise Anna if her mother had deliberately planned it, sitting where the daylight would make her bruises glow. She has one like a plum spreading over her eye, another curved round the edge of her chin, and a sharp red mark across the bridge of her nose. The moment Anna came through the door, her mother removed the sling from her arm to display yet more bruises, pink turning purple, from wrist to elbow.

I know, I'm lucky, aren't I? says her mother, without irony, That's what I told them at the hospital when they were doing the X-ray. The nurses said I must have bones like rubber. They were amazed that nothing's broken. Except my glasses. Look, they're in bits.

She takes the two halves of her spectacles from her lap to show Anna, holding them up and peering through one piece of the frame and then the other.

I can see much clearer now, she says, waggling her finger in the space where the lens fell out.

It's not funny, says Anna, trying to keep a straight face.

It is! It's a hoot. You should've seen it. Like a scene from *The Birds,* all the gulls bombing and diving and me flat out on the pavement. And that chap from two doors down comes running out and says, 'Get indoors lady, they're on the attack!' What a carry on.

So were you just feeding the birds, then, mum? When you slipped?

Only a few scraps. And don't call me mum. I'm Rita to the guests, so while you're here, do me a favour—don't go showing me up.

How many guests are there?

What on earth have you done? says her mother, staring at Anna's head with a look of severe disapproval.

Caught out by this sudden switch, Anna runs a hand over her hair. She didn't have time to dry it before getting on the train, but she thought she'd got rid of the engine oil.

Nothing, why?

Exactly, says her mother, It's about time you had a bit of a cut and blow dry. A nice tint, maybe. Your father went prematurely grey, you know. He said it was all the worry— but genes will out.

There's nothing wrong with my hair, mum. And I like the grey bit, she says, Makes me look . . . distinguished. Not at all like a skunk.

They both laugh at this. Anna's grey is concentrated down one side of her head, a long line of silver in the black.

You'll end up like me, says her mother, They show you all these cards with loops of hair on them, saying, Now Mrs C., would you like the hint of sable or the touch of gold? And guess what?

Anna laughs again. She knows this story well.

It always turns out blue.

*Lilac,* says her mother, Lilac, I ask you. Who in their right mind wants purple hair?

So, says Anna, refusing to be derailed, How many guests?

Her mother ignores the question, craning her head up at the ceiling and tutting to herself. Anna follows her gaze: there's a crack running across the plaster, and directly above them, a series of large, blotchy brown stains. They're sitting in the public room, which has been christened the Nelson Suite. A brass plaque has been put up on the door since Anna's last visit, and a gilt-framed picture of the man himself hangs over the fireplace, but one look at the details tells her it's all window-dressing.

We've got a foreign girl in, says her mother, Danish. Not a *guest,* mind, she's doing the cleaning. She's not much good. Can't understand things. Cabbage likes her, though.

16

The woman who let me in? asks Anna, Blonde, about my age? I thought her English sounded perfect.

Her mother laughs, fingering the broken spectacles.

Your age? She'll never see forty again. And I didn't say she couldn't speak English, just that she doesn't understand things.

So how many rooms does this *girl* have to clean?

Her mother throws her a withering look.

If you must know, there's only Cabbage staying at the moment. He's hoping for a Christmas slot at the Pavilion. Fat chance of that. But now the new wind-farm's up and running, there'll be plenty wanting accommodation round here. They'll be banging the door down. *Men,* Anna, she says, with a wriggle of her eyebrows, Lots of them, engineers and suchlike. So we have to stay open. I can't be *going* anywhere.

The daughter watches the mother as she talks, letting the words—the familiar exclamations, the sudden laughs—wash over her. Looking closely, Anna tries to see what Vernon sees, what a guest, not knowing her, might notice: that white hair, the strong, weathered face, and those dark eyes. An old woman, but tough, for all that. Anna sees the tilt of her mother's head, the slackening under the jaw. She thinks: I do that, now, that tilting thing; I have that way of smiling when I talk. I fold my hands like that. Perhaps it's already too late to front her out.

Anna had got it all planned. The long, snaking train journey up the country had given her plenty of time to reflect. She saw there would be a clear choice: either her mother comes to stay in London, or Anna will have to look after her in Yarmouth. In her head, she's inhabited the cackling laughter and wild shouting at the television, has pictured her mother trailing around after her, the constant interruptions of What are you doing? every five minutes, the endless, pointless cooking and cleaning. In this imagined future, Anna has already stepped back and watched as her mother has taken aim with her water pistol and blown the squirrels out of the trees. She's prepared herself for a fight, but Anna's been too long away: she hasn't really considered that she might not win. Looking at her now, her plans seem hopeless.

But you had a good summer, didn't you? she asks, knowing the answer.

Her mother looks at her narrowly.

A bonanza, she says, Absolute bonanza. What of it?

Well, Anna says, How many guests do you think you'll have this winter?

Can't imagine, says her mother, archly, Hundreds, I suppose.

Expecting this sort of fabrication, Anna agrees.

So it could be really busy, mum. How do you think you'll manage?

I'll manage same as always! I'm a bit bruised, dear, not on life-support. Then there's Cabbage and the Danish girl. And it wouldn't hurt you to put a hand in if you're *really* that concerned about your poor mother. Not as if you've got a proper job to go back to, is it?

It's no more than Anna expects, this line of attack, and brings with it a sharp stab of anxiety. She's been freelance for nine months, having had, one January morning, what her mother would later describe as a blow-out: as if she were a car on the motorway, and could simply mend herself by getting towed to a garage. She'd been teaching at a college in the East End; was employed to cover general art and design, textiles, some graphics work. More often than not she'd be enlisted to take day-release classes—Brick 1, Mech Eng 3—or to supervise a class of schoolchildren who'd come in for the day to make a video. Her mother was thrilled when she'd got the job, *after so many years of faffing about,* as she put it, but her idea of education had been cultivated from repeated viewings of *Goodbye, Mr Chips* and an addiction, in the 'eighties, to *Brideshead Revisited.* It didn't really include teaching family planning to a group of plasterers on a Friday afternoon. And Anna was no wiser than her mother, at the start. It wasn't the security cameras, the passkeys and ID cards, nor was it the cynical disillusionment of the rest of the staff that ground her down: she thought she'd been employed to teach a *subject*. When that subject never actually emerged, she realized that she was there to do anything that the Head deemed necessary. Which mainly amounted to babysitting children from local schools and telling grown men how to have responsible sex. She lasted just one term, until the January morning when she woke up and couldn't move. When she had her blow-out.

She didn't want to tell anyone; not her mother, not even Brendan. Sometimes, when the phone rang and Anna couldn't face the call, she left the answering machine on. She would stand in the kitchen with a glass of wine in her hand and watch the light fade on the garden. Her mother's voice, distorted by the old tape, would end her message with the same question: *And how's the teaching going, dear?*

It was six months before she let on. By then, there were other things to occupy her mother: the summer season was in full flow; people were holidaying at home again instead of going abroad. It was an exceptionally busy time. Profits were up.

With this in mind, Anna broaches her proposal, wanting to get it over with: her mother doesn't need to stay open over the winter, after such a good summer. But the moment she begins to form the words, the door opens; Vernon Savoy puts his head in the gap. The only other time Anna had met him, after a show on the pier at Great Yarmouth, he was sporting a handle-bar moustache. She'd thought it was part of the costume, that and the cravat and the waistcoat stretched over his girth. She sees now it's all part of him. His hair, the colour of pewter, is combed back in a slick from his forehead, but the moustache is almost yellow. His waistcoat is paisley pink and purple, as if in sympathy with the shade of bruising on her mother's face.

Deanna, he shouts, with an air of benevolence that Anna dislikes, We meet again!

The room fills with a scent of sweetness and dust, like dead roses. Afraid that Vernon might be about to do something ostentatious, perhaps attempt to kiss her hand, Anna locks her fingers together behind her back, edging round her mother as he takes up the whole of the bay window. Dropping down on one knee, he grasps the arm of the chair.

How are you, Rita? he says, whispering now.

Safe from his welcome embrace, Anna sits back down and absorbs this tableau: her mother pulls a handkerchief from inside her sling and puts it to her mouth. Now she is the fragile old lady, badly in shock.

I've asked Marta to bring some tea, says Vernon, You'd like some tea, wouldn't you, Deanna?

I certainly would, Mr Savoy, nods Anna, playing her part, And Anna will do just fine, thank you.

If we're into abbreviations, you must call me Vern, he says, plumping up a cushion in the window-seat before lowering himself onto it.

Call him Cabbage, says her mother, back to normal again, We all do. Don't we, Cabbage?

Only you, my dear, he says, with a faint smile, Only you.

Anna squints at Vernon, trying to gauge his expression. Sitting in the window, his face now in shadow, he takes on a hazy silhouette. Anna draws a breath,

I was just about to suggest to my mother, she says, appealing to Vernon, That a short holiday would do her good.

Bones like rubber, says her mother, Did I tell you, Cabbage, what the nurses said? I don't break, me, I *bounce*.

They also said—Vernon picks over his words, searching for the right emphasis—That you'll need some assistance, my dear, what with your hip so badly *bruised,* and your arm out of *action,* so to speak.

He turns back to Anna, and with a jerk of his head, adds, She might enjoy a little holiday. I know I would.

Encouraged by this, Anna begins her speech. She looks from Vernon to her mother and back again.

I thought she might like to come and stay with me for the winter. To recuperate. I've fixed up the garden especially. It's got a bird-table. It's got . . . things. Things—in pots.

The word you're searching for is plants, says her mother, And I believe we have such *things* in Yarmouth also.

Vernon rises from his cushion and takes in the room with a broad sweep of his arm. He's in full character now.

But that's stupendous, he says, so that both Anna and her mother look askance.

Cabbage, there is nothing stupendous about a plant, says her mother.

No, no, my dear. A vacation in London. We could take in the shows.

He makes a giddy gesture with his hands, fluttering them either side of his face, and bursts into song,

*Give 'em the old razzle dazzle! Razzle dazzle 'em!*

Anna shoots her mother a worried look.

It's from Chicago, says her mother, trying to curb her grin, And there won't be any razzle dazzle for you, Cabbage, if I ship out to the smoke. What would you do?

Do? He says, round-eyed.

Well, where would you *go*?

Her mother has removed the sling and is bent sideways over the arm of the chair. She rummages about in a desk drawer, pushing papers aside, searching.

Anna hasn't got room for both of us in that little flat, she says, finally finding the object she's been looking for, And I'd have to shut this place up, wouldn't I?

At this suggestion, Vernon does an immediate volte-face.

Of course, it would be very difficult to leave your home, Rita. And Anna must be quite busy, what with her . . . work, he says, not sure of what it is Anna does, Who'd look after you?

I would! says Anna, I'm not a total imbecile, you know. I *can* look after my own mother.

*I* look after your mother, snaps Vernon, And if I may say so, I do it very well.

So well that she blacked out and fell down those steps?

Her mother is fiddling with the sling, pulling at it with her free hand.

I did not black out, Anna. Will someone help me with this thing?

It was *I* that took her to the hospital, says Vernon, veering between wheedling and indignation, And I'm sure I'm more useful than someone two hundred miles away.

Vernon. *Vern.* I'm not two hundred miles away, says Anna, I'm right here.

Then stay here, darling, says her mother, Stay and look after your old mum.

Of course I will, says Anna, and in saying it, feels a darkness above her, like a trap-door closing, Let's get that sling sorted.

Her mother pulls it from her neck and throws it on the window-seat.

Here you are, she says, opening her hand, Look. I've even found you a key!

# THREE

In the toilets at Victoria coach station, Lewis bends over the sink, scoops up the sudden burst of water from the tap, and splashes it over his face and his head. Under the bored eye of the attendant, he dries himself at the hot-air blower, repeatedly hitting the button with the flat of his hand. He dozed off for the last part of the journey into London, only waking when the coach began its stop-start passage through the capital. He looks into the square of reflective metal that passes for a mirror, marvelling at how he could sleep. It's what the headaches do to him: first, there's the black pain clouding his vision like ink in water; afterwards, a dreamless sleep. On waking, the pain is gone, and time is gone, and whatever has triggered the headache in the first place has also gone, receding so far back into his consciousness, it too becomes dream-like. Lewis always emerges from these episodes in a state of near-euphoria, as if he's been given a second chance at life. That's how he bears it. But seeing himself now, he doesn't look reborn: his face is haggard under the blue fluorescent strip, completely drained of colour. His teeth when he bares them are luminous, as is the scar running in a straight line below his lip. He traces a finger along it, considering his next move: before he can find work, he'll need to find a place to stay.

Lewis goes straight across the road and into the first café
he sees. He orders tea, and because everyone else is eating, a
bacon sandwich. He sits at the window, gazing out at the
traffic and the choked diesel air inside the entrance to the
station. His kitbag is on the floor between his feet. To calm
himself, he does a mental inventory of all his possessions. In
his bag, neatly folded, are one zip-up fleece, one pair of jeans,
three white shirts, two pairs of socks, two pairs of underpants.
On top of these, there's a washbag with a toothbrush, razor,
the half-full dispenser of hand-wash he took from Manny's
kitchen—he liked the smell good enough—and a deodorant
stick. He's out of toothpaste; he didn't think much of Manny's
brand, or the way the tube had been squeezed and bent out
of shape. In one side pocket of the bag is his Swiss army knife
and a book of poems that he's had from way back—since he
was at school. Lewis doesn't often look at it, but knowing
it's there is enough. In the other side pocket are a rolled-over
packet of dried beans and a black felt pouch with a silver chain
inside it: not just any old chain; it belonged to his brother,
and now it belongs to him. His tobacco and lighter and wallet are in his jacket pockets. He goes through the inventory
one more time, listing under his breath and very quickly:
fleece jeans shirts socks pants washbag book of poems knife
beans pouch—and chain. That's it, perfect. He feels the wash
of relief sparkling through his blood. He's sufficiently calm,
now, to eat the sandwich. Lewis resists the urge to lift the
top slice and inspect the meat. Closing his eyes, he finishes it
in two bites.

~  ~  ~

Anna's room for the night is at the top of the house; a space
tiny enough for only the barest of furnishings: a single bed, a
wardrobe, a tray with tea things on it, a bedside table. On
the wall are two pictures, generic guest-house scenes: a pair
of fluffy kittens in a basket, and a painting of a country lane
and a river. The ceiling slopes down to the window, hidden

by thick beige curtains. Anna pulls them back to reveal the view, and feels the wind butting at the glass. On the beach below, it chases the sand into a blur, pushes the clouds across the sky like bolts of smoke. She likes this space, this vantage point, even though the room is cold enough for her to see her breath. She relishes most of all the way it feels detached from the rest of the house—from Vernon's jocular presence, in particular—but her mother has promised her the room directly underneath, one floor down, when she comes back.

More space to settle down in, she said, ominously, More space to spread out. Just needs a good airing.

Anna sits shivering on the bed, turning the key-ring over in her hands. The fob is an oblong of lacquered metal with a lurid picture of Christ on the cross. On the reverse, the inscription says, *Greetings from Greece!* She knows her mother has never been to Greece; Anna assumes it was given to her by a guest, or perhaps someone left it behind. The keys are shiny and sharp, freshly cut. She imagines her mother, scheming, planning, getting keys cut and rooms aired. Anna tosses the key-ring onto the windowsill. Scanning the room, she thinks about what she will need to bring back with her; some books, certainly, and warmer clothes. From far below comes a sound like a piano falling down the stairs, a gale of laughter, an abrupt, barking chorus: Vernon and her mother are singing. Anna listens as the duo wander round the edges of the song, trying to find a tune; at last she recognizes it: Everything Stops for Tea. It's probably their way of dropping a hint. On her way back downstairs, Anna adds ear-plugs to her mental list. She may be slightly deaf, but she doubts she'll ever be deaf enough to obliterate that racket.

~ ~ ~

Lewis does the thing he always used to do on the underground: takes his place in the fourth carriage along. There's no reason to it; just a superstition he has—or used to have—like not walking on the cracks in the pavement, or keeping a hand on the rail of the escalator, or saying touch wood to ward off evil spirits. He's spent the last two nights at a hostel above the bus station, lying on the narrow bunk, listening to foreign tongues and foreign laughter, until now he feels he can be no one again. He senses the change in his blood: it's London, forming like a new scab; sore, but hardening up, covering the raw wound of Wales. The other person inside him, the one Lewis thought he'd left behind, is once more inside his skin. Today, he makes his move. He doesn't know where he's going: he doesn't think it matters.

The tube is packed full of people: workers reading or pretending to sleep, tourists with rucksacks and expectant faces. The young woman standing opposite Lewis has sleek brown hair and chocolate-coloured eyes. She wears a silver necklace with a pendant on it. He can't see what it represents; she clutches it in her fingers, zigging it along the chain when she talks to her friend, a man wearing heavy clothes and a thick woollen scarf. When the man talks, she puts the pendant in her mouth and sucks on it. Despite the fact that he senses a no-go zone all around him—that the other commuters have made a silent agreement with each other to give him more space than they think he deserves—he can't appear *that* dodgy, because over her friend's shoulder, the young woman with the lovely eyes looks directly at him and smiles. Out of old habit, Lewis gets off at Clapham. He walks the verge of the common, taking the scent of wet leaves and car fumes into his lungs. On the fourth bench along, he puts his kitbag on his lap and tips his face up to catch the pale autumn sunshine. He looks like someone basking.

Now, Manny, he says, under his breath, Let's see.

~ ~

What he saw was himself, standing at Manny's front door. He wouldn't normally knock, he would slip along the passage, through the back gate, into the yard, like he used to when he was a kid. But it wasn't a normal situation. He'd been a long time away from Cardiff; he didn't know how this visit would go down. Lewis had already considered the possibility of Carl being around, not knowing how either of them would react. But he hadn't given much thought to Carl's father. He'd found out from a neighbour that his own mother had moved a year or so ago—perhaps Manny would've upped sticks as well, or he might not even *want* to help Lewis find her: Manny might not even want to see him. Lewis was starting to think it was a waste of time.

At his second knock, the nets at the window shivered, low down, and up underneath them poked the head of a ginger cat. It glided along the sill, pressing its body flat on the glass, until Manny's face appeared above it. To Lewis, he looked very old; older than the twenty years' aging he'd expected. But Manny recognized Lewis straight off.

Come round the back, son, he said, with a wave of his arm; as if it were yesterday.

The kitchen door was open, with Manny's boots side by side on the mat. Lewis stepped round them, saw Manny framed in the hallway, his bowed legs and socked feet, wearing a faded lumberjack shirt, and the look on his face made Lewis's muscles spasm. Instead of running away, he said,

You should keep this door shut, Manny. They'll rob you blind.

Aa-hah, said Manny, with a laugh that sounded like a sob, Take me eye,

And come back for me eyebrow, finished Lewis, grinning at the familiar punchline.

Nothing worth nicking, chief, said Manny, stepping up to embrace him. He breathed the words into Lewis's neck, patting his back. Lewis could feel how shrunk he'd become. The greeting was over in a second. Manny covered the moment by turning to switch the kettle on, fiddling about in the cupboard above his head, bringing out an extra cup to join the single one already on the counter. He didn't see how much this embrace had cost Lewis, who was biting down hard on his lip, tasting a long-ago smell: Brut 33.

Instant do you? Manny asked.

Lewis managed a smile.

I'm used to better.

Manny wiped both cups with a tea-towel and chinked them down in the silence. A short, cautious breath; maybe there was a joke to follow, or a change of subject.

Oh, I know, said Manny, It's all cappo-latto-cinque-quento served in a thimble.

With *froth* on top, said Lewis.

They're everywhere now, said Manny, Them cafés. Can't move for them down the precinct. Can't even buy a cup of tea.

Lewis leaned against the cooker. He couldn't be sure of the territory; he'd wait to be asked before he sat down.

See you've got a cat, he said, Thought Sylvie didn't like them.

Yup, that's Ned, said Manny, I've shut him in front, like. Come and say hello.

He put the cups on a tray and nodded Lewis through to the living-room. Along the hall, a metal hand-rail had been fitted. Another was fixed to the wall opposite the stairs.

How *is* Sylvie? asked Lewis, running his hand along the rail, not liking the feel of it.

Manny's voice was low behind him,

She went, oh, two years ago, now. Mind, he said, as Lewis turned his head to take in this news, He'll be round your leg like a pole dancer.

Lewis fathomed the sudden change of subject, and played his part in it.

D'you get them in the precinct, as well? he asked.

Two for one on Friday nights, said Manny, as he squeezed through the door.

Inside the room, everything was much as Lewis remembered it. A pair of easy chairs facing each other, with a low table between them; a high, built-in bookshelf full of ornaments and photographs in cardboard frames; and a tiled fireplace the colour of caramel. Only the television was different: a massive oblong in brushed metal, taking up the whole corner of the room. A sheet of blue smoke hung in the air. Manny invited Lewis to take the opposite chair, which he did, noticing the flecks of cat hair clinging to the cushion. As soon as he sat down, Ned jumped up, clawing a circle into his thighs. Lewis picked the cat from his lap and put it down on the floor. Next to the chair, propped against the hearth, was a wooden walking stick. Below it, a wedge of women's magazines. Two years since Sylvie died. Manny was talking again, so Lewis had to concentrate to take in what he was saying. The old man was hunting around amongst the things on the shelves, slipping his hand behind the photographs. In a twin oval frame, two children stared at him; the girl was about six or seven, but the boy was older. He was wearing a school uniform and an insolent expression. Manny drew out a small bottle and offered it first to Lewis. He didn't recognize the label, but he twisted the cap and smelled whisky.

As it's a special occasion, said Manny.

I am honoured, laughed Lewis.

Not you, sunshine, said Manny, without missing a beat, It's our Ned's birthday!

Lewis knew the uniformed child in the picture, and he knew the uniform: a navy blue blazer with a crest on the pocket of a golden eagle, two-headed. The heads faced in different directions, and the first time he saw the crest, trying on the blazer in the corner of the Co-op while his mother slipped the coupons over the counter, he thought it was a cartoon figure, caught in mid-frame—Foghorn Leghorn on the look-out for Miss Prissy. The tie was shot through with silver and navy diagonal stripes, which, after a few days, the new boys fashioned into tight knots, to be like the older boys. His school shoes were a worry for his mother. She kept saying he hadn't grown into his feet, but for him, the problem was wearing them at all. The men's ones looked hideous, old-fashioned; the sort of thing a teacher might wear. His brother Wayne never had that problem, being small and wiry. No one thought of them as twins. Lewis's mother ironed their school shirts on Sunday nights, and clean ones appeared on the back of the chair next to their bunk-beds on Wednesday mornings. Sometimes Lewis remembered to put his on and sometimes he forgot.

You'll recall our two, said Manny, sensing Lewis's interest in the photographs. He fetched the frame down from the cabinet and stood behind Lewis's chair. He took a moment while Lewis scrutinized the two children.

You wouldn't recognize Sonia now, he said, Here, I've got a recent one somewhere.

He turned back to the shelves and brought down a Christmas card. Inside, there was a photograph of a woman on a beach. She was standing with her arms outstretched and her head thrown back, her dark hair in jagged spikes, like a sea urchin, or as if she'd just dipped her head in the ocean. You could tell she was laughing, even though only her neck and chin were clearly visible. Her shadow cast a sharp angle on the sand. At her back was a cloud of black light hanging over the sea, and a roil of churning waves, almost as inky as the sky. Lit up by a flare of late sun, a line of distant white pinpricks stood on the horizon.

She's pretty, I reckon, said Lewis, holding the photograph between finger and thumb.

She's a stunner. Gets it from Sylvie, said Manny, And her temper and all. She's living away, now, working on some ecology project. Wind-farms in the North Sea, that sort of thing. Gets her brains from her mam too.

It's a good shot, said Lewis, Did you take it?

Manny made a comedy face.

Me? Very likely. Carl took it. He's up there most of the time, back here the odd weekend. Thick as proverbials, them two.

Nice beach, any road, said Lewis, for something to say.

It's over east, said Manny, and with an arid laugh, As far from here as you can get. The edge of the world, she calls it.

Manny took the photograph and stared at it a while longer before putting it back on the shelf.

You don't see much of him, then? asked Lewis, feeling the bite of whisky in his throat.

Ah. You won't have forgotten our Carl. More than I care to, if I'm honest.

Lewis shifted in his chair, feeling the silence.

Still not getting on?

Let's just say we agree to disagree. But, you know—Manny's lips on the rim of his cup made the words almost inaudible—It's not been easy. For any of us.

Lewis kept his voice even.

He's not around, then?

Oh, he pops in now and then, when he wants something. When he's not off doing his own thing.

Lewis sensed Manny's reluctance to continue, but was curious to find out what kind of life Carl was living these days.

What sort of thing?

What does he call it, now? said Manny, playing for time, Oh yeah, you'll like this. He calls it his fun run.

Lewis was unable to keep the irony out of his voice.

Like, a fun run for charity?

And I'll give you three guesses who's the charity, said Manny.

Lewis looked up at the older man. He wore a grim fix on his face, deepening the crescent lines, like brackets, around his mouth.

I take it we're not talking strictly legal, then, Lewis said, pressing on.

Manny didn't answer him. He took another swig from his mug, looked as if he were about to spit it out, and swallowed hard.

He brings back fags and booze. Says everyone's doing it. But as far as what he takes *over,* I goes blind and deaf, me. That's all I knows.

As Manny talked, Lewis stayed eye to eye with the photograph of Carl, wiping off a skin of surface dust to better see the boy. He stared hard at the image, as if he might read something there. It didn't surprise him in the least to learn about Carl's methods of making a living; and he could hardly take the moral high ground himself.

~

Lewis had known Carl's tagline before he knew the owner. It was everywhere you looked: on the electricity substation at the end of the road, a brutal carving cut into the thick green paint; penned twice on the street sign on the corner, inked on the low white wall opposite their new house. *SHARKEY* was everywhere, in blue Biro, black felt pen, penknife, and later—but only for a short while—spray paint. He didn't immediately associate the name with Carl Finn, the boy at the other end of the street whose dad had the taxis. At the time of reading the name, it gave Lewis no other feeling than one of irritation.

Lewis's first actual meeting with Carl passed without incident. He'd been sent to fetch Manny by his mother; she needed a lift, and in those days Manny ran his own taxi firm. Lewis passed lots of houses with cars in the drives, but they were on blocks, or had the bonnets winged to the sky, or were lying dismantled on the scrub grass and the path. None of them looked like a taxi. Manny's garden was a neat square of tarmac, with a polished saloon parked beneath the window. Another car was parked on the kerb. Lewis rang the bell and waited.

The boy that answered the door was small, but already had the start of growth on his face. He was wearing just a pair of football shorts, and he didn't even look at Lewis, who was red and sweating. Carl turned and called upstairs, one word— Dad!—and then retreated, leaving Lewis on the step. They had a dappled glass door shutting off the living-room from the hall; Lewis watched as the boy's shape, in ripples and breakers, receded into darkness. Manny came down the stairs in his socks. It was also Lewis's first meeting with Manny, and he would remember it, as he would remember everything about this father and son. Lewis thought Manny looked how a dad *ought* to look: a bit put out but smiling all the same, his hair uncombed and all over the place. Lewis waited on the doorstep as Manny sat on the stairs and pulled on his shoes. He gave off a smell of stale tobacco and sleep.

Round here, said Manny, We have an ancient tradition called the Siesta. Tell your mam for me, son, tell her there are lots of lifts to be had. She'll find them in the phone book, under Taxi Firms.

Lewis wasn't sure about this speech, but Manny smiled and said, I suppose your phone's not connected yet?

I don't know, said Lewis, We just moved in yesterday.

Manny followed him down the path, grumbling. He pointed out the different houses as they walked.

That's the Robsons' place, Manny said, gesturing with his fob to a house across the road. The render was painted fresh white, and bordering a neat square of garden was the white wall, with *SHARKEY* scrawled across the brickwork. He bent close to Lewis's ear.

We calls them the Snobsons, he whispered, But not to their face, of course. And them opposite you is the Prices'. She's all right but her lads are proper little villains. Take your eye and come back for your eyebrow.

Manny wriggled his own eyebrows as he said it, which wrested a smile from the boy.

So, how're you settling in? All right? Manny asked, Just you and your mam, is it?

And my twin brother, said Lewis. He's called Wayne.

And you are?

Lewis, he said, dying of shame at having to say it out loud.

Manny leaned into him, whispering.

I'll give you a tip, Lewis, as you're new and you look like a good lad. There's *lots* of little villains round here—I should know, my Carl's one of them. Keep out of their way and you'll keep out of trouble. That's it, sermon over. Now, he said, holding out his hand, Are we going to be friends?

~ ~

Trick or treat, mister, the voice says.

It takes Lewis a moment to bring himself back. Blinking in the sunlight, he opens his eyes on three children: two boys, and a girl, lagging behind. The boys wear sweat tops and jeans and sharp white trainers. The tallest boy sports a diamond stud in each ear, and has a half-empty Coke bottle in his hand. His thumb is pressed on top of the neck. The smaller boy is eating a bag of chips, with his Coke nestled in the crook of his arm. Looking at him, Lewis feels a stab of pity. He can't be more than six years old.

You're way too early, son, says Lewis, rubbing a hand over his eyes, Come back in a couple of weeks.

The girl breaks away from the others, sidling round the back of the bench, dancing her fingers along the wood, nearly—but not quite—brushing Lewis's lapel.

Penny for the guy, she says, and all three burst into fits of laughter.

Lewis turns his head to look at her. She's wearing a matching sweat top and jogging pants in pale pink. She too has small white diamond studs in her ears, and blonde hair tied up in a top-knot. She's pretty but her eyes are dead.

Where's the guy? he asks, smiling, trying to share the joke
he doesn't understand, Aren't you supposed to have a guy?
Uh?

I said, where's the guy?

The girl sits now at the other end of the bench, pulling at
a piece of rotten wood and throwing it at the boys. She flicks
a long black strip at Lewis. He senses more than understands
the change in the air.

You're the guy, she says, smiling sweetly, But we don't
want to put you on the fire.

What's a guy? says the youngest boy.

*He's* the guy, she says, Gimp!

You're the gimp, says the older boy, shaking the bottle
and releasing his thumb. A shower of foam shoots across at
her, but the girl is quick, ducking out of the way with a delighted scream and running behind Lewis for protection. He
puts his hands up, catching the last of the spray, shouting at
the boy.

Hey, hey, c'mon! Cut it out!

The boy launches the bottle into the grass.

You've got to give us money, he says, nodding at his small
friend in confirmation, Or we'll report you.

Penny for the guy, repeats the girl, laughing again. She
dances back behind Lewis, whispering something as she passes.

Dirty old . . . guy, she says.

This time, her hand trips along his shoulder, making him
fly up off the bench, whirling, clutching his kitbag and
shouting.

Clear off! he says, feeling his heart banging with fright,
Go fuck with someone else.

They openly laugh at him. Even the little one is brave
now, jumping from one leg to the other and letting out a
high, false giggle that seems to echo through the trees. A
woman passing with her dog stops to take in the scene. She
gives Lewis a long look, as if she will need to remember
him. Cars are queuing on the road that cuts across the green.

Lewis throws his bag over his shoulder and walks fast, not caring that he's heading straight into the traffic, feeling his face and neck burning hot. Something bounces off his back, and again something hits him, and then a third missile flies past his head. Chips. They're throwing their chips at him. They're throwing their chips and they're calling him names.

# FOUR

So, what d'you think?

Brendan pushes back the metal door, revealing his handi-work to Anna. She'd texted him from Great Yarmouth sta-tion to tell him the news, and before she had even got on the train, he'd texted back: BIG suprize @ home.

He led her straight through the garden—which had not been altered—and across the yard to the lock-up.

It's my car, says Anna, Just where I left it.

You mean you can't tell the difference? God, you're going blind as well as deaf. Take a closer look.

Anna walks round the car. The outside has been washed and polished, and there's a new badge on the bonnet. Anna pings it with delight.

New badge, says Brendan, pointlessly, I got the man from Merc to take the old girl away for a day or two. He took that badge off a wreck. He was *very* helpful.

Did he fix the leak? asks Anna, running her hand over the bonnet.

No, he couldn't be bothered . . . Of *course* he fixed it, that's why I called him in the first place. That—and one more thing. Look inside.

Anna opens the door. The interior has been valeted and the passenger seats cleared of debris. It smells of fake pine, but underneath is the more familiar, warm scent that Anna loves: old car.

CD player, says Brendan, Thought we'd bring you into the twenty-first century.

Brendan, it's fantastic. How much do I owe you?

Let's call it a gift, he says, but before she can thank him, he adds, Well, okay, then, let's call it rent.

Rent, she nods, suddenly catching on.

Because you'll want to rent this place out while you're gone, Brendan muses, leaning a hand on the hatch, And I can't think of anyone more trustworthy, and—aw, no!

He holds his fingers close to his face and sniffs them, Is nowhere sacred? Those squirrels crap on everything.

How do you know it's the squirrels? says Anna, Could've been a rat.

Trust me, he says, I know. All my washing got ruined. No wonder you don't use that clothes-line.

How have they been? she asks, watching as Brendan scuffs his hand against the gatepost. Even though she's been gone just a couple of days, she feels a peculiar sense of guilt at abandoning them. Brendan's face fills with horror.

A great big fella came and knocked on the kitchen window yesterday morning. I tried to ignore him, but he kept knocking with his paw—do you call them paws?—honest, what're you supposed to do?

Ah, smiles Anna, That'll be Kong. I usually throw a handful of muesli out. They'll leave you alone once they've had their breakfast.

Breakfast? I'll be getting myself a water pistol, says Brendan, Speaking of which, how's mater?

Mater is as normal as she can be in the circumstances. Some old thesp called Vernon Savoy is 'looking after' her until I go back up.

*The* Vernon Savoy? Brendan's face lights up.

Is he famous, then? Asks Anna.

Is he? He is the *famous* Vernon Savoy. Don't you remember him? *Saturday Night at the London Palladium*?

I didn't do much telly watching as a kid, Brendan, says Anna, Too painful on the ears.

Brendan laughs at this unintended joke.

You're not kidding! And didn't he have a dummy in the act for a while? What did he call him? You know, the butler, with the s-s-stammer. What *was* he called?

Brendan, I haven't got the faintest idea what you're talking about. Vernon Savoy's only famous in my book for sponging off my mother and wearing awful waistcoats.

He doesn't! cries Brendan, And has he still got that ludicrous moustache?

Ludicrous, nods Anna.

It sounds a riot, he says, Anna Calder, confidante to the stars! I bet it's just like The Good Old Days.

They're a complete embarrassment, the way they carry on, says Anna, *You* go and stay with them if you don't believe me. See how long it is before you're sectioned.

Is it really that bad? asks Brendan.

It's worse. But I've been left with no alternative.

They both stare at the car for a minute. A fine drizzle starts to fall, sprinkling them with tiny beads of rain. Brendan puts his arm around her as they turn back towards the house.

Oh, look on the bright side, he says, At least we didn't bother wasting time on that scrap of dirt you call a garden. And give me bedlam over boredom any day.

# FIVE

The idea Lewis had—of returning to Cardiff, of finding his mother again—seems pointless now, in the middle of the day in the middle of a busy London street. He stands on the corner and tries to regulate his breathing. He'd run non-stop from the common until he realized he was drawing attention to himself: a man fleeing down the high street in broad daylight. It wouldn't do. It would look weird. He sees himself as a stranger might; chaotic, dishevelled, wild-eyed: like an escapee from a mental ward. Trying to behave as a normal person would, Lewis tags on the end of a queue of people waiting for a bus, half-sits on the low wall, just like the man next to him, like those two girls further along. His legs are trembling, he has to fight the urge to cry. He rests his back against the railing and puts his kitbag on his lap to stop his knees from jumping. He wants to be no one again, the invisible man, but the confusion—and then the realization—washes over him like sweat: he's run away from one bad situation, and straight into another. For a second, he sees himself as if he's been tied on a long piece of invisible elastic, getting catapulted from one place to the next, only to return twice as quickly. He fights the thought. More like a wrecking ball, he says, under his breath. But if he isn't on elastic, what is he doing in Clapham, directly opposite the Café Salsa, the very place where the rot set in?

~ ~

Lewis had been living in a basement flat off the high street, doing jobs for cash, some house clearance, odd bits of decorating, which was how he first met Vivienne. He'd been employed to paint the interior of the café; there was two week's work in it if he took his time. Vivienne was a fixture, beautiful to look at, always in the middle of a crowd of admirers: would-be poets and bit-part actors and young men in suits, who would twirl their car keys and offer to buy her drinks. She had breakfast in the café every morning, and she'd still be there at lunch-time, chatting on her mobile, scanning the small ads in the paper. During the afternoon, Viv would disappear for a few hours and come back in different clothes: always some black outfit, and heavy pieces of glass jewellery hanging from her ears and her throat. She'd sit at *her* table in the window, in the candlelight, glinting like a scarab.

Viv made the first move. He'd been painting a trompe-l'oeil effect on the back wall: a menagerie of yellow parrots and green monkeys copied from a print the owner had given him. He hated the work; it was vulgar, he thought, but he made no comment because he got paid daily, in cash. She turned to him one morning from her seat in the window, and asked him if he was gay or straight. That was how it started.

Later, she would say she was attracted to his profile; that he reminded her of an actor she vaguely knew. He wasn't pleased with the idea of looking like someone else until he saw a picture, and then he considered that it could be worse. It was Viv, in the end, who forced him to get help with a problem he was hiding, although at the time he didn't take it in.

They'd been seeing each other for a couple of months, casually at first—going out to watch a film or see a gig—and then more intimately, sharing the evenings together at his flat. She was keen to progress the relationship, as she put it: she suggested that they should try living together. No sooner had she vented the idea than her bags were piled up in the hall.

Even though it was her suggestion, from the very first hours Lewis felt as if he were undertaking some kind of trial. Viv brought his problem to the surface in a manner he hadn't anticipated; it grew quietly inside him, a slow inflation of rage. It was the way she had, of untidying the space around her: leaving cutlery on the drainer where the stains would dry in splotches, shampoo trickling like slime down the tiles in the shower, her underwear hanging off the radiators. At first, it induced in Lewis a sense of panic. He told himself to think in broad terms: it was *he* who was abnormal; this was how people lived all the time, surrounded by their mess. He'd seen other people's houses, and this wasn't so bad by comparison. He tried to behave as though it didn't matter: she was beautiful, and glamorous, and as long as they loved each other, it would all be fine. For three months, Lewis managed to persuade himself that this was a fact, stepping around her, smoothing out the jagged edges of their shared life.

In the evenings, when he came home from work, he'd find Viv in front of the television in her pyjamas with her pouch of dope, her glass of wine, her *TV Times,* flicking through stations with the remote control while she talked on the telephone. Or she'd be sitting at the computer, her hair backlit like an exploding star, her collar turned in on itself as she scratched aimlessly at the nape of her neck. She called herself an actress. When she wasn't searching her name on the Internet or watching television or talking on the phone, she was in the bath, surrounded by a mass of guttering candles. At these times, Lewis would stand outside on the steps and breathe the air, the stinking London air, so much sweeter because it didn't proximate to Viv.

He came to the realization he really *didn't* love her one morning when he saw, amongst the thick bangles and droopy earrings, her hairbrush on the dressing-table. The long hairs wafted from it; embedded in the teeth was a coiled mesh of dusty auburn, like the nest of an insect. It made him cringe. His own hair was shorn, every three weeks, by a barber on the high street. He couldn't even touch the hairbrush. He nudged the handle with the edge of a coat-hanger she'd left on the ironing board, until it fell off the dressing-table and into the wastebasket. Liberated by this, he swept his arm across the surface, scattering the jewellery, pots and powder, perfumes and cotton wool buds and assorted debris onto the carpet. It was such spectacular freefall, he felt he could run over the roof. He could knock the walls down, he could rip out the sky. He felt giant.

He woke face down on the bed, opening his eyes to see Viv, scrabbling around on the floor. He couldn't work out what she was doing until he lifted his head; she was throwing things at random into an open suitcase. He didn't know how long he'd been there, but the sky was darkening through the window. He felt the faint breeze of evening on his skin.

She must have been in the room a while, because the wardrobe doors were open and her clothes were strewn all over the carpet, and slumped in heaps against the wall and the bed, inches from his feet. He could tell when he looked at her face that she was angry, but there was another thing he saw there which made him mute: it was fear. He couldn't find anything to say to that. His head felt light and scattered, as if it had been filled with confetti. While she went about her packing, Lewis stared at the mirror above the dressing-table; it hung at a crooked angle, with a perfect smash in the centre, catching the light like a rose in the rain. To the left, the net at the window lifted once in the breeze; it revealed a more angular smash in the pane. He dared not look at his fists.

Viv snapped her case shut and got to her feet.

I'll be round for the rest in the morning, she said, her voice tight, So I'd prefer it if you weren't here. Actually, I think you need help. I've left an address on the table.

But Lewis wasn't planning to stay, either. Early next morning, he took his kitbag, pushed the key through the letter-box, and walked free into the wide, clean air. He didn't take the note with the address on it; didn't want anything of hers, not even a scrap of paper. And it was an easy thing to remember a street name. The last he heard of Viv, she was living with some artists in a shared house in Battersea. He thought it would suit her well.

On his own again, Lewis tried to counteract what he began to think of as his migraine attacks in a new way. He discovered that organizing his personal world relaxed him: the build-up of pressure inside his head abated. He rented a furnished room in a tall, near-derelict building opposite the railway station. Two other men occupied bedsits on the same floor, and another, small space under the eaves was used for storage. The men shared a kitchen and bathroom. Lewis started on his regime by listing everything he could see in his room, slowly, like a breathing exercise. Sometimes he would move the objects into a systematic panorama; it could be alphabetically based, or purely dependent on the estimated age, or actual size, of the object. He liked the concentration this required; he thought of it as environmental mathematics.

After a while, he became convinced that the objects had fallen out of alignment—the lampshade was too far to the left, the ashtray had been slightly uncentred on the coffee table. He had no explanation for this; unless someone else had a key, or there was subsidence: objects did not move themselves. This was how the panic resurfaced, as a growing turmoil, like iron filings swirling around inside him; and all because of an ugly lampshade or a chair in the wrong place. He would need to take action.

One evening, the man who had the bedsit near the stairwell knocked on his door. The sound shocked Lewis: no one came calling, no one ever knocked. The man had come to complain: Lewis's furniture was blocking the way.

It's a fire hazard, mate, he said, craning his head round Lewis and staring into the room, It's a nuisance, no one can get past. The other lads are grumbling.

Lewis stood his ground, puzzled by the expression on the other's face.

I don't know what you're talking about, he said, What fire hazard?

He motioned to Lewis to follow him out onto the landing. The space under the eaves was crammed with pieces of furniture: a bed-frame, easy chairs, a coffee table, a television set, all piled up on top of each other. The ugly lampshade was crushed underneath it all, the stand sticking out into the hallway like a broken limb. Lewis recognized these pieces from his room. He must have put them there.

No offence, mate, but normal people like to have stuff, the man said, Even lifers in prison have a *bed*. If you wanted unfurnished, mate, you should've told the landlord.

Lewis decided that if the man called him *mate* again, in that fake way, he'd have no choice but to hit him.

Weeks later, leaning on the bonnet of a stolen van on the edge of the ring-road and watching as the fire engines screamed past, he made another decision: he needed help. The man was right, as Viv had been right: he was going mental.

~

Lewis had never been to a shrink before. He pictured an elderly man with half-moon glasses sitting behind a large desk; opposite would be a low leather couch, which Lewis would lie down on. Viv had had an appointment with her therapist every Monday for as long as he knew her. But Viv believed in witchcraft too, bought candles from Brixton market with incantations printed on them, burned papery curses in the fire grate late at night. As sceptical as he was about therapy, Lewis thought it must be preferable to Black Cat Bone.

The therapist turned out to be a young woman who insisted he call her just by her first name—Katy. He didn't ask whether she knew Viv, and understood, anyway, that even if she did, she wouldn't tell. They sat facing each other in easy chairs, under a gauze-covered skylight, in a room painted pale green. There was hardly any furniture in it, which made Lewis feel quite relaxed, but during their introductory session,

Katy leaned over and twice touched his arm, for no reason that he could see. It wasn't as if he'd invited it. Lewis regarded this touching business as a behaviour, just like his own—therapists were bound to have them too—and tried to explain that he didn't feel comfortable when she did it. He asked if it might not be part of his problem. She didn't say she wouldn't touch him again; she said she hoped they could agree in the first instance not to focus on 'problems' and not to resort to 'labels'.

But Lewis was keen on labels: he actively craved them. When he told Katy at the next session that he was having difficulty visualizing the *problem*—unable to find a better word to describe what it was he was suffering from—she relented. She rattled out a line of jargon.

It may be that you're suffering from a form of anxiety disorder instigated through childhood trauma and augmented by lack of closure, she said, Or, just as likely, it may be nothing of the sort. That's what we're here to find out.

Immediately he could see the words lined up, like beads on a string; he could taste them. When he told her this, repeating the phrase with the exact same intonation she used, she simply raised an eyebrow, as if to say, See, that's trouble with labelling, isn't it?

Over the next few sessions, Katy tried to encourage him to put things back into his environment. She called them 'unblocking exercises', which made Lewis think of drains.

Start small, she said, Any ordinary object will do. But make it something you'll be bound to notice, like a picture. For example, you could put a framed photo on top of the television.

I don't have a framed photo, said Lewis, I don't have a television.

In another session, Katy asked him to concentrate on what he was hoping to achieve when he removed things from his environment. He supposed that it had something to do with his visual memory, his need to ensure that everything remained in its place. He told her as much:

If I can't know where everything is, then I get rid. That's it. The less there is, the less I have to remember. The less to forget.

But he didn't tell her what he really thought: that a life without objects is easier to bear, because objects store memories, and memories are like quicksand. They suck you down into a place that no longer exists, where events happen beyond your control. And no matter how hard you try to change the memory—make the rain fall and the sun not shine, make that bend in a leafy lane a straight, clear road—you can't. You can't undo. You can't not see what you've seen. Not once in all this did he mention Wayne.

Better to get rid, he told her, Wipe the slate.

Lewis understood that people forgot things all the time: their house keys, their cigarettes, their mobile phones; and he understood too, that it was perfectly normal. His brother Wayne was a forgetter. In turn, Lewis had become the one who could be relied upon to be responsible: he was the one who had to remember. Perhaps he took this too literally. But being unable to forget hadn't got him into trouble; not until he took that flat in Wandsworth. He had yet to learn that all space gives you is nowhere to hide.

## SIX

The advert had described the flat as a 'studio apartment'. After the shared house, and the other tenants complaining about the 'fire hazard' he'd supposedly created under the eaves, Lewis liked the sound of a studio. He had a mental image of a cool, white, empty cube, with light flooding in through an enormous sash window. He would not be sharing with anyone else, and if he did well in his new job with FoodToGo, he'd have no trouble managing the rent. Lewis thought that anywhere would be preferable to the YMCA, and was elated when he saw the outside; a shady courtyard with a view of the common in the distance: not like living in the city at all. But he took one sure look at the interior, and let out a slow breath: it was brimming with *things*. He saw at once the life of another person, locked into every object, peeling away from the walls in the afternoon grey.

He placed his kitbag on the cooker and the doorkey back in the lock where he knew he could find them both again, and then he set to work. He stood in the centre of the room and made an inventory. Not on paper or out loud, but in his head, where it wouldn't interrupt the words coming out of the woman's mouth. She was telling him about hot water and council tax and a rent book which she would go and buy from Smith's next time she went shopping. She was asking him if everything was alright, which required a nod, and then she was leaving through the door which led onto the yard, which he could also enjoy any time he liked, she said.

Lewis remembers it as the worst place, because until then he had deluded himself into thinking that his desire for nothingness was a *lifestyle* choice. This was supposed to be a fresh start in a new home; immediately it made him feel ill.

When the landlady had gone, he stood in the centre of the room and completed the inventory.

Two armchairs, table, five dining chairs in differing styles (that's four too many) a television set on a coffee table, a second coffee table under the window with a lace doily on it and in the middle of that a heart-shaped pomander with a gold thread attached so if you held it up it would twirl, and if put your nose to the holes it would stink of old. There was a corner cabinet full of . . . stuff. He couldn't remember the word for bric-a-brac even though he searched for it, stumbling over tête-à-tête and bring-and-buy: this troubled him. An assortment of pictures and embroidered hangings covered the walls. The carpet was obscured by two hair-matted rugs. Floral curtains. A clock in the shape of a teapot saying Time For Tea. Everything spoke to him of a life once lived. It was unbearable.

He set to work in the kitchen, but he was so vexed that he might have missed something in the studio area, full as it was of things, that twice Lewis had to stand between the rooms and go over the inventory again. The kitchen was worse: hundreds of jars with crusted lids under the long counter, and Tupperware boxes covered with a film of greasy dust. There were stacks of plates with geometric designs in orange and brown; and in the cutlery drawer, an armoury of stained metal implements. He couldn't countenance the bottles in the cupboard. Even though he knew he should rinse them out and recycle them, that it would please his landlady to see that he was taking care of the environment, he couldn't do it. He took a breath, and threw the bottles and jars into a large black sack, and when that was full, into another.

After the kitchen, he would set his sights on the studio; but the kitchen and the plastic sacks and the surreptitious carrying of them down to the end of the lane, the endless indexing—all this exhausted him. The teapot clock said half-past seven. It was still light outside, but Lewis thought it would be reasonable to go to bed. He lay down in the dusk and listened to the falling birdsong.

By the Friday, he had almost finished. He left one table, one dining chair, and a telephone point about which he could do nothing. The kitchen was bare now apart from a fridge-freezer, cooker, saucepan, and kettle. On the worktop, in a straight line, Lewis had washed, dried, and placed a plate, a knife, a fork, two spoons (one large, one small), and a single cup and saucer. Nothing there he couldn't count. There was one thing that bothered him. The bed in the studio was small and suited his needs, but along the wall was a large leatherette sofa in bruise pink. The landlady, when she came to collect the rent, stood in the kitchen and tried to keep her face. She had said he could make it his home, she had said that. Lewis would use it in evidence. It was previously her mother's flat, she'd said, it would be completely understandable if he wanted to thin things out a bit. The landlady kept her face, right up until he said he wanted to get rid of the sofa. She had managed to find space for everything else he had discarded. The sofa would have to stay.

Something to sit on, she said, When you want to relax.

He could have said he didn't want to relax, but he said, instead,

I lie on the bed to relax.

This is—was—a furnished let, she said, A new tenant might want a sofa, even if you don't.

The words frightened him; Lewis saw them as a kind of threat. So he tried to live with the sofa.

At work, he made an effort not to think of it. But all the time, while he was arranging the boxes of finger food and mini cartons of cold soup and meat pieces on sticks that had to be Trayed and Cling-filmed as per instructions—Twenty on each platter, no more, no less—he saw the sofa, breathing in his space. After his shift he moved it into the hall, so he wouldn't have to look at the shape of it in the dark.

FoodToGo had employed Lewis because he said he could drive a van, because he was very clean—presentable, said Mrs Dunn, at the interview, You are very Presentable. And, because they paid minimum wage minus deductions for training and uniforms, they had a rapid turnover of operatives. He was trained, in fifteen minutes, to unwrap the food from the boxes and place it onto metal trays, adding a garnish of parsley at each end (Very Important, she insisted, Don't forget it). Lewis had to count each item of food before covering the tray with cling-film. He was good at this. Finally, he had to tick off the list of completed items—The Menu—which were bound for this party or that private view, and sign it.

When the training was finished, Mrs Dunn gave him a set of keys and showed him the van. It was old, and the inside smelled of stale fat. She saw him eyeing the rust and the dents, his look of distaste as he sniffed the air.

You won't even notice it after a while, she said, with a laugh.

I'll notice this, said Lewis, waving a hand at the skeleton hanging off the rear-view mirror.

You're meant to, she said, It's a little aide-memoire. No speeding, no boozing on the job, no stupid driving—or that's how you'll end up.

Lewis was about to tell her he didn't need his memory jogging, but then she bared her teeth again,

Besides, he reminds me of my second husband, she said.

She gave him a map of the area so he wouldn't get lost, although none of the food was hot, nothing would go off if he did get lost and was, say, half an hour or so late. When he arrived at the venue, he was to unpack the trays, set them out on whatever surface he was instructed to use, remove the cling-film, and disappear.

The idea was that he would then go on to deliver another Menu to another party, but it was a small business, and often Lewis found himself at a loose end, hanging about outside, waiting. Sometimes he went to a pub, but when the noise was no longer bearable, he sat on a wall, took out his book, and read. He tried not to worry about the sofa, although occasionally in the dead time he went back to his flat just to stare at it, like a drunk coming home for a fight.

He spent his first week's wages on food; bought a loaf of organic bread and wrapped it up, two slices at a time, in the cling-film he'd stolen from FoodToGo. He put them in the freezer. He bought dried beans and UHT milk. He bought apples and put them on the windowsill opposite his bed, where the view beyond the common was of a distant hill and some trees. To the left of the view was a tall, grey office building. Lewis wanted to remove this from the picture. He cut out a triangle shape from the back of his rent book and stuck it on the glass. It was dark green. From the bed, it could have been another hill.

FoodToGo sent him across town to a gallery where an artist was having a show. When he arrived, two people were waiting, looking at their watches but smiling with relief. They were pouring wine into stem glasses, and offered him one while he set about unwrapping the trays. He accepted, and steadied the wine on one of the trestle tables set up to take the food he'd brought. There was something odd about the trays this time. He counted the sausages on sticks: twenty on each tray. He counted the chicken nuggets. Twenty. The sandwiches. Twenty. He went back to look at the sausages, and saw they were of different sizes: they looked unbalanced. He ate one, pushing the little wooden stick into his back pocket, but the balance was still unbalanced. He ate another. He had recently become vegetarian, but they tasted good. He ate another. His pocket was filling with sticks. While the two hosts sat behind the tabletop in the foyer, Lewis ate another and another. The more he ate, the less balanced it looked, even though he tried moving them around, angling them, making a pattern. He finished the sausages and put the tray back in the box, spread out the remaining trays to disguise the lack. There was a raw feeling in his throat, like heartburn. The sausages, when they came back up, were as pink as the sofa.

FoodToGo had to let him go. Mrs Dunn was plain in her disapproval. Certain items had gone missing, she said, and there had been a complaint. Not about the sausages, or the mess in the toilet afterwards, but the way he helped himself to the wine. As if he were a guest, for God's sake! She told him to drop off the keys when he'd completed his last delivery. She would post him a cheque for the days he had worked.

Lewis drove straight to the flat. He spent the day lying on the bed, sometimes sitting up with his back against the wall so that he could admire the view, which was how he happened to see the change. Outside his window, a lake had appeared. He was not fooled by illusion. Someone had placed an empty glass on the sill; the lip of it was in his picture, catching the light as water does. Later in the afternoon, some time after he'd fallen asleep, other changes happened. Someone's building a bonfire, he thought when he first saw them, then later reassessing his impression, he realized they were chairs, stacked upon each other in a random pattern. Just outside his window, in the yard. In his view. A man was carrying more chairs into the space, until there were forty, or fifty perhaps, in all. He asked the man what was going on, and was told the chairs were going to be restored by the woman's boyfriend. The view from his window was now of an abandoned glass, and chairs.

He lay in his room another full day before he walked up the hill towards the council building. He had no idea what he would do next. The building was small enough to be hidden by a rip of paper from his rent book, but massive up close. On the ring-road, he saw a petrol station where he stopped in and bought a sausage roll and a red canister, which he filled with petrol at the pump. Back in the flat, he put the apples and the bread from the freezer in his kitbag, stored the beans in one side pocket, and put his book of poems in the other. The remainder of the milk he poured down the sink. The keys to the van were in his pocket. Lewis dragged the sofa through the door and out into the yard, and piled some of the chairs on top of it. He arranged the other chairs in a pattern around the sofa, the backrests facing inwards, the legs kicking the air. Then he reversed the van up to the gate, offloaded the stale trays of food, throwing them onto the pyre he had created. When he finished, he drove back up the hill to the council building, got out and leaned against the bonnet. He took the sausage roll and ate it in two bites. Felt it burn.

Lewis told the therapist about it, start to finish. He was precise, and exact, kept his voice plain. He omitted to mention the blaze, or stopping at the edge of the ring-road to call the fire brigade. Nor did he tell her about stealing the van, having decided that the less she knew, the less she'd be able to tell the police if they came calling. It was their last session, but she wasn't to know that, either. Immediately, Katy jumped to conclusions, fixing on the canister and the council building. She asked him, in an indirect, meandering way, whether as a child he'd had issues with authority: his father, for instance, or his mother's subsequent boyfriends. It was something she did; always trying to interpret the information he gave her as a key to his past life.

I just wanted to burn it all down, said Lewis, attempting to bypass the scatter of language which would get them to the point of the session, All of it. The sofa and the chairs—even the building that spoilt the view. Every single thing. Normally, I don't get to do what I want.

It was then the discussion turned to things he wanted. That was how it went with her, one minute you'd be talking about a bad feeling you had, sitting on a hill, eating a sausage roll, and the next you'd be listing all the things you ever desired in your life. You'd be giving yourself away. Katy was good at that; so good, so slippery, it felt like it was *his* idea to go and find his mother.

If you wanted to, she'd said, You could certainly put that wish into practice. It would be a form of *exposure,* of course. You couldn't be empty any more; and you'd be making yourself quite *visible.* But perhaps there's something preventing you? Perhaps there are some things you feel the need to run away from? He could have said, You might feel the need to run away, too, if you knew my mother. But after twenty years, Lewis reckoned he didn't know her either; how could seeing her again make matters any worse?

He had driven to Cardiff with a strange feeling of weight-lessness, as if he had shed his earth-bound skin. Everything that pinned him down was at last behind him—London and Viv and the bedsit near the station and the sofa in the flat in Wandsworth, Katy and her talk—all that would be ancient history. He would reconnect—he repeated the word aloud, as Katy had suggested—with himself. He would find his mother; he would make his peace. But then he found Manny instead. He'd trusted him. That was his first mistake: right from the off, Manny knew more than he chose to let on.

# SEVEN

The van was parked half on, half off the pavement. Manny eyed the rust on the bonnet and over the wheel arches, and the numerous dents in the bodywork. While Lewis made a pretence of unlocking it, Manny made a pretence of not noticing, folding and unfolding the slip of paper in his hand.

Why don't we try the phone book first? Manny suggested, Give her a ring? She might have moved again. She always was a bit of a wanderer, your mam.

Lewis could hear the caginess in the old man's voice. He chose to ignore it.

Itchy feet, he said, And I've tried to phone. So let's go and find out, shall we?

Manny wouldn't budge. He stood at the open door, staring across the seats of the cabin, and waited until Lewis slid in.

Are you sure, son? he asked, and at Lewis's nod, hauled himself into the passenger seat.

Lewis reached his arm through the window and peeled a parking ticket off the windscreen. He handed it to Manny.

What am I supposed to do with this? Manny asked.

Dunno, said Lewis, It's not actually my van.

Rented?

On loan, Lewis replied.

What about this fella? asked Manny, flicking the plastic skeleton which hung from the rear-view mirror, Hitchhiker?

Lewis gave a pained expression, then sighed.

It's a reminder. Sort of. Long story.

Manny said nothing, but sat upright, shaking his head and tutting. He appeared very Gallic doing this, or perhaps, thought Lewis, perhaps it's just the beret that does it. The beret looked brand new, as did the large patent leather holdall which Manny wore slung sideways across his body. He had the air of a geriatric dispatch rider.

What d'you keep in there? asked Lewis, mainly to avoid the subject of stolen vehicles.

Manny didn't reply, just flipped the clasp and held open the flap. He angled it in Lewis's direction, gave an artful smile.

See? He said, triumphant. Lewis took his eyes off the road for a second and glanced across.

I don't want to upset you, mate, but it's empty, he said.

*I* know that, said Manny, Do you think I'm gone senile? But *they* don't, do they?

Who?

Them robbers down the precinct. It's my decoy. They lie in wait, you know. Scagheads. Pension day, it's like high bloody noon.

Should you be drawing a pension if you're still working? said Lewis, with half a smile to show he was joking.

I've paid my tax, said Manny, not smiling with him, Here we are now.

The house where Lewis's mother lived was exactly the same in style as the house they'd rented twenty years before, except, at a glance, he could tell that she'd decided to settle. The garden had a clipped front lawn, neat rows of flowers in the borders, a giant yellow butterfly pinned to the outside wall.

Manny flapped his hand at Lewis as he slowed to a halt.

Round the bend! he shouted, ducking as if he were about to be shot, Don't let her see us in this!

Lewis sighed, scraping the van round the corner, parking it next to an overgrown hedge.

Manny ran ahead of him, crabbing along the hedge, peeping over into next door's garden, then racing up the path.

He looked faintly comical in the open air, and he knew it, grinning widely at Lewis before stooping to look through the letter-box. Manny stared for a good long while, made a pantomime of cupping his ear to the door, then turned on his heel and trotted back.

She's not there, he gasped, winded by his efforts.

How d'you know? asked Lewis, We could see round the back.

Post on the mat, said Manny, pushing a hand to Lewis's chest, C'mon, chief, we'll try again later on.

Lewis moved the hand away and stepped up the side path. There was a bicycle leaning on the wall next to the back door, which was slightly open.

Mam? he called, and feeling Manny's protestations behind him, called again, louder, Mam, are you in there?

Who's asking? said a man's voice. It came from the stairs, followed by quick footsteps.

Who's asking *me*? Lewis shouted back, blinded by the darkness of the inside, I'm looking for my mam!

Well, I'm her bloke, grinned the man emerging from the shadow, So I suppose that *could* make me your dad.

~ ~

Lewis's Real Dad is dead. So whoever the man with the builder's tan and the goatee thought he was, he wasn't Lewis's father. He was just having a joke. Lewis's 'dads' went like this:

## DAD #1:

Dead. As a child, Lewis didn't often think about his real father; he was too busy coping with

## DAD #2:

Errol was Lewis's uncle-dad. Lots of their friends had them, even the boys who had real fathers at home had uncle-dads lurking around. Errol was self-employed, which meant he was on the dole, and spent a lot of time lying on the couch. Lying in Wait, he called it, for the Right Moment. Lewis's mother once made a comment, picking his socks up off the carpet, that it was more like lying in state. You only had to say the wrong thing once to Errol to not make the same mistake again. It was a lesson the whole family learned.

Errol claimed he was in the SAS. He had to make himself available at all times, he said, but the closest he ever came to the SAS was watching *The Dirty Dozen* at Christmas, lying on the couch with a box of liqueurs in his lap. He'd be chewing at the sides of his moustache and shouting, You don't do it like that! And, Never in a million years, Telly-boy! Only Lee Marvin made him happy. There's a real man, he'd say, You wouldn't mess with him.

It was messing with a real man that got them into trouble. That's what his mother had said, when they were packing their bags in the middle of the night. She was leaving Errol for a real man, only Errol mustn't find out, ever, and no one must know their business because he'd come after them. They were going to make a fresh start, in a house she'd found across town. She tried to make it sound like a thrilling adventure. Wayne was happy enough that they were leaving, but Lewis remembered the first time his mother had mentioned Errol: he'd been a *real* man too, in those days. Lewis was beginning to distrust real men, and anything that was made to sound like an adventure; he knew they weren't at all thrilling, and he knew that there was nowhere, really, to run.

Errol found them on the second day in their new house. Lewis and Wayne were putting up posters on their bedroom wall, arguing about who was going to have the top bunk. Lewis knew he would get his way; he was the oldest, and bigger, but Wayne was good at putting his case; he was more agile on the ladder, he would suit the top bunk. Lewis was, he reasoned, always restless at night, and occasionally sleep-walked.

Wandering about on that top bunk, it could be hazardous.

Better all round—Wayne was saying, when he stopped mid-sentence. It was just the one scream. The boys stared at each other. Standing at either end of the bunk-bed, they felt, through the floor, a thud.

Downstairs, Errol was lying on the carpet, streaked with blood. There was blood on the wall above him and on the door-frame. Lewis knew it wasn't Errol's blood. It was a facility he had, for seeing things precisely, as if someone had showed him a film still. What Lewis saw, then, was someone else's blood, and Errol in a faint: what Wayne saw was murder. He stood over Errol with an air of thrilled satisfaction.

Quit ya jibba jabba! he cried, raising his fist to the ceiling, and in a mock-American accent added, I pity you, fool!

Lewis carried on through to the kitchen. His mother was bending over the fridge, so at first he didn't understand what had happened. He'd already taken in the strings of blood in a trail over the floor and the worktop, and a zing in the air, like an electrical charge; it was the smell of panic. His mother had one hand wrapped in a tea-towel and the other gripping a pack of frozen peas. She was biting it open, pulling at the plastic with her teeth. She looked at him and passed the packet across the worktop.

Open that for us, babes, she said, in a calm voice, the one she used when she was doing something ordinary, like cooking their tea.

And then run down and fetch Manny. Tell him it's Della, she said, Tell him it's an emergency.

Behind Lewis, Wayne was over his euphoria; Errol was coming round. They could hear him groaning.

What's he done to you? Wayne shouted, his voice going up at the edges.

Nothing, said their mother, Now will one of you go and fetch us a taxi before I bleeds to death!

At the hospital, she presented the packet of frozen peas to the casualty nurse, who was already shooing her to the front of the queue. They went on through the double doors and out of sight. Lewis and Wayne and Manny sat in the waiting-room and said nothing, until Manny saw Lewis's face, like plastic melting, and said,

Don't worry, son, they'll sew that finger back on. She kept it nice and cold. Shall we get us a drink from that machine?

~ ~

Manny always was good at evasion; back then, it was about his mother's finger—or maybe he didn't understand that sometimes truth was a better option. As they walked back to the van, Lewis had the distinct feeling of being a child again, and that Manny would happily lie to comfort him. But he was no longer a child. He didn't care for comfort.

Manny sighed heavily behind him. It might have been out of frustration at the way Lewis had behaved, or in sympathy with the reception he received. Either way, Lewis didn't care. He had to resist the urge to turn about, push past Manny, and run back inside; he would have knocked the boyfriend flat if Manny hadn't stopped him. Neither of them spoke as they climbed in the van, but Manny let out another sigh, loud and long.

Something on your mind? asked Lewis

No, chief.

What did he call himself again?

Gary Barrett, said Manny, He's local.

You know him?

Not really, said Manny, then after a beat, He drinks in the Old Airport with our Carl. They do scuba club on Tuesday nights.

Lewis did a double take.

Your Carl? Scuba? Fucking *scuba*?

Manny grimaced.

I know, son. Unbelievable.

And this Gary Barrett, said Lewis, D'you think he was telling the truth? About her?

Search me.

Lewis pondered this. The man was polite enough after the initial encounter, but he wouldn't tell Lewis anything about where his mother had gone or when she'd be back.

It's not really my place to say, he said, But I'll tell her you called. Leave us your number, just in case she wants to get in touch.

It was the *just in case* that made Lewis's blood pump in his neck. That, and the feeling he had, that his mother had been upstairs, standing behind the bedroom door, listening.

Manny watched the skeleton dangling off the rear-view mirror, swinging his head in time to the rocking motion it made. Now and then he'd flip a finger at it, making it twirl.

Does he glow in the dark, then? he asked. Lewis shrugged.

Like I say, it's not really my van.

He turned the radio up, and they sat together, staring ahead, listening to the music. Manny turned it down when the disc jockey started to talk.

Can't stand all that yakking, he said, finally.

Lewis didn't respond. They remained silent until Manny started to fidget again. Lewis could tell he was building up to something; he waited for it to work itself out.

You could always stop with me, Manny said at last, Just for a bit, until you've sorted something for yourself. And since Sylvie went—it'd be company. After a fashion, like.

Thanks, said Lewis.

You'll want to think about it, of course, said Manny, offended, I expect the offers are flooding in.

How old is Gary Barrett, do you think? Lewis asked.

Manny shrugged.

Don't know. Mid thirties? About your age, I reckon.

Exactly, said Lewis.

And that's what's eating you?

Yep.

Well, you know, son, squaring up to her boyfriend—however old you think he is—isn't going to get you in her good books. You can't just go barging into people's lives without a by-your-leave. Not after all this time.

Lewis snorted, jabbing his foot so hard on the accelerator that Manny jerked forward in his seat.

After all what time? said Lewis, It's stopped still for her. For a minute, I thought it was Errol standing there.

Errol, said Manny, clutching the seatbelt across his chest, Which one was he?

When we first moved round yours. Errol came to look for us. You took us to the hospital, remember?

Manny stared out of the passenger window, nodding his head.

Gary wouldn't do anything to hurt her, he said, turning to look at Lewis, He's soft as butter, that one.

Thought you didn't know him, said Lewis, his words tight in his throat, Only, sounds to me like you two could be mates.

I told you to leave it, said Manny, You won't heed a warning, that's your trouble. Always has been, always will be.

I see, said Lewis, That's my trouble. So, what would you warn me to do now?

Go home. Forget it. Get on with your life. That's my warning, chief. Do you hear me?

Loud and clear, *chief,* said Lewis, pulling up in front of Manny's house, I believe this is you.

As Manny stepped out of the van, Lewis wrenched the plastic skeleton off the mirror.

Give that to your mate when you see him, he shouted, throwing it at Manny's back, Tell him that's *my* warning!

# EIGHT

Get on with your life, Manny had said. But this is his life, sitting on a wall in Clapham high street and staring at the window of the Café Salsa; this is his elastic, inescapable joke of a life. The buses come and go, blocking his view, unblocking it, and the people get on and new queues form around him, and still he sits on the low wall, hugging his kitbag. He had left Cardiff in rage and panic: he wasn't thinking straight. Lewis shuts his eyes, trying to block out the street noise all around him, trying to think in a direct white line. A metal grind of gears fills the air, a man's sudden swearing, a long blast on a car horn. Unbidden, an image swims into Lewis's head: of the night they went to recce the house. There were himself and Carl in the front of the van, Barrett poking his head between the seats, and Carl, reaching down into the footwell. Lewis had kept his eyes on the road, but now, as the blackness clears from his vision, he sees Carl again, surreptitious, examining something in his hand, and talking, all the time talking, driving Lewis insane with his talk.

He didn't see what it was. It happened so fast, a blur of trees lit up white in the headlights, a sudden, dense blackness, and, finally, the heart-shaped lake appeared before him, opening out in a spill of cold moonlight.

Biting on his lip, Lewis reaches into the side-pocket of his kitbag, feels beneath the split bag of beans for the black felt pouch where he keeps Wayne's bracelet. He knows, without removing it, knows by its weightlessness, that it's empty.

~ ~

He couldn't have known, the first time he saw the bracelet—the first time he had ever coveted anything his brother had—that he would eventually be its keeper.

His mother was late home from work again. Lewis was preparing their tea in the kitchen while Wayne watched *Top of the Pops* in the next room, letting out exaggerated boos and whistles whenever a band was featured that he didn't like. Lewis had peeled and chipped a stack of potatoes, and was washing up when he tuned in to the sound of voices. In the living-room, his mother was kneeling on the floor next to the couch, while Wayne sat, hugging his knees, at the far end. He looked upset, but Lewis couldn't see why, at first, because there was his mother, looking worn and lovely, holding out a silver bracelet and saying, Just like the one Mr. T wears, love. Look, the links are dead thick, aren't they?

He wears *gold,* said Wayne, staring at the television, And he don't have crap written on it.

Seeing Lewis in the doorway, his mother got up off her knees and handed him the bracelet. Lewis felt how heavy it was, and how cold.

Smart, he said, reading the inscription. On the front plate, *Wayne* had been inscribed in a swirling flourish.

Yeah, said Wayne, unable to keep the sarcasm from his voice, Until you turns it over. I'm Wayne on the front and retard on the back.

Lewis flipped the plate: in large capitals, the word EPILEPTIC was etched. In the kitchen, his mother was firing the spark gun repeatedly at the gas ring, talking to herself.

You does your best . . . I don't know. I asked the man about it down the market, and he said a bracelet was the thing, yeah, because they checks the pulse first? And they knows to look? But he—she gestured with her head to the other room—He won't have it, will he? I can't take it back now it's been engraved. What am I gonna do with him, babes?

She had her back to him, she hadn't even taken her coat off. Lewis didn't want to hug her, or speak to her, even. He wanted to say, What about me, like a petulant child, What did you get me? Anything? Did you get me a *single thing*? But instead, he hung the bracelet on his wrist and waited for her to turn round to face him.

It's a bit loose on me, even, he said, not looking at her, Say you takes these links out, makes it a bit tighter so the name don't flip over, like . . . ?

His mother called Wayne, who dragged himself into the kitchen like a deep-sea diver emerging from the depths.

What?

Your brother's had an idea, she said, About the bracelet. We'll make it tighter, see, so only you'll know what's on the back.

I'm not wearing no bracelet, he said, his face purple with shame.

It's called a *chain,* said Lewis, That's what Mr. T calls them; he calls them his slave chains. Says they're to remind him of his ancestors, and what they had to go through.

Yeah, but who's my slave? muttered Wayne, fingering the chain despite himself.

I am, said his mother, I'm shackled to the pair of you. Now. Is it sausages or burgers, my masters?

~ ~

The memory is so close he can taste it. He would've liked a ring with a skull's head on it, like the ones in the window of the Oriental shop. He would have been content with a cross and chain, even if it wasn't silver or gold. In the end, he was happy to have nothing, because the bracelet was only to keep Wayne safe; and in the end, he was unhappy that he got the chain, after all. He got his very own slave chain.

Through the jumble of thoughts in his head, another emerges, sudden and hot as chip-fat: the therapist had suggested that what he wanted was to be invisible. She said he wanted to be invisible and empty. Lewis had bought the theory, until now: if that was the case, he argued, then he'd got quite far on empty. The new knowledge comes like a wash of light inside him: No, she was wrong. He doesn't want to be empty, that's just how he *feels*. That's the very thing he doesn't want. He isn't running away from anything, now— he's running to. He's running to wherever Carl is headed, and he'll get his brother's chain back, with interest.

Thick as proverbials, said Manny. The edge of the world, he said, Over east. Doing a *fun run*.

Lewis gets up from the wall and walks. He'll go over east, then, and he'll find Carl. And this time, when he gets hold of the slippery little bastard, he'll bait him, and land him, and gut him like a fish.

# NINE

Anna doesn't know what to take. Brendan keeps reminding her that Yarmouth is only a couple of hours away, and she has calculated the mileage for herself in the road atlas spread out on the kitchen table. It just feels to Anna like a very distant world. She senses that she ought to take everything. So far, she's packed a couple of boxes with bits of work she has to finish, her camera, a pile of unread books taken from a larger pile of unread books—the remainder of which she kicked under the bed—and a hot water bottle. She runs her hands over her collection of glass in the dining-room. It's a motley group: two large jagged cuts that look like pieces of an iceberg, a row of misshapen paperweights, unearthed bottles in blue and green and brown, fragments of leaded lights from a Victorian window. Anna decides to leave them be. Her mother would think them ugly.

You'll need clothes, you know, says Brendan, seeing her struggling along the hall with her computer and following her like a handmaid with the trailing leads, As I have it on good authority that they *do* wear clothes in Strangerland.

Anna tries to ignore him. Normally, she would enjoy the banter, and even make fun of the situation and her place in it: noble and selfless daughter going to look after mad old widow in the middle of nowhere. They could have had some fun with that. But Anna can't begin to fathom her place in this situation, let alone mock it. Her final trip to the car is with two armfuls of clothes swept off the rail in the bedroom. She dumps them in the boot, on top of the boxes, the books, the computer, and the map, which Brendan retrieves for her, causing a subsidence of clutter in the back. They stand in the yard and scan the houses opposite. No one else is on the street. Anna runs her hand along the ridge of the open car door, feeling the stickiness of the rubber sill under her fingers.

What did you tell Marie? she asks, searching for a last way out, Did she give you time off, just like that?

Brendan grins.

I told her that I've got to look after my elderly mother for a while. Well, it's nearly true!

And she'll keep your room for you?

Brendan waggles his head to mean maybe, maybe not. He sighs.

Of course she will. No one understands her like I do. We have a *bond*.

So that's it, says Anna.

That's it.

No excuses.

Nope.

I feel sick, she says.

It'll be the thought of driving all that way, says Brendan, fanning her with the road atlas, You just take it easy.

And you look after my squirrels, she says, feeling tearful and ridiculous.

It's for a few weeks, Anna, he says, They won't even know you've gone. I promise I'll give them breakfast *before* they have their shower.

Anna ignores this renewed attempt at levity.

Have you packed some CDs? he asks.

A few, she says, scowling, I think they're in the boot.

He hands her a plain paper bag with a CD inside.

Well, here's a new one. Something to get you through the wilderness, he says.

I don't know if I can do this, she says.

Brendan comes close and holds her, squeezing her tight. He doesn't say she can.

~

*I'm travelling in some vehicle,* sings Anna, and, jabbing the pause button before the next line of the song, pulls into the car park. Situated on a stretch of asphalt, propped up against a ramshackle garage, is a low, rendered building advertising itself as an All-Day Eatery. It's the first stopping place Anna has seen since she got lost coming off the A14.

And I'll be sitting in some bloody café any minute now, Brendan. Thanks for nothing, she says, so loudly that two lorry drivers standing in front of their trucks stop their conversation and stare at her.

Joni Mitchell, she says, striding across the forecourt.

I'm *Tony* Mitchell, says the shorter of the men, which earns him a shove from his friend. They don't speak again until Anna is under cover of the awning, peering at the sign on the door. It says Open 24/7, but when she tries the handle, it's locked.

They're closed, says the man who called himself Tony, Shut for good now the by-pass is open. But you can get stuff in the garage.

Food, says the tall man.

Is that what it is, says Tony, I did wonder.

Anna looks about for signs of life. Through the plate window, a teenage girl is reading a newspaper.

Thanks. I just wanted some directions.

To?

To Great Yarmouth.

The men point in different directions. Tony is all for sending Anna onwards, cross-country, to take in the scenery. The tall man thinks she ought to retrace her steps and use the new by-pass to get on the A143,

Because that's what it's for, he says.

The bleep of a phone ends the debate. Both men pat their pockets and inspect their phones.

Yours, they say, in unison.

Anna pulls out her handset and flicks the button. It's a single-word message from Brendan: W-W-Walter, it reads.

Walter, she says, at a loss as to what it means. Moving back to her car, she turns and waves at the two men.

Thanks for your help.

Walter, calls Tony hopefully, I've got a mate called Walter!

## TEN

At Victoria station, Lewis boards the coach. When the driver asks him where he's going, he stares at her, his mind blank.

All the way, he says, To the end.

Toilet's out of order, she says, So we'll be making an extra stop after Stanton.

It's all the same to him. Lewis takes a seat at the back, sprawling along the row. The out-of-order toilet is located down some steps a few seats ahead of him: whether it's the sickly smell of chemicals, or his presence—staring people down as they approach—the area around him remains unoccupied. He doesn't have to *look* any particular way to put people off; Lewis knows how to appear unfriendly. When the bus pulls out of the terminus, he throws his jacket over his head and crosses his arms over his chest. To anyone else he's a worker on the night-shift, getting his head down for a few hours. In the sweet leather darkness, Lewis pays another visit to Manny.

He'd spent his time in Cardiff at the old man's house. Despite the bad way they'd parted after going to find his mother, Lewis had run out of ideas. He realized he had a number of choices: he could stay, and make at least one more effort to see his mother, he could go back to London; or he could go anywhere in the world. Anywhere in the world turned out to be Manny's back door. He didn't seem at all surprised to find Lewis standing there for the second time that day, with a clutch of beers in his hand.

Peace offering, said Lewis, holding the four-pack out to Manny, From the prodigal.

Not *my* bloody prodigal, thank God, so you can forget the fatted calf, Manny said, It's fish and chips. And you're buying.

The worst, reasoned Lewis, would be having to sleep in Carl's old bedroom. He tried to put it from his mind, but Manny wanted the preliminaries over before they went to the takeaway and 'settled down' for the night. He took Lewis upstairs, nodding at one closed door,

That's mine and Sylvie's,

and another, which had a china plate on it with what looked like a faded insignia. Lewis peered at it, trying to read the words. Sonia Eloise Finn was written in tiny, elaborate lettering.

Sonia's room, said Manny, She invented the middle name. Always a bit above herself, that one.

He pushed open the door of Carl's bedroom. It was dark enough, but from the sliver of light that bled round the edge of the curtains, Lewis could make out a divan in the corner with a red duvet, posters on the walls, the wallpaper lurid despite the gloom.

You'll find it's not been altered, Manny said, I don't believe in decorating for the sake of it, and there's nothing wrong with this.

He passed a hand over the wall,

Bloody expensive, too.

There's plenty wrong, Manny, said Lewis, eyeing the repeated pattern of the Liverpool FC crest that covered the entire top half of the wall. Beneath a white dado-rail, the paper had been painted scarlet. It was stained here and there with fingermarks and smudges.

He always was a stinking little glory hunter. Suppose he's a Man U supporter now?

When you've quite finished taking the mick, said Manny, You'll find clean sheets and that on the chair, look. Duvet's not been used in yonks, so give it a bit of a shake-out.

Manny moved into the room, turning the pillows over and banging them together. Lewis remained on the threshold.

If it's all the same, Man, I'll sleep downstairs.

Not on the settee, you won't. Sylvie'd be rocking in her grave. And the lad's not stayed in donkey's years, so you won't *catch* nothing. It's either this, or you're in with me, said Manny, And no offence, youth, but you're not my type.

~

They went to get fish and chips from the takeaway in the next street, Manny walking past the neighbouring houses with a pronounced limp that Lewis hadn't noticed during the day.

What's happened to you? he asked, looking down on Manny's beret and the thin straggles of hair poking out on either side.

Nothing, said Manny, Just act casual.

When they got to the end of the road, Manny resumed his normal walking style.

I'm suing Snobson, he said, You'll recall the Snobsons? Them with the picket fence and the airs and graces?

Lewis remembered them; he remembered their son, Sam, most of all.

Well, that boy's gone right off his nut now. Gone to live with the gyppos over the rec. So April just gone, old Snobson, he buys himself a dog from them. For *protection*.

Manny grabbed Lewis's arm, leaned to one side, and pulled up his trouser leg. He pointed to a faded, semi-circular scar on his calf.

Not just any old dog, now. A—hang on, what d'you call it?—a Bedlington lurcher. Well, excuse me if I don't curt-sey. Nearly had me for his lunch. But Snobson reckons I was trespassing.

Lewis coughed back a laugh.

And were you?

Nope. I was just disposing of some rubbish they'd dumped in the garden—and looking up into Lewis's eyes, gave the answer—An old fireplace, if you must know.

From *their* garden, said Lewis.

Manny paused outside the takeaway and studied the menu in the window. Lewis remembered it as the Fish Plaice, but that was years ago. Now it was the Hong Kong Chinese, with laminated pictures of various food items tacked on the glass.

I was doing them a favour. Being neighbourly. It *looked* like it was put out for the rubbish, and what am I? Mystic Meg? In my book it's called finders keepers.

They're worth a lot, those fireplaces, said Lewis, Especially cast iron. Especially with the original tiles.

Manny turned and stared, as if Lewis were a stranger who'd accosted him on the street.

What would you know about it?

Two men edged around them and went inside. Three young boys followed on their heels.

I used to work in reclamation, said Lewis, Y'know, ripping stuff out of schools, hospitals. Are we going to get some food, Manny, or just stay here and look at the pictures?

You? In reclamation? That is a laugh.

Only I might just starve to death standing here listening to you going on.

That dog took a chunk out of me, said Manny, pointing to his shin, It's got to be a crime. You can have chinky from here if you'd rather, he said, pushing the door open, Or a curry.

The phone was ringing when Manny let them back into the house.

You get that, son, he said, And I'll bring these through. Leaning back in the doorway, he shouted down the hall, If it's insurance I've got it, double glazing don't want it! Lewis turned, the receiver on his chest,

It's definitely some sort of scam, Manny. This twat calls himself your son.

Manny dropped the parcel of chips on the table and ran down the hall.

I can see that leg's really giving you jip, said Lewis, handing over the phone.

~

They ate their supper from the paper, then passed the time smoking, drinking beer, and when that was gone, Manny's whisky. After what had happened in the morning, Manny was careful not to mention Lewis's mother, so they talked about nothing in particular, avoiding the past and skirting the present. Lewis knew Manny wouldn't mention Carl first; he'd have to bring it up.

What did he want, then? asked Lewis, nodding towards the phone in the hall, Trying to sell you knock-off?

Says he's got some business down the bay. He wanted to know who you were, said Manny, staring crookedly at Lewis.

Lewis stared evenly back.

What did you tell him?

I told him the truth. He was very complimentary about you, n'all, as it happens. Said he might pop in, for old times' sake.

At this news, both men fell silent. Manny turned the television on, and they watched the end of a period drama about a stern mill owner who falls in love with a penniless employee. Manny pulled a face and made tutting sounds.

My Sylvie loved this sort of tripe, he said, Anything with a bonnet and a bustle, she was glued.

You miss her, said Lewis.

Aye, I do. But I don't miss that, Manny replied, leaning over to turn the sound down. He produced a pack of sticky playing cards from a drawer, and they played brag into the early hours, using matches for money, until Lewis declared himself bankrupt.

That's a hundred quid you owes me, by my reckoning, said Manny, giving the cards a final flourish, Unless you wants double or quits?

Lewis drained the last of the whisky in his mug,

Go on then. My choice of weapon.

Reaching into the pocket of his jeans, he took out a ten-pence piece.

And I thought you were skint, Manny deadpanned.

Your shout, said Lewis, balancing the coin on the edge of his thumb.

Tails, no, hang on, heads. No. Tails.

Sure? Lewis raised his eyebrows and flipped the coin. It twirled through the air, catching the brass edging of the cof-fee table with a bright chime and rolling to rest between Manny's feet. They both bent over to look at it.

Quits it is, laughed Lewis.

Manny's voice was creased with dismay.

It took a dint on the way down, he cried, Surely that's a re-throw?

Don't be a bad loser, Manny. After all, what did you al-ways say to us? It's not the losing, boys, it's the taking part.

Manny hooked his mug in his finger and grumbled his way to the kitchen.

You know where the bathroom is! he shouted, in a tone he imagined was stern, And the bed. I'll see you in the morning.

Lewis wasn't ready to face Carl's room again. He reached over to the remote control and turned up the volume on the television. Manny put his head round the door.

I've marked that whisky, he said, then, seeing the expres-sion on Lewis's face, he put his hand on his shoulder.

Just help yourself, son. I'll give you a knock in the morning.

Lewis stared up at him.

You got some work on?

Said I'd meet Carl at the Old Airport, said Manny, Noth-ing to trouble yourself about. You can come too, if you fan-cies a trip.

I'll sleep on it, called Lewis, hearing Manny's footsteps on the stairs. To himself he said,

But not up there, in that cunt's pit.

~  ~

The rain sits in bright drops on the window of the bus: finding his own eyes staring at him shocks Lewis back into reality. The driver has pulled into a lay-by banked by a clot of dense bushes. She calls out, Diss, anyone for Diss? Against the blackened leaves, Lewis looks at his reflection again, sees himself doubled and slightly out of register, his eyes glittering and untrue.

Thought you were going to the end, she says, as Lewis steps off the coach.

# ELEVEN

When Anna can no longer bear the sound of the buffeting wind, she switches on the radio. The traffic news cuts in immediately, giving out information on local tailbacks, diversions, and accidents. The announcer warns of gusting rain and gales spreading from the east. Searching for a station, she hits another button at random, and Joni Mitchell resumes her singing. Anna lets the scenery sweep away on either side of her. The sky directly ahead is thunderous black, but in her rear-view mirror, a clear twilight blue. She doesn't recall the last few miles she's travelled, or dusk falling. A lorry bearing down from the opposite direction flashes its beams at her, and Anna puts her headlights on. Round a winding incline, aware of the glare and dip of another set of lights coming towards her, Anna almost doesn't see the figure cutting its way through the landscape. He's too near, walking the cats' eyes at the edge of the road, so she has to pull out into the middle of the carriageway to avoid hitting him.

Tosser! she shouts.

In her rear-view mirror, she glances back: he's carrying a kitbag over his shoulder and holding out his thumb.

Never in a million years, she says.

# TWELVE

The last thing Anna wants, with a headache and a bad night's sleep to haunt her, is breakfast with Vernon and his waistcoat. She tiptoes down the stairs and pauses at the dining-room door, listening hard for signs of life: cornflake munching, heavy breathing, anything to warn her of his presence.

Coast is clear, says a voice behind her, which makes her jump. Marta comes through from the kitchen, carrying a tray loaded with coffee and toast and boiled eggs.

Hi, says Anna, Am I the last?

Actually, you're the first *and* the last. Mrs Calder and Mr Savoy don't normally take breakfast down here. They have it *in their rooms,* Marta says, with a delighted, whispered emphasis, as if this fact is a great secret.

Who are the eggs for? asks Anna, following Marta into the dining-room.

For you, if you like. Certainly for me.

Marta collects some cutlery from a box near the door and sits down at a window table. Anna pulls up a chair opposite. She watches as Marta shells an egg, dips it into a pile of salt on her side-plate, and bites the top off. Marta has a fresh look, with clear, pale skin and her hair pulled back off her face. Her eyes in the morning light are mineral blue, framed by prominent laugh-lines. Anna sees that her hair isn't blonde, as she first thought, it's the colour of blanched almonds. Her mother was right about her age; Marta has the vigour of a younger woman, but close up, she could be fifty. Anna decides she likes her, but the sight of the egg disappearing so quickly makes her feel nauseous. Outside, on the road, the trees are bending under the onshore breeze.

I think I had too much of that brandy last night, says Anna, waving away the offer of toast, I'll stick to wine in future.

They are great brandy drinkers, laughs Marta, Every night, chink chink! Down the hatch!

And the odd spritzer for elevenses, continues Anna, like a mantra, A little something in their afternoon tea . . .

Yes, and then it's cocktail hour. They're very—Marta searches for the word—Sociable.

I'm not sure that's the way I'd put it, says Anna, and seeing Marta's quizzical look, changes the subject. She doesn't want to discuss her mother's habits at this hour, and Marta is a stranger still.

How long have you been here?

Marta takes a second egg. This time she slices it, and puts a layer on a piece of toast. She chews and thinks.

Since the summer. My son Kristian is an engineer on the Velsters project? You know, the wind-farm up the way here—Marta nods towards the window—So I decided to take a holiday.

A holiday? In Yarmouth?

Yarmouth is Great, says Marta, shaking her head to acknowledge the old pun, But really, I missed my son, and I've no one back home. So I'm here, for a while.

But you're here, says Anna, tapping her finger on the table-cloth, You're working here, as my mum's skivvy.

Marta considers the word, says it aloud to herself. Her accent is faint, with a slight, yawing resonance that Anna likes the sound of. She gives Anna a puzzled look.

You know, my mother's chief washer-up, cook, cleaner, and cocktail mixer, Anna says, before it occurs to her that she may have made a mistake; Marta would be doing it for the money, same as anyone. In trying to correct herself, she flounders.

Not that there's anything wrong with the job. I mean, you just don't strike me as a . . .

Skiffy, says Marta, laughing, It's okay, really. I was going to leave, go back to Randers, and then your poor mother—she leans closer to Anna, dropping her voice—Actually, I have been concerned. Before the fall, maybe a month before, I found her in the garden, gone.

Gone? Anna whispers back.

Blank, blanked out. That time I said I would call a doctor, but she said there would be no need, because you would be coming here to look after her.

Anna nods over her coffee, and then, taking in the measure of this, echoes the phrase.

She said what? That I would be coming here?

Sure.

Anna has to clarify what she's just heard. She says the words slowly and deliberately:

A month before she fell down the steps.

Hmm-mm, Marta shrugs, Maybe six weeks. But she *knew* you would come to stay. She was very looking forward to it.

You do know my mother's a scheming bitch? Anna says, half-smiling.

Marta nods her head over her cup and gives Anna a lit-up grin.

Of course! It's a privilege of age, isn't it? To be scheming. And you are her only child, and very far away. I am a mother too, you see. That's how we're like. Sometimes it's essential, to scheme.

~

The wind is so strong, it almost takes her off her feet. Anna clings to the skinny trunk of a young tree, feeling her coat ballooning at her back. She tries to gauge the best way to avoid being blown off the sea wall and onto the shingle below.

It's an ice-clear day; the gulls scroll across the sky like rips of paper, the nearest ones dipping and teasing their way through the air currents. Anna crabs down to the sand, the sharp grains peppering her eyes and face, until she is at sea level. With the tide out, the sand is soft and difficult, then firm, then suddenly hard under her feet. She feels a child-like urge to run across it, running and yelling all the way down to the sea. She breaks into a self-conscious jog, slowing up as she reaches the shoreline. The waves are black and grey and rolling indigo.

There's no one on the beach. She walks towards the west by instinct, surveying the stretch of sand ahead of her for signs of human life: a dog-walker, fisherman, kite enthusiast. Perhaps it's too early, still. She considers that it might always be this empty. The wind at her back is hounding her, it whips her hair into her eyes and presses her coat into the back of her legs. For relief, Anna turns about, and with her head down and her body pitched forwards, walks directly into the blow, passing her mother's house on the road above her, passing the thin trees and the concrete wall, and further still, out beyond a bank of grey stone buildings high above her eyeline. The sand glitters silver here, and then gradually rust-coloured, as if it has bled. The groynes rise from the surf like a row of ancient chines. Climbing on the nearest one, Anna sees, for the first time, the wind-farm. She can't believe she hasn't noticed it until now; she would have seen it easily, had she been looking. Standing on the iron ridge of backbone, oblivi-ous to the gale sucking the breath from her mouth, she counts as best she can the tall white turbines, counts the long clean lines of them. She watches as their rotor-blades turn in uni-son, flashing sunlight over the sky in swift, repeated strikes. Anna hadn't realized that they were actually out there, in the waves, in the middle of the sea. No one said they were in the *sea*. She thinks it's a miracle: how beautiful they are, how massive they must be up close. And they must make a noise, surely. She turns her ear towards them, and hears the water gurgling through the struts beneath her, and the gulls crying, the wind flailing the sand.

~ ~ ~

Lewis spent the night in a deserted caravan in a field just outside Ditchingham. The cold didn't bother him, but the wind did: sucking the plastic on the windows, rocking the frame of the van, making an eerie, high-pitched whistle which sounded, in the darkest part of the night, like someone calling his name.

This morning, after a two-mile walk, he's hungry and thirsty and his body twitches with lack of sleep. The first shop he sees is an old-fashioned-looking grocery store. Inside, the air is warm and damp; he senses he is visibly sweating.

Lewis takes a packet of ham slices and a round of cheese triangles from the cold cabinet, and a loaf of bread from a basket below the counter. He puts them on top of the newspapers, gets a bottle of Lucozade from the fridge, and two cans of beer.

Is this bread for you? asks the woman serving, Only if it's for you, we've got fresh bread over there on that shelf.

Isn't this fresh? says Lewis, poking the wrapper with his finger.

It's just past its sell-by, says the woman, We keep it for people who like to feed the swans. It's half-price.

Lewis shrugs, and pays for the food. In need of a shower, he considers asking the woman whether there's a sports centre nearby, or a swimming pool, but then thinks the better of asking; it might seem a strange request. Instead, he buys some Rizlas and a pouch of tobacco, and considers the alternatives: where there are swans, there will be water.

Opposite the shop is a long swathe of green with a walled-in war memorial under some trees. As he gets near, Lewis can see the river running full, and people feeding the birds. It looks organized, the groups separate but intent on doing the same thing, as if they're actors in a silent movie. Couples stand on the grass bank, children bend too close to the water for Lewis's liking, and one or two individuals have positioned themselves on the benches. A middle-aged man straddles the low wall around the memorial; his hand is full of grain, which he throws down for the pigeons, but his eyes are on Lewis. Finding himself an empty bench towards the far end of the bank, away from the man, Lewis puts together a sandwich, positioning the slippery ham on a slice of bread, then folding it in half. He attempts to peel the foil off one of the cheese triangles and, failing, puts his lips to the torn opening and pushes the contents whole into his mouth. He drinks the Lucozade and takes a bite from the middle of the sandwich; the crusts are too chewy to swallow. He launches them into the water, and a volley of gulls swoops down, screaming and flashing their wings, followed by a parade of swans gliding away from an elderly couple, who have been feeding them at the river's edge.

Cupboard love, cries the old man, and Lewis nods and moves off. As soon as he's vacated the seat, the couple sits on it, making themselves at home. Looking back, Lewis sees they are surrounded by the swans, their long necks bending like hairpins as they snatch at the bread. The sight makes him shudder: he won't be bathing in the river, today or any other day.

# THIRTEEN

The house is deserted when Anna gets back. She feels it in the dead air of the hallway, in the absence of fuss and clamour which has surrounded her since she arrived. Now she stands with her scarf in her hands, listening. Nothing, she can hear nothing. After the battering of the wind outside, Anna is glad of the sensation of blocked silence. She knows it won't last, and sure enough, as soon as the rush of the sea in her head dies away, there is noise again. She removes her coat and hangs it over the newel, angling her head to one side, like a bird detecting a threat. She goes first into the kitchen, where a radio is playing at an irritatingly low volume, and switches it off at the plug. Everything is orderly here; the dishes are stacked, a tea-towel has been hung to dry over the cooker. Two trays sit side by side on the counter, one with teacups on them, the other with three cocktail glasses. She picks one up and holds it to the light. It has a faded transfer of a fawn on it, and *Babycham* written in a blue swirl on the base. She remembers these from her childhood; they were brought out at Christmas, or for guests. They look vulgar now, slightly shabby. They don't belong here, she thinks, they belong there, in the old house. They belong *then*. Continuing the search for other noises, climbing the stairs and stopping to listen, she pauses to sit on the top step, putting her face to the uprights and peeping through them. The hall does remind her of the house they lived in when she was a child, with its wooden flooring and coloured glass in the door. She takes a deep breath and holds it, as if preparing to dive into the space below. Anna sees herself small and distant, falling through the air.

~ ~

The party hadn't begun, but Anna's mother told her that she had to go to bed. Anna was set to reason with her: it wasn't bedtime. It was far too early. It wasn't even *dark*. None of these logical arguments had any effect on her mother. She was wearing heavy perfume, a tight black dress and high heels; she was wearing her rings. Anna took her mother's hand as she was led upstairs, imagining the weight of those jewels on her own fingers.

It must be a very special party, said Anna, rolling her thumb over the surface of the rings, Is it Christmas?

No, said her mother, It's dad's work. His *colleagues,* she said, with a derisive catch in her voice, And yes, it's quite special for grown-ups—turning Anna at the bedroom door—But boring for little ones. Sleep is much more exciting.

Her mother wrinkled her nose as she said it. Anna knew the lie for what it was. She would have to strike a deal.

I'm sure I'll sleep better, she said, eyeing her mother from the pillow, If I could be *Modom.*

This made her mother smile. She sat at the side of the bed.

Okay. But only for a bit. I've got the drinks to do, she said, splaying her hands flat so that the rings glittered against the pale eiderdown.

Anna pondered the gemstones: her mother wore an assortment of large dress rings on her hands, two square ones on the left and an oblong and oval on the right. The oval looked pure and brilliant against her mother's olive skin, but Anna already knew it wasn't a real diamond, and discarded it. She didn't care for the square-cut rings, either, which were spoilt, in her eyes, by the fussiness of the settings.

87

I think I'll try . . . that one, she said, pointing at the one she always chose.

Ah, said her mother, The tourmaline. What a surprise.

Remembering her role in this game, she removed the large oblong from her finger and presented it to Anna.

An excellent choice. Would Modom care to try it for size?

Anna loved the whiteness of the metal, thick and flat as a belt, but she loved the stone more. The tourmaline was heavy, blue-green, and so clear, she could see her skin through it. She squeezed her fingers together to hold the ring in place.

I'd like to think about it, she said, in her madam voice, Leave it with me.

Her mother gave her a look; no messing around, it said, but just as she put her palm out to demand it back, the sound of the doorbell stopped her.

I'll be up in a minute. You can wear it 'til then.

But her mother didn't come up in a minute. Anna put the tourmaline to her eye and looked at how green the world was. She held it to her cheek and felt the cold stone grow warm. She pressed the imprint of a square into the back of her wrist. She licked it, tasting perfume, and ice, and what she imagined was the sea.

When she woke, hours later, the ring had slipped off her finger and down into the folds of the bedsheets. She had forgotten all about it by then: there was another thing, strange sounds—voices—that made her get out of bed and go onto the landing. It was dark and cold, but it would be alright: she could see her mother and father in the hall below. Framed in the leaded lights of the front door, they looked like figures in a stained-glass window. They chinked glasses softly, they kissed. Anna held her breath; she would like a drink too. She wanted to call out, but watching made her throat feel tight. At a sound from the dining-room, they pulled apart, her father's head jerking sideways so she could see his profile in a square of emerald-shine. As they bent towards each other again, her mother began to laugh. But it *wasn't* her mother's

laugh; it was low, and jittery, and the woman, in a long floating dress, didn't look like her mother; she was the wrong
shape, she had the wrong hair. As if she had broken a spell,
Anna found her voice, and called out, once: Mum. Her father jumped forward just as Anna pitched into the air, catching her as she tumbled down the final flight of stairs. She heard
a smash as he dropped his glass, and her own small scream of
shock. He carried her back up to her room, pulled the blankets over her. He put his fingers to his lips, laid them on her
head.

In the morning, there was no sign of the broken glass, even
though Anna remembered to look for it: just her mother on
her knees in the hallway, polishing the wooden floor, polishing and whistling a tuneless air.

~ ~

Anna pauses outside her mother's room, feeling again the taste
of tourmaline on her tongue. She can't recall how old she
was, or if that was the first time she'd seen her father do such
a thing. All the doors on this floor look the same, the woodwork painted in old cream, brass fittings in need of a polish.
Only the china name-plates are different, which her mother
had made up in deference to her favourite actresses: the Grable
Suite, the de Havilland Room, and her mother's own room—
her little joke—the Hayworth. On the second floor, the
names are of actors; Anna's room is Bogart, and across the
hall, Vernon inhabits the Cagney Suite. She finds this alloca-
tion strangely appropriate. There are two more rooms up a
final flight of stairs; a twin-bedded room, and the tiny one
she slept in on her first night. Both are vacant and unnamed,
their doors wide open to the world.

Anna can hear noises inside her mother's room, sounds of
a certain cadence, an electrical flatness, which tells her it's a
television left on. She knocks on the door and tries the handle
immediately. She has not been inside since her mother first
moved to Yarmouth, nearly ten years ago. Anna remembers

the wallpaper, although it wasn't on the wall, then. Her mother had got a catalogue from Laura Ashley and had been advised that Antique French was the style to go for: she loved things that sounded foreign and looked expensive, especially if they were half-price. This particular pattern, cod—Louis Quinze in prickly flock, was remnant stock.

Anna angles past the bed and turns the television off. There's hardly any space to move, the room's so crammed with furniture. Much of it she remembers: in the corner, there's a battered leather recliner which her father used to stretch out on after his day at work, stained on the arm-rest with pale, repeated circles. Anna traces them with her finger, feels a breathless pain at the proximity of him. She bends close to the head-rest, to find his smell, close enough to see the thin layer of dust. It's all in here, as if her mother couldn't bear to share it with anyone else: pictures and plates crowding the walls, china figures carrying a pitcher, or cuddling a dog. There's the heavy wardrobe with the ornate keys still in the locks; she's even kept the matted sheepskin rug which used to lie in front of the hearth. Now she's inside, Anna can't resist the temptation to pry. She would like to see her mother's rings again. Blocking the light from the window is the dressing-table, a mess of toiletries scattered around a mirrored box. This too she remembers from childhood. Everyone thought it was a great joke that when you lifted the lid, it played the tune from *The Godfather*. Anna's mother kept cigarettes in it, long thin sticks in rainbow colours, which she'd put in a holder and angle away from her body, blowing white plumes up to the ceiling. This is how Rita wanted to be seen, as the Hollywood actress she might have been.

Standing at the window with her fingers on the lid of the box, Anna looks down on to the street, and catches sight, now, of her mother. She is sitting in a wheelchair, with Vernon at her back; they're waiting to cross the road. She's wearing a beige overcoat and a Burberry scarf, a green tartan blanket over her legs, and brown lace-up bootees. Her hair is blowing straight up from her head. She and Vernon are squinting up at the house.

~

While Vernon stows the wheelchair under the stairs, Anna helps her mother into an armchair near the fire.

Are you cold, mum? she asks, Shall I light this fire?

Don't worry, Cabbage'll do it in a minute. Got myself some new glasses, says her mother, Look! We went to the mall. Eighteen pounds. What a bargain.

Did you get your eyes tested? asks Anna, trying to adjust the cushions, ignoring the way her mother jerks like a child away from her, Only you can't be too careful . . .

*At my age.* I'm only seventy, you know. No, we got them off the counter in Boots. They're only for seeing with. Will you stop fussing there? I'm quite comfortable.

Seventy-six, mother, says Anna, And you have to take more care of yourself. Get your doctor to give you a check-up.

Vernon stands in front of the mantelpiece and rubs his hands together, as if in anticipation of some delight. He's grinning at the pair of them. His waistcoat is yellow today, with a maroon fleur-de-lys motif running through it.

Shall I spark it up? he says, bending over the fire and pressing an ignition switch.

Oh, says Anna, I did wonder.

Just like the real thing, says her mother,

But without the mess, finishes Vernon.

He takes his place in a chair on the other side of the hearth, then jumps up immediately.

Ah! I nearly forgot, Marta's afternoon off. Shall I make some tea, or would you like something more . . . invigorating?

Anna's mother gives him a delighted smile.

Go on, Cabbage, she says, Invigorate me.

Anna takes the opportunity of Vernon's absence to sit in the vacated seat.

That's Vernon's chair, you know, says her mother, sensing a confrontation, He'll be back in a minute.

Anna's spirits had lifted after the walk on the beach, but now, with their performance about to begin again—Vernon hanging on every word, and her mother being so winsome— she can feel frustration blooming inside her.

Why am I here, mum? she says, sounding like an interrogator, What am I doing here?

Ah, the eternal questions, mocks her mother, Who am I? Why am I here?

No, I'm being serious, says Anna, Why do you want me here?

Her mother puts her head to one side, and looks at Anna through her new glasses. They are large ovals of transparent plastic, tinged with pink. Her eyes behind them are huge. Anna is reminded of Mr Magoo. After a few seconds of reflection, she wafts a hand in Anna's direction.

You're too serious, that's your trouble. You need to perk yourself up a bit. And I may be old and forgetful, but I seem to recall that you *wanted* to be here. Unless you're tired of us already?

Anna stares at her mother, unwilling to acknowledge the truth of this.

I do want to be with you, she says, But Yarmouth. It's so . . . *empty*.

Snatching her glasses off her face, her mother gives her an affronted look.

What do you mean, empty? Empty of what? What should it be full of?

Anna shrugs.

People? Things to do?

And you call yourself an *artist*. Have you seen that view? says her mother, pointing at the window, And there are plenty of things to do if you're bored with the scenery. You could go to the cinema, or, or the theatre—stop laughing, my girl, I'm serious!

Anna covers her mouth with her hand, but she still can't hide the smirk.

What's on at the theatre, then, mum? Ibsen? Chekhov? Is the RSC on tour? Or maybe something with a bit more *razzle dazzle?*

When was the last time you went to the theatre? her mother snaps, Seeing as London has so much to offer.

Anna falls silent; she was joking, but she can see she's caused real offence.

What I mean is—

When?

Anna hangs her head.

About three years ago. I find the acoustics difficult, she says.

I knew there'd be some excuse. You don't have to lecture me about Isbin and all that rot. I was simply making a suggestion. If you're really interested, Cabbage can fill you in. He's the theatre buff. You can exchange snobberies with him.

They sit in silence, listening to the steady click of the gas fire. Anna would like to cross the space between them, sit down on the rug in front of her mother, and lay her head on her knees. The image brings her up short: the time she could do that has passed. There will be no next time. She can't remember when she last embraced her mother, or was held by her. That time must be over, too.

S'getting dark, her mother says, Nights are drawing in. Cabbage'll pull those curtains in a minute.

Anna nods at her.

I know you don't like him, she continues, her voice growing so faint, Anna has to angle her head to hear, I know you don't *approve,* but he's a decent sort. He's not your father . . .

She exhales, a sleeping sigh, almost, her words trailing after each other,

. . . But he's alright. Really.

Her mother stares at the window in a benevolent, serene way.

Do you miss dad? Anna asks, holding her own breath.

Her mother says nothing; she's still staring, so Anna has to look over her shoulder, expecting a sight at the glass—a rare bird, a sudden fall of snow. It's only dusk creeping in. With her face turned away, it's easier for Anna to speak.

Do you, mum? Do you miss him?

Anna glances back for a reaction, just in time to see her mother come round. It's as if her spirit had left her body and has suddenly flown back in. The switch from blank to animated is uncanny.

Where's Cabbage? her mother says, Why are you sitting in his chair?

I'm here, says Vernon, standing at the door with a tray of drinks, I'm always here for you, dearest, you know that.

# FOURTEEN

At a place called Horsewater, Lewis decides to rest awhile.
He can guess why it's so named; there's nothing more to the
village than a few rendered cottages, a flint church standing
on a triangle of land, and a wide, shallow cut down to the
water—presumably the original drinking place for horses and
cattle. He crouches on the lip of the river-bank, creeping
closer to the edge until he gets used to the proximity of the
water running below him. He removes his shoes and socks,
takes a deep breath, and plunges his feet into the flow. It's so
cold, it burns after only a few seconds. Lewis looks at the water
for a long minute before taking the hand-wash out of his bag.
He pumps a few blobs of it into his palm and smears it over
his face. He has to bend quite low to get the foam off, soaking his clothes in his hurry to get away. When he opens his
eyes again, he sees the surface of the river, the flies hanging
in the sunlight, and a black swirl of weeds straggling in the
current. Manny would be wondering about him, worrying,
even. He pictures him, sitting alone in the living-room, smoking cigarettes, watching dramas with the sound down, waiting for the phone to ring. Or he'd be dragging the vacuum
cleaner over the carpets, drying his mug with a tea-towel;
keeping the place nice because Sylvie liked it that way, as if
she'd just popped out to the shops and would be back any
minute.

~ ~

Manny had his good blazer on and a pair of brown slacks. On his feet, cream-coloured loafers with a gold chain across the bar.

You look very dapper, said Lewis, Off down the precinct, are you? Spot of lap-dancing?

Manny grinned at him,

You and me, sunshine, are going for a liquid lunch. So get your pulling clobber on and be quick about it.

The Old Airport was a ten minute walk away, cut into a bank of red brick amenities which marked the end of the old estate and the beginning of the new one. It had a peeling poster outside advertising Kris's Karaoke night, and a Cantonese restaurant above it. On the bench in front of the pub, a man was slumped, his head on his chest and a can of lager nestled between his knees.

Look at the state of that, Manny whispered, nodding over at him, That's Son of Snobson. *Told* you. Off his trolley. Calls himself *Magic* Sam these days. Says he does healing—you'd have to be pretty desperate to let that article near you. Have to be at death's door.

Manny shook his head, but Lewis had already pulled away and was walking over to the bench. Close up, he could see that what he had thought was a paisley-patterned shirt was in fact bare skin, covered with intricate tattoos. The men exchanged a few words while Manny waited, holding the door open and sighing.

He was a good kid, said Lewis, Do anything for anyone. Seems alright to me.

The interior of the Old Airport gave no clue to its name, apart from a small clip-framed photograph of a biplane wedged between the optics. It was early enough in the day for them to be served without a wait, early enough for them to be the only customers in the bar. Lewis headed for a nearby table, but Manny caught his arm. He looked anxious as he levered him through a side door.

Thought we'd get a game of pool, he said, And bury a hatchet or two while we're at it.

Inside the room, under an oblong of white light, Carl and another man were in the middle of a game. A line of coins was neatly positioned on the edge of the table. Manny reached into his trouser pocket and added two more.

Mind if we joins you, lads? he said, putting his pint down on a table next to the window.

You'll know our Carl, he said.

Carl nodded once in Lewis's direction and then continued to line up his shot.

And this here's Gary Barrett. I believe you've already met.

Gary came round the table and held out his hand to Lewis.

No hard feelings, mate, he said, when Lewis shook it.

Barrett's tan was darker than Lewis remembered, and the goatee was newly shaved off, leaving a pale reminder around the mouth. He wore an earring that Lewis felt sure he wouldn't have forgotten; a large gold hoop; and had *Ich Dien* tattooed on his forearm in blue ink. It was the first afternoon the four of them spent together, and without incident, except for the phone calls Carl took on his mobile. Manny would have to have been blind not to notice Carl's to-ing and fro-ing to the toilet, but in the end he even joked about it; after the fifth call in as many minutes, he nudged Lewis.

I'm gonna get me one of them mobiles, Manny said, A proper baby-magnet.

Barrett laughed so hard at this, he choked on his beer.

*Babe*-magnet, Man, he said, You sounds like a paedo.

He repeated the joke to Carl on his return from the toilet.

Certainly is a hot-line, said Lewis, eyeing Carl steadily.

Carl stared back.

Business is booming, he said, and then, almost as an afterthought, added, I don't suppose you'd be interested in some spare dosh? Cash in hand, like? No strings?

Animated by this proposal, Barrett got to his feet, pointing his pool cue at Lewis.

Can you drive? he asked, and looking at Manny, Didn't you say he had a van?

Carl shifted back in his seat and stared at his shoes.

Shut up, Gaz, he said, I can drive myself.

Lewis tried to catch Manny's eye, but he avoided him, leaning back and grabbing hold of his pool cue and saying, I'll show you how it's done, Gaz, just rack 'em up.

Didn't realize I was so interesting, said Lewis, Can't have much round here to talk about, if I'm a topic.

My dad said you're a decorator, said Carl, I was thinking about this job I've got on. I could do with someone who knows how to make good, you know, decent tosh-up, like. We're doing a recce tomorrow, if you're interested.

Lewis said nothing, all the while watching Manny, but by now his face was closed. He busied himself chalking his cue, blowing on the tip, firing the white ball up and down the table until Barrett finished loading the triangle.

Look and learn, now, chaps, Manny said, bending under the light and taking aim.

~ ~

Lewis dries his feet with his socks, and rummages through his kitbag, looking for a clean pair. He forces himself back again to the last time he saw Carl. He'd dropped Manny off at Splott market, and picked up Barrett and Carl from Barrett's flat on Moorland Road. He sees the journey minutely: Carl is up front, while Barrett sits on the spare wheel in the back, sticking his blunt head between the front seats like an eager dog. He can't recall what was said; he could only be certain that he wouldn't have made small-talk with Carl. The job was about money, and only money. But this would have been the first time they'd been together in a vehicle since they were kids; something would have been said.

There's a patch of dead space in his head when he tries to picture arriving at the house; he can't see the driveway and he can't see the lake. But he knows that it's a heart-shaped lake and he knows there was mud on his boots. On his return to Manny's, he had a few drinks. He had a good few drinks. And Manny didn't ask about the decorating job, because— the idea comes sharp as a gash to Lewis—because Manny would have known that there was no job. Just a way of parting Lewis from his van. In fact, Manny had asked him nothing about anything; he *must* have known.

Emptying the coins from his pocket and counting out a handful of change, Lewis retraces his steps to the church. At the far end of the triangle, where a narrow track cuts away from the main road, is a red telephone box. Lewis has little hope of it working, but the inside smells of fresh disinfectant, and when he puts the receiver to his ear, there's a dial tone. He slots the coins in and punches in the number before he's had time to think of what he'll say. Manny answers on the second ring.

It's me, says Lewis.

Where are you, son?

Lewis stares straight ahead, at a waterlogged sheet of paper stuck behind a square of Perspex. The surface is covered with a frenzy of scratches.

I'm in a phone box, he says, smiling at himself.

Have you seen our Carl? asks Manny.

No, says Lewis, Haven't seen my van neither. Funny that.

Listen, son, Manny says, sounding breathless now, and so close, Lewis could put out a hand and touch him, Believe me, I don't know what he's up to.

He'll be doing a fun run, I expect, says Lewis, Where *exactly* over east, Manny? Where does your Sonia hang out?

This has got nothing to do with Sonia, says Manny, his voice raised, Just leave her out of it. You'll get your van back, I swear. On Sylvie's grave.

Lewis lets out a quick laugh.

I don't want the van back, Manny, I want my brother's bracelet back. Oh yeah—and I want your prodigal.

You're welcome to him, with knobs on, but I don't know nothing about a bracelet.

Lewis leans his head against the glass panel, contemplates the sky.

Where over east?

Let me meet you there, says Manny, his voice agitated, We'll sort out Carl together.

You're gonna meet me? Where? says Lewis.

There's silence, Manny's staggered breathing down the line, then the pips.

Son. Listen to me. Our Sonia's a good girl. She wouldn't—

I'll tell her when I see her, says Lewis, shouting as the pips grow louder in his ear, I'll tell her what a good girl she is. See you at the edge of the world, Man.

Lewis replaces the handset. He puts his fingers on the Perspex, tracing the names and obscenities like Braille.

# FIFTEEN

Whatever the brochures are in Vernon's hands, he makes a show of hiding them as soon as Anna enters the room. Like all his gestures, it's heavily staged, drawing attention to itself. Anna decides that if he can't behave normally around her, she'll just have to ignore him. But she waits in the doorway, unsure of what to do; clearly, they've been discussing something private. Her mother is leaning over to her left, almost lying across the chair, rubbing her hip and smiling sweetly at Vernon. Her face is bright pink and shining in the firelight. Vernon makes a fuss of putting the papers down by his side, exchanging a sly look with her. On a tray placed between them is a lone *Babycham* glass, a bottle of sweated gin, and a bowl of melting ice-cubes.

Would you care for a drink, Anna? he asks, lifting his own, full glass in salute, I'm afraid we started without you.

Like a pair of fire-dogs, says Anna, No thanks, Vernon, I'll wait until dinner.

What *is* for dinner? asks her mother, suddenly alert to a new idea.

Should I be making dinner? Anna cries, in a panic. It occurs to her that perhaps it's been mentioned at some point, and she's forgotten, or misunderstood. It's easily done, the way these two meander in their talk.

Of course not, says Vernon, Not unless you want to, that is. I usually make dinner at the weekends. We're having Welsh rarebit. You can just *relax*.

I'm not here to *relax,* Vernon, she says, aping his tone, I've come to help my mother. Apparently. So perhaps we can discuss what I should be doing, now we're all together. I wouldn't like to get in the way.

Her mother makes a waving motion in the air.

Oh, Deanna, give it a rest! Tell her, Cabbage, tell her to cheer up. You don't have to do anything. Just keep me company.

You've got Vernon for company, argues Anna, and sees out of the corner of her eye Vernon's head doing a satisfied wobble as she says it.

I want you *here,* says her mother, pressing her finger into the arm of her chair, As I was just saying to Cabbage, it's not as if you've got anything to go back to. Not as if you've got a *boyfriend*.

Her mother makes to get up, and then, remembering her infirmity, sits back again and pats the seat beside her. Close up, the bruises on her face are more livid, blossomed from the gin and heat of the fire.

And? asks Anna.

And? And so, while you're here, enjoy yourself. We worry about you, you know. Down there in London, all lonely. Who knows, you might even meet someone. A nice divorcé, or a widower. You can't be looking for unmarried men at your age. Bound to be something wrong with them.

Anna glances over to Vernon, who seems totally absorbed with the olive in his glass.

We can go out together, Anna, finishes her mother, *On the pull.*

As she says it, she starts to giggle. It's clear that her mother is already quite drunk, and that it won't be long before the conversation reverts to its inevitable template; first the reminiscences, closely followed by regrets, then tears. Anna understands the kind of drunk her mother is, and how quickly it all goes bad.

That's a great idea, says Anna, Let's go on the pull. We can hang out round the clock tower, get a few bottles of cider down us, and go for a *spin* with the local lads. We might land ourselves a real catch.

Anna's mother shoots Vernon a look.

You see? She's terribly stuck-up. Always has been. I think she must have got it from her father. He was such an awful snoot, my Len. Do you know, Cabbage, he wouldn't call me Rita in company?

Vernon shakes his head in wonder at this revelation.

He'd call me Darling. How silly is that? He said Rita sounded common. And serviettes were napkins, the toilet was the lavatory. What a rotten snob!

I think you've had enough, mum, says Anna, appalled at hearing this, and in front of Vernon, who strikes Anna as the biggest snob she's ever met.

He used to say that too. You're a proper little chip off the old block, Deanna. Sour-faced killjoy . . .

Her glass tips gently to one side, the gin splashing over the rim, then spilling in a long line onto the carpet. Her face takes on the same vacant look Anna saw earlier.

Time for a snooze, I think, says Vernon, leaning forward to save the glass. They both help her up to a standing position, but she squirms away from them.

Don't manhandle me, she says, I can manage!

Anna holds her mother's elbow as she inches her way up the stairs, lifting her right leg with her free hand, positioning it on the next tread, before easing herself up on her left.

Like Jake the bloody Peg, her mother says, cackling into her shoulder, You should let me do it my way!

Your way? asks Anna, raising an eyebrow, Go on then.

Her mother nudges Anna out of her way, and bending over, puts her weight on her hands. She crawls up the flight on all fours, stopping to catch her breath at the top of the landing.

Howzat! she cries, triumphant.

Just as well there aren't any guests, says Anna, stepping up behind her, You look like a bat.

An old bat, says her mother, That's right, you be cruel. See if I care.

~

Once Anna has got her mother to lie down, she makes her way back to the Nelson Suite. A close darkness has settled in the hall and the dining-room, giving the house a gloomy feel. Now, she could have that drink.

I don't know what to do for the best, Vernon, she says, as a way of beginning.

He's standing in front of her, fingering the pockets of his waistcoat like a naughty child: she's not at all clear of how she will phrase what she has to say, only that something needs to be said. He sits back down, gesturing to Anna to take the other chair.

I'm clueless, he agrees, frowning at a piece of fluff he's found, But all ears. Fire away.

I don't think it's such a great idea, the drinking. Do you? she asks, It can't be good for her. Especially with the medication she's on.

Vernon puts his chin on his chest and takes a deep breath. He starts to say one thing, then stops himself, running his hand over his head to flatten the stray hairs.

We always have a sherbet or two in the p.m., he says, in a piqued tone, Oils the engine, you know. We find it quite acceptable.

Anna stares at him. It's not so much his appearance she dislikes, it's this way he has of talking, as if he's auditioning for a part in a play.

But she's not well, is she? She should be taking it easy. She should be resting.

Not too much excitement for the old girl, is that it? A trip to the shops, a couple of gins—it could kill her! he says, his eyes wide and mocking.

Well, yes, says Anna, finding her way through his antagonism, Why go to the shops today? It's freezing cold out there—it's blowing a gale.

We would have asked you to come with us, says Vernon, smiling oddly, She wanted you to. But you'd gone out on your own, vanished into thin air.

He says it with a rising tone, as if he could make it happen simply by conjuring the right voice. Anna recognizes his petulance: she's being called on to explain herself.

I've come here—I've been summoned here, to look after her—

Vernon cuts the air with his finger,

No one *summoned* you, Anna, the choice was yours, was it not? I merely thought you would like to be kept informed of her state of health. Perhaps your conscience is playing tricks on you.

I don't have a guilty conscience, she says, feeling the heat of the lie, I just want to do what's right. And for that, I need some support.

Leaning across to switch on the table-lamp, Vernon is calm again, his voice low.

And your mother needed new glasses, he says, straightening up, She can't see a thing without them. Bumps into the furniture. Or did you not notice that small detail?

Anna understands that this gesture—the switching on of a lamp—is something he automatically does, as does anyone in their own home: an action that requires no thought. It isn't meant as a slight, but his proprietorial air makes her furious. Vernon knows all there is to know about this house and her mother, what she likes to do, and when. It has the precision and regulation of a life *well-oiled,* and she is fluttering around

behind them. Behind *him*. And now, because she has misman-
aged the whole conversation, he's on the attack.

I have been looking after your mother—Vernon continues
—And she me, let's not forget that, she has looked after me,
too, for nearly ten years. I think we've managed pretty well
so far.

Do you pay my mother rent, Vernon?

Slowly, he eases himself out of the chair, looking up from
his brogues and directly into her face. Stage left, she thinks.
Here's the big speech.

It's probably none of your business, he says, mildly, But as
a matter of fact, I do. Anything else?

Else?

Anything else you'd like to know, only I usually take a
nap myself before dinner—if that meets with your approval.

Anna blinks hard. Is there anything else? She's finding it difficult now to fathom what it was she wanted to say. She didn't
start out to make an enemy, but she can't see a way back.

Are you two an item? she asks, sounding ridiculous. Even
Vernon laughs at this.

Ah, he says, You'd like that, wouldn't you? Another stick
to beat her with. That's not really any of your business either, is it? But we have been thinking of a holiday, if that
makes us an *item*. You gave her the idea, you know; she's
very taken with your suggestion of a short break. Just not very
taken with being cooped up in your flat.

Vernon pauses, staring at her with a round-eyed, innocent look.

Then I'll go with her, says Anna, As I've apparently nothing better to do.

He bends down behind the chair and pulls up the stash of
brochures. Holding them out to her, he smiles broadly.

We so hoped you would, he says, Somewhere warm, we
thought—for her arthritis. We picked up the brochures today,
only you seemed in such a brown study earlier, Rita said not

to mention it. I've marked the places. We thought Crete might be nice at this time of year.

He pauses at the door, turning to deliver his final line, before leaving her alone.

Rita will absolutely love it. An excursion *en famille*.

*Sur mon corps,* whispers Anna, to the empty room.

# SIXTEEN

At the booth inside the Fun Palace on Yarmouth promenade, Lewis gets ten pounds' worth of change. His skin smells of hostel, and a greasy slick coats the roof of his mouth. He shouldn't have had that breakfast; he can feel the fat bubbling in his stomach, and the taste of burnt coffee on his tongue. He thinks he knows what will cure him. The coins in his hands are warm and sweaty, the thought of what he will do with them makes his jaw set tight. This is how it feels at the beginning—a magnesium flare in his blood; at this point, the end is never a consideration. He positions himself in front of the Super Sweeper penny-falls, and rolls the two-pence pieces into the slot, mechanically, one after the other until his hand is empty. He hasn't lost the technique; he believes the faster he gets rid of the coins, the more chance he has of winning. After a while, the automatic gesture becomes part of him again, like blinking, like taking a breath.

Lewis graduates his gambling: two-pence, ten-pence, fifty, a pound, working up from the penny-falls to the whirling, flashing fruit machines. He began to play seriously as a teenager, him and his brother Wayne bunking off school and getting the train to Barry Island, where they were less likely to be seen by anyone they knew. Wayne would initiate the trip, and then spoil the day; wanting to pick up some girls, or chance their luck in a pub, or get into a fight. And it was

Wayne who insisted that they should take his mate Carl with them, show him how to work the machines.

As Lewis pumps the coins into the slot, it's not Carl Finn he's thinking of, but his brother. It's Wayne he's remembering, and Wayne he's trying to forget: the green eyes lit up in the flickering glass are his brother's eyes, and the sound of the coins falling in a rush into the tray below is his sudden, mocking laughter.

~ ~

That face will get you into bother, she said, so that Lewis could almost believe she was flirting with him. She was Miss Hepple, and he was in love; and Wayne had to go and spoil it.

She wore long tasselled skirts and embroidered blouses with the top two buttons undone. According to the other boys, she smoked hooky cigarettes in the store-cupboard. She was the art teacher, and the first time Lewis saw her, she had a tidemark of purple paint, from wrist to elbow, that he couldn't take his eyes off. Every time she raised her hand to write something on the board, or smooth back her long brown hair, he saw it. He needed to keep checking after that, and was pleased to find that she almost always had marks of various colours halfway up her arms. Wayne said her first name was Valerie; she'd told him so herself. Lewis could believe this was true. Although he looked much older than his brother, a foot taller, nearly, and broad to Wayne's narrow frame, it was Wayne who was blessed with charm. Lewis had inherited features he presumed belonged to his father: a downward, brooding curve to his mouth, a suggestion of surliness. Wayne, thirty minutes younger, was fairer skinned from birth and remained so, and his mouth was wide, laughing, full of crooked teeth, just like his mother. The boys shared their father's eyes, she'd told them once; green with irregular hazel flecks. According to her, they had inherited other traits from their mysterious father: Wayne had words at his disposal, many of them, and was quick with his hands, despite the tremor. That wasn't inherited, she said; that was down to lack of oxygen. Lewis had taken up too much space in the womb, and too much time being born. He gathered from this that he had inherited his father's selfishness.

At secondary school, they were separated into different streams; Wayne would get easily bored, his mother said, but Lewis would get on well enough if left to his own devices. Which is how Wayne eventually came to be in Carl Finn's class, sinking like a stone to the bottom. Remedial, they called it, although, if anything, the boys in the group were too forward, too full of everything. Lewis wasn't surprised that Wayne knew Miss Hepple's first name. He wouldn't have been surprised if Wayne had tried it on with her; he'd certainly got more than his fair share of girlfriends. At fourteen, Lewis hadn't kissed anyone.

It took him two months before he got up enough courage to stay behind at break-time and ask if he could help her tidy up. It had been snowing; out in the playground, the boys would be having fights. Wayne had spent that morning assembly passing notes, trying to organize a battle with some other lads in Lewis's stream: he'd written Snobs v Sharks on the sheet, and you were supposed to sign up. Carl Finn and Sam Robson had put their names underneath Wayne's, but Lewis was happy to have a reason not to take part. Sam was alright, he thought, but he'd already had enough of Carl, and his effect on Wayne. He didn't like the way the two of them egged each other on. Wayne could find trouble in an empty room; he didn't need Carl to encourage him.

Miss Hepple showed Lewis how to pile all the colour palettes into the sink, running the tap until they sank. Some of the paint hadn't been mixed properly, and pockets of powder bloomed to the surface. The water swirled green and blue and red, black spiralling through yellow. He put his hand in and pulled it out again immediately; it was freezing cold.

Just rinse them, she said, You don't want to be stuck in here all break-time.

She leaned over him to dig out a block of soap from a cardboard box on the windowsill. Her smell was sweet and bitter, like biting into orange peel. It made Lewis's tongue tingle.

And don't forget to wash your hands afterwards, she said, her face so close to his, he could see the pores of her skin.

Later, when he looked at his arm, trying not to think about the cane coming down on his palm, he saw, running from wrist to elbow, the marks of a rainbow.

It was Wayne's idea of a joke. Lewis found him at the edge of the playground, with Carl and Sam. They had their jumpers pulled halfway up, and were carrying something in the folds.

What's going on? He shouted, chasing Wayne's back. His damp hands were stinging in the air, the knuckles bright red. His brother was laughing and out of breath. Over-exciting himself, his mother would say, if she could see him. He followed them round the corner, and understood what they'd been doing. On the car park adjoining the football pitch was Miss Hepple's 2CV. The car park itself had been cleared of snow, but it didn't stop the boys finding some: the driver's seat was full of it. They'd undone the poppers on the flap, and had been piling it in through the sun-roof.

We're going to fill it up, c'mon! shouted Wayne.

She'll shit herself when she sees it, said Carl, piling more snow into the gap.

Whose is it? Asked Lewis, although he already knew. There was a hot feeling in his chest.

Come *on,* said Wayne, You're such a chicken!

As he flashed a look at him, Lewis saw his eyes, sharp as the sun on the snow, shining too bright, and knew what was going to happen. In a slow second, Wayne paused, looked troubled, as if he'd got something stuck at the back of his neck, had been hooked on an invisible line. He let his hands drop, jerked once sideways, then sank to the ground. Lewis was ready for this. He cleared a space around his brother and let him make his own particular shape in the snow. Carl stood still, amazed at the sight unfolding, but Sam had run for help. He came back with the teacher on duty.

It was Wayne's idea of a joke, but it was Lewis who paid the price, standing with Carl and Sam in the headmaster's office. He had only ever seen the headmaster on stage in assembly, or the back of him as he disappeared into his office. Everyone feared him, because of the rumours of his time spent as a governor of a Borstal, but it was common knowledge that no one got caned any more. Now he was close-up, Lewis could see he was shorter than he looked on the stage, with a pink face and a rill of shimmering sweat along his hairline. He gave them a lecture, and as the three boys began to relax, he searched in a cupboard behind his desk, and pulled out a thin strip of wood.

Lewis worried about Wayne, who had been taken to the sick-bay, and then driven home. Counting the strokes—one, two, waiting for three—he hoped their mother would be back from work. He wondered if Wayne would tell her what had happened. Lewis's palm was turning pink now from the thin whip of the wood. At three strokes, he wondered if anyone had removed the snow from the inside of the car, or whether it would be slowly turning to liquid, soaking into the fabric of the seat, dripping into the footwell. He wondered whether Miss Hepple would ever trust him again.

You can put your hand away now, the headmaster said to Lewis, Unless you'd like another three?

Lewis looked up and saw that the caning was finished.

What do you say? This to Carl.

Thank you, sir.

The headmaster repeated the question to Sam, who also thanked him, and then to Lewis, who said nothing.

The two other boys, holding their left hands in their right as if to press the pain away, were staring at him as if he too were about to fall down in a fit. He hadn't felt the caning at all, but here was the proof, coming up red across the centre of his palm, blue-edged along the thin web of skin between finger and thumb.

What do you say? The headmaster repeated.

Lewis couldn't trust his mouth.

He says, thank you, sir, said Sam, shooting a glance at Lewis, He's lost his voice, sir.

The headmaster turned on Sam in a swift rage.

Are you trying? To be funny?

Sam, brave despite the threat, shook his head.

No, sir! It was the shouting, sir. He was shouting for help. For his brother.

The three of them marched back down the stairs in silence. It was Sam who broke it.

He would've done you again, he said, He's a sadist.

Lewis nodded. He wanted to say something to Sam, to thank him, but knew better than to do it in front of Carl, who was walking between them, breathing heavily through his mouth. His skin looked green in the ceiling lights of the corridor, the muscles in his face working as if he were chewing gum. Finally, he spoke.

Tell your fucking spaz of a brother he's in deep shit, he said, raising his palm to emphasize the point, Tell him he owes me.

# SEVENTEEN

Anna paces the car park. She counts forty-two steps to the door of the Little Chef, and turns about; thirty more steps take her to the massive grey dump-bins pushed against the fence, another fifty-one back to the car. It's a blustery morning; the wind carries intermittent sheets of rain. Squall, her mother called it, when she said goodbye to Anna this morning.

You'll need a mac if you're going out in that squall, she shouted, Shall I lend you mine?

Her mother was standing at the top step, hanging on to the edge of the door. She was wearing a moth-eaten towelling robe, and her hair was stuck up from her pink scalp in wayward tufts. Her bare feet looked blue.

Go on in, mum, it's freezing, she called back, You've got no slippers on!

As she made to drive off, Anna felt a flare of embarrassment: she was back at her first day at secondary school, and there was her mother, standing at a different door on a busy street, shouting, Mind the road, Anna, watch out for the traffic.

The same cry again today:

Watch out for the traffic, that A11's a bloody death-trap!

Except back then, her mother wouldn't be seen in public without full make-up on. Over twenty-five years later, and now even her bare feet are acceptable.

There are four cars parked near the entrance, but none of them belongs to Brendan. As soon as she arrived, Anna went inside to make sure he hadn't got there before her. She stood at the Please Wait to Be Seated stand and craned her head over the banquettes. Two family groups sat at either end of the room, as distant from each other as physically possible. A lone diner watched a television high overhead in the far corner. Outside again, Anna went across to the petrol station and bought ten cigarettes and a box of matches. She sat on a low wall and lit one, pulling her mother's coat round her, scraping her feet along the mud slick at the side of the verge, waiting.

She's still trying to smoke it when Brendan arrives, screeching to a halt in the middle of the car park and jumping out of the car. He fetches a large bag from the boot, which he slings over his shoulder. As he approaches her, laughing, he pretends to fall over with the weight of it. When he reaches Anna, he pulls her close into his body. From a distance, they could be taken for lovers. She presses her face against his shoulder; he smells of warmth and the city. She wants to stay right there as she is, breathing him in, but he pushes her backwards and holds her at arm's length.

You look great, he says, That sea air's doing you good.

Whether it's his jovial tone, or the fact of seeing him, Anna can't tell: it's too late to stop the tears. He wraps an arm round her and guides her towards the entrance. His pace matches hers exactly.

Nice raincoat, he says, as they take a window-seat, Is that what passes for fashion, then, in Yarmouth?

A man in a suit on the opposite table turns his head from the television screen to examine Anna. When she stares back at him, he smiles and looks away.

It's my mum's, she says, feeling the tears falling again.

If I'd known I was going to get this sort of reception, I wouldn't have bothered coming, says Brendan, I usually make women laugh. Not cry.

I'm sorry to drag you up here, she says, pulling a paper napkin from the dispenser and blowing into it, But I couldn't face the whole trip down there and then the whole trip back again.

That's plain enough, he says, keeping his eyes on her, I'm surprised you got this far. What's happened?

Anna tilts her face to the window, thinking of an answer. It's fogged with steam, and someone has wiped a circle in the centre, which is re-misting; the cars on the forecourt look as if they're melting. She would like to give Brendan an explanation, a dramatic tale, but she can find nothing.

Is it your mother? he asks, Is she worse?

No. She's fine. She's fit as a fucking flea, actually, she says, so loudly that the waitress approaching them with the menus turns on her heel and walks quickly away again. Anna and Brendan look at each other, shamefaced.

That's it, y'know, B, it's so tedious being with them, with their singing and cavorting and the way they

Finish each other's sentences.

Exactly, she says, smiling with relief.

Brendan holds his hand up to stop her, leaves the table, and finds the waitress. Anna can't hear what he's saying, but she lip-reads an apology, and some extensive flirting behaviour that she's seen many times before.

It's what parents are for, though. To drive you mad, he says, carrying on exactly where they left off, You can't stand being with them for a minute, but you love them to bits from afar.

I don't love Cabbage to bits, she says.

You what? asks Brendan, giving her his full attention.

That's what my mother calls him, says Anna, Your famous Vernon Savoy. She calls him Cabbage.

Brendan mock-swoons.

She is actually perfect, your mother. So how come she's let you out? I don't see any ball and chain.

She's a sweetie, really, says Anna, Bad-tempered, foul-mouthed, scheming—but still my mother. But she has her ways, Brendan. These chains are invisible.

Anna crosses her wrists on the table to show Brendan her imaginary shackles. He wraps his hands around hers and pulls her close.

I brought your stuff. Well, most of it. What I could track down.

He rummages on the floor beneath him and pulls up the bag, lifting it for Anna to take.

All there, I think. I had a hell of a job finding your passport. Under that bed, he says, pointing a warning finger at Anna, Are unknown terrors.

Did you pack my bathers?

Bathers! What are you like? Your *swimsuit* and flip-flops and beach towel and that rag you describe as a sun-dress—Brendan closes his eyes in distaste—Are all there.

Anna opens the bag and looks through it, pulling out a length of tie-dyed silk.

This isn't mine, she says.

It is now. It's a present. Call me psychic, but I thought you might just be going on a beach holiday. And that's a sarong. It's what normal people wear on the beach. *Not* a fleece.

Well, here, she says, rummaging in her pocket and drawing out the pack of cigarettes, I didn't get you anything. But you could have these?

Ahh, nearly new, says Brendan, And my second favourite brand. Thank you. So, what's the destination?

We're going, she says, To Crete. But what if it's cold? I'll need my fleece.

Does it get very cold, then, in Crete? In October? And who's we?

Me and my mother. And unless I can stop him, Vernon frigging Cabbage.

At the mention of his name, her mouth turns down again. She hangs her head, staring into the depths of her bag.

I can't go if Vernon goes, Brendan. I swear, I'll do something . . . irrational.

That'll be a first, he says, Not like you to do something irrational. Remember Joseph? Did he have two wives, or three? Now he *was* a bad choice. And that one with the piercings and all the cats?

Anna shudders.

Don't remind me. And my mother keeps banging on about me not having a boyfriend. If she only knew.

Brendan straightens an imaginary tie.

I could be your boyfriend, he says, Just say the word.

Anna isn't listening. She's gone back to a year ago, to a flat stinking of antiseptic and a bedful of cat hair. There was more cat hair on the furniture and on her clothes; slippery boluses of grey matter on the worktops or behind the curtains, and wherever she trod, sharp granules of cat litter. Roman, as he called himself, was tattooed and idle, and stuck all over with ornate pieces of bright metal. A new piercing every week.

That *particular* choice, she says, not wanting to say his name, Had more holes than a pin cushion.

Brendan grins.

But you weren't to know, Anna. Well, not at first. And lots of people actually *like* body art. And let's face it, you're not the tidiest person in the world, he says.

He's about to launch into another anecdote when he sees her face creasing up. Anna pulls another napkin from the dispenser.

You said it, B: I make bad choices.

Don't start that again. You just need to get out more, he says, And I mean that in the nicest possible way. Any man would be lucky to have you. Even in that flasher's mac.

The compliment is fleeting: Brendan smiles broadly over the top of her head, to the waitress bringing coffee and pancakes.

Go back and tell your mother you'll only go if Vernon *stays,* he says, holding up a sliver of pancake to her mouth, That's what you need to do. Tell her you want some quality time with her alone. Two girls together and all that claptrap. She'll buy it, he says, Trust me.

He takes another forkful, feeding himself this time. Still chewing, he says,

And as you're never going to have me, can I suggest that I'm allowed to vet the next man you decide to fall in love with. Are we agreed?

Agreed, she says, But there's not going to be any *next man*, Brendan. I'm done with them for good. I'm going to take up a hobby; something safe. Something really dull.

Fly fishing? He offers

Too many men about.

Macramé?

Anna puts her head on one side as if considering the suggestion.

I quite like the sound of macramé.

Bell ringing?

Bell ringing, she says, Now what could be duller than that?

~ ~ ~

Lewis rests his head against the side of the fruit machine, his hand poised over the slot; he's listening for backing. If he can hear the coin drop, then the hopper will be full. He knows this can be a good sign—he's been watching this machine for a while, and it hasn't paid out—but the music is so loud, and the other machines are making so much noise, he knows he hasn't got a hope. He loses the pound in three swift hits of the button. Not a single hold.

Pulling another ten-pound note from his wallet, he queues at the booth for more change. *It's not the winning that matters, it's the taking apart.* It became Wayne's catchphrase. After they'd lost their paper round money, Wayne would look for something to vent his rage on; bus shelters were good, for the tremendous shock wave of noise the glass made before it shattered into a million tiny squares, or kicking off wing-mirrors in the car park behind the supermarket, or dropping bottles off the cliff edge and watching them explode like bombs onto the concrete path below. Changing his mind, Lewis pockets the money and turns away from the booth.

Outside the Fun Palace, the sky has darkened and the wind has come up, not as cold now, but carrying a threat of rain. Lewis sits in a shelter facing the sea and returns the note to his wallet. As he does every time, he sees the top edge of the photograph he keeps at the back, just the sharp white rebate, and a hint of a head. He doesn't need to look at it. The picture is of himself and Wayne as pageboys.

You can run away to the end of the earth, his mother said, But you can't run away from love.

Errol moved back in with them a week after the fight (which his mother would always insist was an accident), and they were engaged the following month. They got married on Bonfire Night. By Christmas, Wayne had had his first grand mal.

In the photograph, Errol and his mother are wearing matching beige outfits, with the boys on either side of them, awkward in their suits. Wayne's got the sleeves of his jacket rolled up like Don Johnson; the bracelet on his left wrist catches the sunlight. Errol's sweating and grinning: his moustache has gone and his head is shaved, so he looks for all the world like a buttered new potato. Lewis's mother is holding her hand up to show off her ring—a thick gold hoop jammed solid with a row of gemstones: an eternity ring, bought instead of an engagement ring because they were in it for eternity, she said, and eternity means Forever. Her little finger is smaller than it used to be, and cocked a bit to the left. Apart from that, and the missing nail, no one would ever know. Manny was wrong about them sewing it back on; they said it wasn't worth it, just the tip. And Lewis realized that his mother was wrong about eternity: it doesn't last forever, it only seems that way. Errol was gone by Easter.

Lewis doesn't need to look at the photograph, because he knows every minute detail of it. And he doesn't keep it out of fond memories, nor as a souvenir of how things used to be. He keeps it because it's the only picture he has of Wayne. By the summer, his brother was dead.

# EIGHTEEN

Anna finds her mother at the back of the house. Despite the chill in the air and the drizzle, the French windows are open. Standing quite still in the fading light, her mother appears not to notice her. Every now and then she'll say something to herself, soft cooing noises that have no meaning. They remind Anna of long ago; the sounds are comforting, warm.

My little dove, says her mother, without moving, Have you flown back in?

She turns to smile at Anna.

So you have, she says.

Anna would stay in the doorway, but her mother beckons her over.

I don't want to disturb you, she whispers.

Not disturbing, her mother says, But watch, now—they're stocking up for night-time. Listen to that!

At the far end of the garden, beyond the long wooden bench and the jumble of terracotta pots, are two large bird-tables. Black shapes arrow on the dusk, shadows dip and weave in and out of the trees. Anna turns her head to hear a flurry of twittering and chirping, almost an angry sound.

Are they fighting? she asks.

Her mother gives a silent laugh.

Trust you to think that. They're telling each other, I'm going to bed!—and, I live here!—and, This is my branch, this is!

So they *are* fighting.

Her mother catches hold of Anna's coat and leans into her.

How's your friend? she asks.

He's fine, says Anna, He said to say hello.

They stand and watch in silence for a moment.

You should invite him up, her mother says, It would be nice to meet him.

He's not really that sort of friend, mum.

Who says so? You? Or him?

It's complicated.

Her mother sighs, and Anna waits, expecting her to say, It always is, with you. Instead, she says nothing for a moment, so Anna becomes more aware of the fingers gripping her coat, and her own hand on her mother's arm, and the fine rain blowing in around them. She looks at the side of her mother's face; at her eyes, bright against the darkness. This would be a good time to take Brendan's advice.

He's heard of Cabb– Vernon, says Anna, easing her way into the subject, You didn't tell me he was famous. Or that he had a dummy for a partner.

Walter, says her mother, That's what he called it. They were quite big at one time. Walter had a stutter; it was so funny. You couldn't get away with it now, of course. But to be honest, he wasn't very good in the end. His mouth went a bit funny.

Who? asks Anna, not quite following, Vernon, or the dummy?

Vernon, you daft girl! That's why he grew that moustache. He'd go mad if he heard you calling Walter a dummy. He was his *partner*. Ventriloquism, she says, through pressed lips, Is an art form.

They both laugh out loud, making the birds flitter off the tables into the trees.

Aren't you cold? Anna asks.

Not for long, eh? Soon be on the beach. Soon be getting a tan.

She turns at last to look at Anna.

I've told Cabbage he can't come, by the way.

The relief is so immense, Anna feels as though she could kiss her. She puts a hand up to waft away a stray hair on her mother's head. She would like to kiss her, to hug her; she almost does.

Don't get silly, her mother says, turning back into the room, I've not given in to you. It's just that he's got to stay here and look after our guest.

You've got a guest? says Anna, unable to keep the disbelief out of her voice, A proper, staying guest?

Yes, proper and staying. And paying too, I hope. He's in the dining-room now if you want to go and say hello. His name's Mr Caine, she says, delighted with the fact, But he's much more handsome than the real one.

Her mother twinkles at her, then frowns, flicks an invisible speck from Anna's lapel, and finally takes a step back in order to look her up and down. It's a ritual Anna dreads.

Sight of them, says her mother, Your father would've hated that.

Anna follows her gaze down to her shoes; the leather is scuffed and dull and the edges are caked with mud.

Why don't you go upstairs and make yourself a bit more presentable first, she says, Comb your hair and that?

~

It's always the bloody same. Nothing's changed, nothing ever will.

Anna talks to herself in the mirror as she drags the comb across her head,

She has to go and spoil it. Every single time.

Anna keeps her memories of her father under water. She doesn't know how long after he died that she started to do this, or if it's normal, even, but she understands and in some way approves of the simplicity of the connection; her father died at the age when she began to learn to swim.

~ ~

On Saturday mornings, he'd sit at the turn of the stairs in his socks, and polish all the shoes. Under the sink he kept an old orange-crate, filled with Kiwi and Cherry Blossom, outgrown clothes cut into neat squares, yellow dusters with huge black finger dints, and two kissing brushes for the final shine. He'd start big and end small, the same every time, which meant that Anna would have to wait, one leg snaked around the other, for the moment when she could slip her feet into her red sandals. He'd bend over to do the buckles for her; he always sounded out of breath.

Years later, when her mother decided to move to Yarmouth, Anna helped her pack up. She found his relics buried beneath another, newer, box under the sink. She sat where he had sat, and examined the rusted Kiwi tin with the polish cracked and dry, a fragment of a dress she wore as a child, a piece of her mother's apron, the remnants of his old striped shirt. Holding a yellow duster to the light, she found his fingermarks. She put her own finger against the smudges, and saw him again, on Saturday mornings, sitting at the turn of the stairs, in his socks.

Her mother wanted all that thrown out. She liked the convenience of the new products. She didn't like the dusters and the smell of polish and perhaps she didn't like the memory. So Anna did as she was asked, stamping on the edge of the box until it broke into splinters, throwing the kissing brushes on top of it, and the tins, and the cloth with his fingermarks; tipping it all in the bin for the dustmen to take away.

~ ~

With her hair combed and a change of shoes, Anna stands in the doorway of the dining-room, rubbing her palms down the sides of her jeans. Vernon's broad tartan back is the first thing she sees, his hands gripping the edge of the far table, his body swaying over it like a drunk in a bar. She can't see round him, but she can tell he's trying to be amusing, relating some anecdote he thinks is funny. Her mother plays a flourish at the piano, craning her neck at the assembled group like a Salvation Army band leader summoning the troops. On cue, Vernon throws his arms wide and claps his hands together.

A song, Rita, that would be marvellous!

Marta comes into the frame now, budging Anna out of the way. She moves towards the group with a tray full with food: soup, mounds of cut bread, and cheese. The man will be expected to eat surrounded by these watchful eyes, amid the singing and piano playing and general clamour. Anna can hardly bear to look. She hangs back at the edge of the frame, dead still, mouth open, feeling a deep burn of embarrassment creeping up her neck. It's just like being a child again, called on to perform. Marta is no better: smiling and wiping her forehead with the back of her hand, as if to say, It was a huge effort, this heating up of soup and slicing bread, but worthwhile, because, look, we have a guest! As Vernon edges past, Anna sees the man sitting at the table, catches his eyes and the look he gives her—a desperate appeal, frightened, almost— and she turns away.

~

She spent the evening in her room, lying on the bed. She tried to tell herself that her sense of embarrassment was out of proportion; all she had to do was go in and shake his hand, make an effort to disperse the crowd. It would have been an easy, sociable act, and a kindness: if it were not for the man himself, the sight of him there. He wore an expression on his face which stopped her breath. From the first glance, Anna saw it: a look of desolation which couldn't be combed out or polished off. She understood in that second how they shared this quality. So she ran away. It seemed the only option, but it mortified her still.

As the evening drew on, the shame didn't leave her, it just grew more intense, until Anna had convinced herself that not only was she completely inept, but a few days with her mother had already sent her hysterical. Worse, she was hiding in her room like a sulky teenager. Brendan's voice came back to haunt her: You need to get out more. If only he were here. Brendan knew how to make people feel at ease; he always made things look so smooth and easy.

From below came the sound of singing, raucous laughter, clinking glasses. Too late now to make an entrance; there'd be questions, wry looks from her mother, some witty crack from Vernon. Sulky teenager or not, Anna decided she'd rather stay put.

At last, she hears the sound of Vernon's unsteady footsteps on the stairs. She sits on the end of the bed, watches the strip of light under the door flicker as he passes, hears the door to his own room, opening and closing. There's another sound, as if he's clearing his throat, then a faint rush of water. Anna pulls on her mother's raincoat and steps onto the landing. Everything is quiet below. In the dimmed light from the hall, she negotiates the stairs like a prowler, moving swiftly through the French windows and out into the garden. The night is thick as a bag. She stumbles, banging her toe against the edge of the bench and muffling a yell. Feeling her way onto it, wiping off a slick of water with her hand, Anna sits on the edge. She searches for the cigarettes in her pocket, then lets out a groan as she realizes she gave them to Brendan. She finds her mobile and jabs at the keypad. When she hears the message—her own wavering voice telling her she's not at home—she tries another number.

C'mon Brendan, answer the phone. Come on. Talk to me.

Faint movement at the corner of her eye, a darker object in the shadow of the trees. She straightens up, telling herself it will be a fox, or a neighbour's cat. It's too dark to see. The man peels himself out of the blackness. Coming closer now, he's glittering with raindrops. He's staring at her.

You *can* smoke inside, you know, says Anna, trying to keep her voice even, It's a hotel, not a hospital. Despite all appearances.

Lewis stares at the burning tip of the cigarette between his fingers as if he doesn't know how it got there.

I prefer it out here, he says, taking a step nearer, It's good, after rain. Do you mind if I sit down?

Don't suppose I could have one? She asks, gesturing to the cigarette.

You *can* smoke inside, you know, he says, half-smiling.

Lewis reaches into his jacket and takes out the pouch of tobacco. Clamping his own cigarette between his teeth, he begins to roll another, nail-thin and perfect. Anna watches him do it, stumbling over her words as she tries to explain herself.

It's just—it sounds silly, she says, lowering her voice, But my mother . . . she doesn't like me smoking. And anyway, I've given up. Nearly.

Giving up's easy, he says.

Yeah, says Anna, I've done it loads of times.

They both laugh at this familiar joke.

So. You must be Anna.

Mr Caine, I presume, she says, blinking rapidly, I'm sorry. I should have introduced myself earlier. But I hate a crowd.

I hate a crowd, parrots Lewis, as if pondering the fact, Me too. And *what* a crowd. Are they like that every night?

A wind picks up from nowhere, sweeping the clouds over the tops of the trees to reveal a fat brown moon hanging in the sky.

Careful, Mr Caine, that's my family you're talking about.

When he glances at her, she's no longer smiling. With her head angled slightly away from him, and her dark hair covering her eyes, she reminds him of an animal. He likes it that she isn't smiling; he likes that he can't read whether she's joking.

No offence, he says, handing her a roll-up, Just the fat guy, he's got a lot of lip. Under that moustache.

Vernon, she sighs, Ah, well, you can insult *him* all you like. He isn't family. And won't be, if I have anything to do with it.

Lewis bends near to light her cigarette. In the light from the flame, he steals a glance at her face; her mascara smudged and the sockets dark-ringed, the eyes behind the stuck lashes burning. The whole look of her is perilous. He knew it the first time he saw her, standing in the doorway, wiping the sweat from her hands and bracing herself, he knew then: she is for him. Second time around, and he's surprised at the sensation: it's not the sudden jarring he felt earlier. The feeling now is almost peaceful. Almost like a drug. Almost bearable.

He your mother's boyfriend?

Now Anna does smile again; crooked, ducking her head. Lewis likes that too.

He would say *companion,* she says, mimicking Vernon's voice, He's such a pretentious old fart.

She takes a suck on the roll-up, watching Lewis as he turns away from her to cough into his fist. She sees his knuckles, the cracked grazes across them.

Don't hold back on my account, he says, Say what you feel.

Anna takes a deep breath.

The great parasitic loon! she says, and then laughs.

He's not one of the guests, then?

Listening to him talk, you'd think he runs the place, she says, glancing at Lewis from under her fringe, Well, to be fair, he probably *does* run the place. And you're the guest. Singular.

Lewis makes a little frown of surprise.

I have had the pleasure of listening to him talk, thank you. And sing. They're very into their showbiz stuff, aren't they?

You mean you haven't noticed the film posters, or the piles of sheet music on the piano—or the door plaques?

The what? He says.

I'm in Bogart, she says, with a slow blink, But I believe your room's not named. My mother will be out at the crack of dawn getting one made up in your honour: the Michael Caine suite.

Forgetting who he's supposed to be, Lewis is mystified. Then he remembers.

The Caine *Penthouse,* I think, he says, grinning with relief.

I'll let her know you've got a preference, says Anna, and then, as a new idea occurs to her, her face lights up.

Who would you rather be, she asks, Caine or Bogart?

Bogart, naturally, he says, without thinking, How about you? Erm, Lauren Bacall or Elizabeth Taylor?

Liz Taylor, Anna says, But only in her Richard Burton period.

Lewis considers this. Out of old habit, he flicks the cigarette ash into his hand. Realizing what he's done, he tips it away onto the path.

That's cheating, he says, It's all or nothing.

He was Welsh too, wasn't he, says Anna, bending to catch his eye. Lewis pitches the dog-end of his roll-up on the path, then gets up and retrieves it. He changes the subject.

Inside or outside? He asks.

Anna hesitates.

Inside or outside *what*?

I mean, where would you rather be—as a preference?

Outside, definitely, she says, pleased with her choice, What about you?

Same, says Lewis.

They're quiet for a second, then Anna catches a breath.

Okay, she says, chewing the inside of her lip, Tea or coffee?

Tea, says Lewis, watching her closely.

She continues,

Wine or beer?

Beer, he says, In Cardiff they have a beer called Brains SA. Anna is delighted with this fact.

They do? What's the SA stand for?

Lewis laughs,

They call it Skull Attack, he says, But that's more to do with how you feel in the morning. You like wine, I guess.

Yep, and gin, and lager, says Anna, But only out of a bottle. Is that where you're from, then, Cardiff?

Lewis says nothing to this.

Okay, says Anna, feeling the moment sink and not wanting to let it, Stockings or tights?

This brings a laugh like a choke from Lewis.

You serious?

Anna nods.

Depends, he says, I mean, if you're robbing a bank, the last thing you want is an extra leg flapping round your head, getting in the way of things.

Like your gun, offers Anna.

Like your bag of swag, corrects Lewis.

I meant on a woman, actually.

In any other situation, Lewis would see the question as clear flirtation, but when he looks at Anna, her face is earnest.

What do you wear? he asks.

Socks. And pop socks in summer.

Pop socks. Do they still call them 'pop socks'?

I do, Anna grumbles, Anyway, I was just checking out a theory.

Which is? asks Lewis, raising an eyebrow.

That men who prefer stockings are—obviously—more basic in their desires than men who prefer tights.

She tries to say this lightly; it's intended as a joke, but Lewis shakes his head at her, suddenly serious.

No, no, you can't pigeonhole a fella on the basis of something he says. You can't say he's basic just because he's responded to a direct question, and maybe he's got the answer wrong, but that's because the only *right* answer exists in your head. You can't do that. It's not fair.

Sorry, she says, glum.

Anyway, pop socks are just short stockings, aren't they? He says, trying to make amends, They'd be perfect for a bank job. Pop them out of your pocket, pop them on your head!

Anna inspects the end of her roll-up.

Look, it's gone out, she says, holding it up again for re-lighting.

Lewis draws his hand from his pocket.

Nothing lasts forever, he says, leaning close.

Their fingertips touch as Lewis gives her the lighter. She sees him flinch, as if stung from the contact. The lighter is warm from where he's stowed it in his fist. She turns it over and over in her hand.

I'll roll a loose one next time. Just for you.

I'm honoured, Mr Caine, she says.

They are silent for a moment, looking out over the garden, trying not to look at each other. It's so quiet, Lewis can hear the grass ticking, stretching itself upright after the downpour.

My name's Lewis, he says, with his head down, Just don't let on to anyone else.

Anna hears perfectly well the effort this takes. She nods, looks fully at him, says nothing.

# NINETEEN

Lewis leans against the wall and stares out to sea. Despite what people say about sea air, it doesn't give him an appetite, nor a good night's sleep. He had lain awake for hours in the darkness, listening to the wind buffeting the window, police sirens in the distance, the raucous laughter of a group of young women passing on the road below. Towards dawn, he got up, and showered and shaved. He has decided that if he can do nothing else, he can at least walk: this will make him tired. But now he finds, once again, he's unable to rouse himself.

The wind has fallen away to nothing; he's amazed to find that he's enveloped in a diffuse and even light, as if the day's been preserved under tissue paper. He expected to be greeted by a scene of devastation, but apart from a few pieces of scattered rubbish marking the tide-line, there's no evidence of a storm. Ahead of him, a monochrome sky and a monochrome sea meet on an invisible horizon, so it's all one: a giant sheen of brushed metal hanging from the heavens. Even the sand at his feet is drained of colour. He tells himself it should be easy to move in this; like sleepwalking.

Lewis tries to stay parallel to the shoreline, but as he gets nearer, he sees the waves, steady and gentle, a milky frill skirting the sand. The sound they make is like breathing. The air feels sticky on his skin. Grains of light scatter in his vision. He wills himself to be calm.                              .

When he reaches the groynes, he sits in the lee of a rusted post and rolls a cigarette. He takes out the match-box he stole from the raincoat in the hall; it has a motif of a leaping deer on the front, and a telephone number on the back. He doesn't recognize the code. Lewis tries one match, then another; each one fizzes wetly against the strike. He takes a third between his fingers and rolls it warm, flicks it with the edge of his nail. It flares at once, leaving a small yellow scorch on the tip of his thumb. Thick bolts of mist come in off the sea, so he can't tell smoke from air; they clear, to reveal the wan shore and the water, then crowd in again, wiping the view away. With his head against a horizontal strut, he looks at the world sideways; now he can't tell up from down. He wants to take the time to think about Anna, but when he goes over their meeting last night, he feels a knot of anxiety, caught like a bundle of wire in his ribcage. If she *knew* him, she wouldn't want to. Fact. He tries to recall what they talked about, but the memory is like a silent film—brilliant, sharp images, and no sound. He has spent the waking hours of the night trying to relive it, and still now, he can't get much beyond the weather, her mother, the names of film stars. He feels as if his memory is living an independent existence inside his head. The memories he'd like to forget trail him like scavenging dogs; all the good moments are lost in his need to escape them.

It's my mind, he says quietly, I should be in charge of it.

There is another anxiety: the idea that he can spend half the night sitting in the cold dark with a woman he's only just met, and feel as though he knows her intimately. Now he considers it—to him, it didn't *feel* remotely cold and dark. It felt light, and warm, and she was funny. She was lovely. He can believe he imagined the whole thing. If he saw her again, it would just be ordinary; she would just be anyone.

Looking up, he catches sight of a figure in a windcheater and jeans: it's as if he has magicked her. Anna, on the far end of the groyne, clambers awkwardly over the post. She's singing to herself. Lewis can't make out the words, but it sounds military: it sounds like swearing.

Morning, he calls, turning his face up at her as she jumps onto the sand. She doesn't appear to hear him. Lewis is afraid she might walk straight past. He searches his mind for something to say; anything, to keep her. He tosses the box of matches into her path.

Shit! she says, suddenly aware of him, You scared me!

She bends down, picks up the matchbox, and throws it back hard.

Sorry, he says, Story of my life. Are you alright there?

Anna takes a few steps towards him, then falters. She turns sideways to inspect her closed fist, as if she's caught a secret.

Look what I've done, she says, spreading her hand for him to see. There is a gash across it like a second lifeline. In her other hand, she has a crumpled tissue smeared with blood. She gives him a rueful smile.

Come here, says Lewis, patting the sand next to him, Let's inspect the damage.

She kneels; now he can see her face more clearly. Her eyes are sharp with pain, or maybe irritation; her skin glows pearl. To Lewis, she is exquisite. He feels the wire in his chest unravel. Taking her fingers, he flexes them slightly, traces below the wound with his fingertip until she grunts at him to stop. She pulls her hand away and closes it against her heart.

That's nasty, he says, How did you do it?

Anna turns her head and stares out to the east, peering into the mist.

I was looking for something. I tripped. Those groynes are practically buried out there.

Looking for something . . . in the fog?

Anna thinks she knows the coast well enough now to correct him; she uses a word she has learned from her mother.

It's not a fog, she laughs, It's a fret.

Ah. So what's the fret?

She doesn't respond directly. She came out to photograph the wind turbines this morning, as she has every morning since her first sighting of them; she's annoyed to find they're not visible. She nods in the direction of the sea, thinking about her answer. They have to be seen to be believed; she won't put her trust in words.

Nothing, she says, Another time.

Another time, says Lewis, And we'll find that groyne and punch its lights out, yeah?

Another time, I'll show you what I was looking for. If you're still here.

She sits down beside him, dragging her hair from her eyes. Now and then she opens her hand, half-glances at it before curling it back in her lap.

Stings, I expect. You'll want to lick it, he says, wanting to lick it for her.

After a second, she spreads her palm, tentatively dabs it with her tongue.

He's been trying not to stare at her mouth; the colour is too true in the even light, but now he gives in and watches.

This weather's pretty awful, she says, tasting blood on her lip, Like drowning.

No, thinks Lewis, it's not like that at all. He follows her eyeline into the distance, then glances back at her face. He finds he can't not look at her.

Better than that racket last night, he says, Couldn't sleep for the noise.

Oh. I didn't hear anything. Is it the bed? Is it creaky? she asks, solicitous now, Because we can always put you in another room.

The bed's fine, he says.

She looks him in the eye.

But you didn't sleep?

Rust never sleeps, he says.

Anna hooks a strand of hair behind her ear. She doesn't know how to answer that. She heard it too last night, this strange way he has of talking, as if he's learned the language from a textbook.

It's almost as though the sea isn't there, she says, gesturing into the mist, As if you could just get up and walk to Holland.

Why would you want to do that? he says, with a wild look that makes her grin, Tell you, I want to be able to *see* where the water is.

You like to swim? she asks, I never really got the hang of it.

Me neither. Which is why I like to see the water. Know your enemy, he says, with a bitter laugh.

But the sea isn't your *enemy,* she says, Surely you don't think that? And it has to be more interesting than this—she waves her hand, dismissive—This nothingness.

Actually, I think it's unreal, he says, looking about him, Like sitting on a cloud.

She breaks the moment with a burst of laughter.

How would you know? she cries, Spend a lot of time up in the clouds, do you?

Your mother told me you two are going on holiday, he says, wanting to hear her laugh again, So you'll find out soon enough. When you're on that plane and you're looking out of the window, don't be surprised to see me. I'll be the one smoking a fag.

And using *my* matches to light it, she says, nodding at the box on the sand.

Nah, he says, They're no good. They got damp, see?

He hands her a match from the box, holding it while she strikes; it flares immediately, a bright, sulphurous pink.

I'll bring you back some duty-free, if you like, she says, close enough now for him to touch her.

A present? he says, And you barely know me!

He leans forward, nudges her with his shoulder. He loves it when she nudges him right back.

I'll *sell* them to you, she says, If you're still around.

They're silent again, and close. He wants to say, Yes, I'll be right here where you left me, but he knows he can't. Anna opens her hand; the wound is gummy and the blood has dried. Specks of red glitter her palm.

Do you think I'll have a scar? says Anna, offering up her hand.

No, says Lewis.

How did you get yours? she asks, gesturing to the white line under his lip. Instinctively, he puts a hand up to caress it. He can't find the words to say, so he remains silent, but she feels his breathing change—more rapid, shallow—and when she looks into his face, it's closed. Anna stands up, brushing the sand from her jeans.

Are you coming? she says, Only, I need to get a plaster on this cut. And some coffee.

Lewis hears the invitation in her voice. He can tell by her expression that she expects him to say yes. It would be good to spend the day, get to know each other.

I'm staying put, he says, deliberately making his voice un-friendly, Catch you later, maybe.

She walks on without saying goodbye. From the corner of his eye, he sees her turn round once, twice, to look at him, then give up, her pace quickening along the beach. He gets to his feet, feeling his voice tight, and calls, Anna, Anna, stop!

But she doesn't stop and she doesn't look back.

~ ~ ~

From the sky, the land below is gauzy, soft as a dream. Sonia leans against the window of the helicopter cabin, shielding her head in the crook of her elbow, trying to see. It's like looking through a lace curtain. Most of the view is wiped away, except for one or two sharp patches of clarity, as if a hole has been punctured in the mist. She can just make out the lamp-posts on the promenade, like a row of spent matches. In a flaw of clear air, Sonia sees a figure moving swiftly up the steps, only to be swallowed again beneath the fog. Tight beside her, Kristian has his eyes closed and is breathing through his mouth. His face is very pale, and when she touches his hand to comfort him, she feels his skin, clammy with fear.

It's getting worse, says the pilot, We're turning back.

His voice through the headphones is tense. Sonia can't see from her angle whether he's angry about the weather or about Kristian, suddenly deciding to come along for the ride. She pats Kristian's arm.

We'll be down in a minute, she shouts.

Kristian's face remains rigid at this news. A minute is still too long for him; under his breath, he's muttering something not even he can understand.

The platform is shrouded in mist, blowing off the sea. Sonia braces herself for a sharp set-down, but they sit perfectly on the landing pad, and she barely has time to unclip her harness before Kristian is clambering over her, trying to open the door. When the pilot slides the hatch, Kristian pushes past him and is sick on the grass.

Alec, I'm so sorry about him, says Sonia, He's not been up before.

And he's not going up again, says Alec, Next time, it'll just be you and me. Understood?

Sonia is thrilled by the sternness in his voice, and what she hears as the hint of a future date.

Yes, sir, she says, fighting back the urge to salute, Just name the day.

She puts her hand on Kristian's shoulder and watches Alec march away.

Very handsome, Kristian, wouldn't you say?

Kristian gets up, teary-eyed, from his crouching position, and gives her a weak smile.

Sure, he's handsome, he says, And quite severe. I kinda like that.

Me too, says Sonia, I kinda like that very much.

# TWENTY

Lewis is sitting on the bench in the garden, has been sitting here all night long. But this time it's not his usual, vacant torpor: this time he's waiting. At the far end, a blackbird dots along the grass, pausing now and then to check on him. Lewis is content to watch. The sky is different again this morning, soft and blurred for a while, then kindled by a sharp, dazzling light. It's all the seasons in one go, he thinks. There's a chill in his bones, a welcome numbness. He's wearing his leather jacket and his black jeans. Lewis begins with the jacket, mentally searching the pockets; he has already actually searched them. There are four in all, two on the outside, and two built into the lining. The left outside pocket contains his pouch of tobacco, and a new acquisition—a key on a garish fob, found in the far corner of his windowsill. The right pocket, to his amazement, gave up the crumpled tissue Anna was clutching on the beach. He doesn't remember taking it from her, but he keeps hold of it in the palm of his hand. The blood smears have dried dark brown; when he puts the tissue to his nose, he gets a perfume he can't define. It makes his pulse quicken. The more he tries to find the scent, closing the tissue over his nose and mouth, the more elusive it becomes. He has his wallet in one inside pocket, and nothing in the other. He has searched his kitbag—he won't bother to search again: his lighter has gone. At one time, losing it would have been important, it would have sent him awry, but finding something belonging to Anna is more than fair trade.

He has made up his mind to see her before she goes. He came down last night after he heard the rest of them go to bed, and sat alone on the bench, telling himself that if she came and found him here, it would be *her* doing: it would not be something he had caused. And she didn't come down. He was certain she would. He waited, watching the moon move across the sky. He smoked his roll-ups. At some point at daybreak, he felt his body jerking, the muscles twitching with fatigue. He felt his arm fall loose at his side.

In another life, Wayne grabs his hand and says, I'm here, brother. Sleep now, yeah? So finally, Lewis slept.

~ ~

The fits came more frequently, despite the medication. There was never any warning. Lewis would be going with Wayne to watch the Bluebirds play on a winter evening, joking, laughing, their breath pluming out before them, and all at once, Lewis would be on his own. Behind him, Wayne would be in the road, kicking up dust. Or they'd be out shopping on a Saturday, arguing about what to buy their mother for her birthday, and Wayne would be persuading him, bringing him round to the idea of the china plate with the poem that they'd seen on a market stall, when the talk would suddenly stop. Wayne would be making shapes with his mouth, but there'd be no volume, only his lips moving minutely, as if chasing the words. The fits were never predictable, and never quite the same: some came invisibly, a series of small flickers across Wayne's face, a lostness in his eyes; some came like a storm.

Lewis learned to dread the moment, and then quickly got over the dread, and went about the business of taking care of his brother. Usually there was no event or reason; they'd be lying in their bunks at night and Lewis would sense that

Wayne was fitting, could even feel his own limbs twitch, as if he were attached to his brother by an electric leash.

It's not like that, said Wayne, when Lewis asked him about it, That's just something you heard the doctor say. It doesn't feel electric to me at all.

This time, Wayne was lying on the gravel. The shadow of the slide fell in a slant across his body. Small children stared from the safety of the roundabout, the ones nearby reined in their swings like ponies, and watched, gaping. Lewis tried to think what brought it on: the cigarettes they stole from their mother's handbag, the cider they'd been drinking, the pair of them messing about on the top of the slide; it must have been something they were doing—something wrong. Wayne had been shouting at the top of the slide, gleeful, careless, and then he dropped like a rock, landing on the gravel below with a dull thunk. He'd vomited, which wasn't unusual, but he hadn't wet himself. After each episode, Wayne would be ashamed; he'd heard enough descriptions to make him feel that way, but at the moment of recovery he was calm, his pale face tranquil.

What is it, then? asked Lewis, What is it like?

He was cradling his brother's head in his lap, wiping Wayne's face with his sleeve. Where the gravel had bit into his cheek there were speckles of red, pricking the skin like measles. Lewis checked for blood, for broken bones; as far as he could see, there was nothing. But at the second when Wayne let out his cry, of joy—of disbelief—Lewis had felt his own body falling from a great height, and a collapse deep inside his chest.

I feel something too, said Lewis, wanting to be his brother at that moment, But I don't see what starts it. I don't *get* it.

Wayne looked up at the trees that bordered the playground. It's them, he said.

Lewis could see nothing but the leaves, trembling in the breeze, and spangles of sunlight winking through them.

It's that, Wayne said, fluttering his fingers, That light. It makes me feel weird and then . . . nothing. I'm gone. Like that alley at the back of our house. That stuff the ground's made of—it's too glittery. It's way too glittery.

Lewis knew the alley; they always avoided it, after the first time.

What does it feel like, then, if it's not electric?

Wayne turned his face away.

I can't tell you, he said, I'm not there. It's before that's really bad. The second I know I'm going, I've already gone. That's the worst.

He looked up at his brother.

But it's always nice to come back, he said, with a faint smile, See your ugly face again.

~ ~

Lewis feels a pain in his chest at the memory of it. He takes out his tobacco and rolls a loose cigarette: he will give it to Anna. If he sees her.

When he lifts his head, the blackbird has gone, and he finds himself eye to eye with a squirrel. Sensing movement, it freezes, holding its position perfectly and keeping its eye on Lewis, who in turn holds his. After a moment, the squirrel darts up to the bird-table, steals a crust, and jumps a length into the trees. Behind him, Marta coughs.

Don't tell Mrs Calder, she says, But I like to watch them. They're very cute.

She smiles as he turns, placing her hand on the back of the bench and craning round him like a nurse in an old people's home.

Can I get you some breakfast? she asks, Only Mrs Calder and Mr Savoy are eating down here this morning, what with the flight and everything. So it's no trouble.

He waves away her offer.

Not for me, thanks, he says, I'll get out of your road.

Anna's mother catches him just as he's about to leave. She's wearing thick make-up and a sweet, dense perfume. She stands too close, hanging on to the open door, trying to block his escape.

Mr Caine, she says, I hope you're not running away again?

He's down the steps and gone from her sight before the door closes.

## TWENTY-ONE

Anna's mother leans over for a refill, waving her cup in front of Vernon's face. He stretches across the table and snatches it from her with the air of a reluctant minion.

Well, what if he *is* a spy? she says, Good luck to him. As long as he settles up, what business is it of ours?

I didn't say he was a spy, mum, says Anna, trying to keep her voice level, Only that he likes his privacy. If he doesn't want to have breakfast, that's entirely his choice.

They are sitting round the window table in the dining-room. Anna has her back to the door, her head angled slightly to catch any sound in the hall. Outside the window, the sky is a soft, vaporous blue.

Tea? cries Vernon, and then seeing Anna flinch, lowers his tone to a stage whisper.

You know, Anna, Rita only thinks he looks like a spy because he puts her in mind of Napoleon Solo.

There's a petulant edge of jealousy in his voice. He pours a slosh of milk in the cup, holds up the teapot with an enquiring look. When he sees Anna's response, he thumps it back down on the table.

Napoleon what? asks Anna, distracted.

Her mother laughs.

Never mind, dear. Cabbage is peeved because I happened to say I thought our man was attractive.

He'll attract the flies, I'm sure, mutters Vernon, which makes Anna's mother laugh again.

Actually, Cabbage, he scrubs up very nicely. I thought he looked quite dashing this morning, she says, Didn't you, Anna? Rugged.

If you say so, mum, she says.

He didn't mention where he was going, she continues, looking slyly at her daughter, Perhaps he's gone for a stroll on the beach.

Anna pretends not to hear. She'd been avoiding Lewis, spending the time in her room making last-minute adjustments to her packing, not really caring about any of it, but in need of something to do. She tried to put some detail in her notebook about the wind-farm, but the words wouldn't come, and the sketches she made were hopeless. She'd told him her room was called Bogart. He could have come and found her. She stayed up there the whole evening, waiting for a knock on the door. After a while she began to seethe, thinking he owed her an apology. A longer while later, and she decided it would just be good to see him before she went away. Waking fully dressed on her bed in the early hours, she saw how ridiculous she was. Now, the feeling is the same: her heart is heavy as a plumb. She was sure they shared something—a real connection—plainly, as usual, she was wrong.

I was saying, Anna . . . that Mr Caine, says her mother, He's got a proper film star name. Don't you think?

I *think* I'll take a walk before we set off, says Anna, pushing back her chair, Get a bit of fresh air.

We'll have nothing but fresh air by this time tonight, says her mother, shooting a knowing look at Vernon, And that taxi's booked for ten sharp. Don't go making us late!

~

Left, left, I had a good job and I
    Left,
    I left my wife and fourteen kids

Was I right?

After a while, Anna stops marching and stands, hands on hips, alone on the long stretch of beach. She has been walking in the direction of the wind-farm, trudging across the wet sand and climbing over the groynes, for what feels like miles. When she set off, the air was clear; she had good sight of the horizon. Now the weather blows thick and thin, clearing its throat of yesterday's fog. She tells herself it must be a trick of light, the way the turbines looked so close; they seem no nearer now than when she started. And there's something missing about them today, but she can't fathom what it is. She thinks perhaps their spell on her is broken. Only when she's turned round and walked a good mile back towards home does she realize what's wrong. She turns again to check. They look even more flimsy now, as if they're dissolving into the landscape. Soon they'll be invisible. She stares hard, opening her eyes wide to let in the available light. Sure enough, the blades aren't moving: they are as still and sharp as knives, forming a line of crosses against the sky. Anna shakes her head at herself. How could she not have noticed? She feels it like an omen, as if time will stop too, until she comes back. The thought gives her courage. She will find Lewis and talk to him. She's got nothing to lose by telling him how she feels; it will be awkward, but she does awkward very well. What would Brendan say, if he were here? *Any man would be lucky to have you.* Anna tries to ignore the other voice inside her, reminding her that Brendan is capable of saying just about anything, but it grows more persistent, louder than the waves and the gulls, and the gusting wind singing through the groynes. She hits on a new song to march her back, crunching her feet into the sand, blocking the doubt with a rousing chorus,

Ars'ole, ars'ole, ar soldier I shall be—

When she raises her head, she sees Lewis, walking in her footprints. Against the white sky, he's sharp as an X-ray.

What kind of navvy taught you that? he says, feigning shock. Anna smiles at him.

Kids at school, she says.

Nice school, says Lewis, closing the gap.

Yeah. But not nice kids.

She is at his shoulder now.

How not nice? he says, his head on one side, mirroring hers.

She has to stretch up to kiss him. Slips on the sand a little so his arm catches her just at the elbow to hold her there. His other arm closes round her, pulling her body in line with his. It's awkward and perfect. He tastes of silver.

Afterwards, her blood will run quick with the memory of it. But right now, she tells him how he tastes.

He holds her to his chest, puts his lips on her hair. He takes her hand and slips it with his into his pocket. His skin is sandpaper rough. He leads her fingers deeper, so she looks up at him, widening her eyes in mock outrage at where she might be led. She finds the cigarette he has rolled.

For you, he says, laughing, In case you don't get on with those foreign fags.

Actually, I've given up, nearly, she says, But if you still want that duty-free, I'll be back next week.

I don't know if I'll be here next week, he says, There's something I've got to find.

Anna tries to say it lightly:

Something or someone?

Both, he says, But it's not what you think. It's a problem, he says, It's a problem I've got—

Anna puts her head up to kiss him again, feels his grip tighten. She'll tell him she can help him with the problem, whatever it is; and then, without warning, she feels an abrupt change coursing through his body. He slackens his hold on her, raises his head to the horizon. She's lost him. Unable to read his face this way, Anna touches his chin with her fingertips.

They say a problem shared is a problem doubled, she says, but he doesn't respond to the joke. He's still looking beyond her, so she has to turn her head, see what it is he's seeing. The turbines stand like a row of needles—pinpricks of light—glinting at them in a patch of hazy sun.

That's what you were looking for yesterday? he asks.

The wind-farm, says Anna, Only, it's really beautiful when it's clear. You have to see it on a good day.

This is a good day, says Lewis, For me, any road.

Me too, she says, not sure if she has grasped his meaning.

# TWENTY-TWO

You can't unsee what's been seen. True. But nor can you see what isn't there.

Lewis perches, naked, on the edge of the bed, talking himself through it. There's traffic on the road below, and children screaming down on the beach; he hears a buzzing noise from out of sight, cutting the air like a saw. Every small thing reminds him of before. He takes a shower, despite the age of it, turning round underneath the head to make the most of the drizzle of water it gives. He likes the bathroom for its lack of colour, of objects, familiarity, resonance: there's nothing in here to catch him out. The room itself isn't bad either, although he's had to make some adjustments: he hasn't moved the picture of the kittens above his bed, but the one opposite, a scene depicting a bridge over a river, was directly in his eyeline. He's flipped it over, so that only the pale brown paper of the backing and the edge of the frame is visible. Even though he knows what's on the other side, not having to catch sight of it makes him feel better.

He lays back, placing his hands against the damp skin of his chest and counting slowly as he breathes: One, Anna, two, Anna. His last glimpse of her was through the window, from high up. The glass was old and wavy, so his view of the street was as if under ice. The scene rippled below him: Vernon helped her mother into the front seat of the taxi, while Anna opened the back door, glancing up just before she slid inside the car. Her oval face tilted, she looked worried, and beautiful, to him. He felt a swell of grief in his throat. He waved at her. Catching sight of him at last, she lifted her hand in the air, as if in salute. He put his fingers on the glass and kept them there until the car was gone.

She's still beautiful to him now. Lewis shuts his eyes and presses his palms into them, presses hard enough to make them ache in their sockets. He would want the last thing he sees to be the image of her standing nervously in the doorway, or marching towards him on the beach, her face taut with an unknown fury. He tries to hang on to the fact of her, counting her name over and over, but as soon as he forgets to concentrate, his mind, like a sickness, rises up against him.

~ ~

There had been a song in the charts back then, some old punk in heavy metal get-up. Wayne used to drive him mad with it, singing at the top of his voice.

*It's a nice day to start again, It's a nice day for a—white wedding! It's a nice day to—START AGAIN!*

I'm gonna batter you if you *start* again, said Lewis, shoving his brother sideways. Wayne did a mock fall, then laughed, kicking up his leg and missing Lewis by an inch. They were waiting at the bus stop near the substation, waiting for a surprise, said Wayne. It was a sunny day—the kind of day when Lewis's mother would stand at the kitchen sink and count out Wayne's medication. She'd watch him, with the pills going sticky in her palm, as he swallowed, pulled a face, breathed heavily into the glass of water, retched over the sink, pulled another face, then swallowed the rest of them. She kept her eyes on him, aware of the tricks he pulled; hiding them under his tongue until her back was turned, then spitting them into the drain out the back. When he was done, she made him open his mouth wide so that she could see they were gone.

This morning, their mother had a new job to go to, and was heading for Manny's house to cadge a lift into town.

Make sure he takes his pills, she said to Lewis, And get yourselves some tea if I'm not back by six.

She held out a five-pound note, which Wayne, passing at just the right moment, snatched away and stuffed into his pocket.

I'm telling you—don't forget them pills, she said, as he grinned back at her from a safe distance, And I'm telling you again, that money's for your tea. *Not* fags.

Lewis followed his mother to the door. He had an urge to put his hand on her shoulder, to wish her good luck, but was aware of Wayne in the background, watching. Too old, at fifteen, to give her a kiss, despite Wayne, he half hugged her anyway.

Daft bugger, she said. Turning at the door, she pointed a finger in Wayne's direction.

Remember, mind, and then to Lewis, as she always did, she said, And you. Look after your brother.

Wayne was sitting in the shade at the turn of the stairs, wafting the money over his face, passing it across his mouth, smelling it. He rolled it up, pretended to smoke it like a cigarette.

Mam said not fags, said Lewis, sprawling on the step below.

Quite right, agreed Wayne, shifting sideways and pulling something from his back pocket, Why waste it on *buying* fags . . . when we've already got some!

He produced a gold pack, dented, already opened. He flipped the lid and counted.

She's only had three, he said.

She'll be back for them, said Lewis, craning his neck to get a view of the door. Wayne shook his head.

Manny don't like the punters smoking in his cars. Might get ash on the seats. She won't find out 'til she gets there:

'Ooh, Ill just have a quick ciggie before I clock on—and—bugger. Forgot 'em! I'll just have to borrow one.'

They both laughed at the impression. Wayne put the cigarettes back into his pocket, and with a swing on the stairpost, leaped over Lewis. He lifted his sweatshirt off the back of the chair.

You coming or what? he said.

Where to? asked Lewis.

Thought we'd take a trip. A little jaunt, he said waving the five-pound note.

They walked out into a morning of pure sunshine, the first hot day of the summer.

Wayne and Lewis had been standing at the very end of the road, where the houses gave way to allotments and fields, for over half an hour. The buses turned round here to make their journey back through the estate and on into town. From the top of the bus, you could see mounds of earth, like giant ant-hills, erected by the council to stop travellers settling on the wasteland. Further in the distance, the river showed only as a strip of brown on green. But they weren't getting the bus today; they were waiting.

From where the brothers stood, the only thing of interest was the electricity substation, housed in a prison of black railings. They'd been bent and busted to allow access to the fields beyond; a red rut in the grass marked a path. Carl's tag—SHARKEY—was carved on every side of the building. The word was irregular close up, as though a rat had been nibbling at the paintwork. Wayne ran his hand over it as he waited, occasionally looking up and down the street, while Lewis looked anywhere but at Wayne. The sight of his brother's fingernails tracing the letters put him on edge.

Wonder why he decided on an 'e' there, Wayne said, inspecting the grime on his fingertip.

Wonder why he decided on Sharkey at all, Lewis replied, Didn't he used to call himself Fish, or something?

Wayne grinned at him.

Yeah, but fishes smell, whereas sharks . . . bite, he said, snapping his jaws together, Where the fuck's he got to?

He's got to right here, said Carl, who had crept up behind them from the track side, C'mon, crip, what's keeping you?

Wayne vaulted a mound of battered grass and followed Carl round the back of the substation. It had a new padlock on the door, hanging open, and an enamelled yellow plate above it with a symbol of a man falling backwards; a zigzag pierced his chest. Danger of Death was written underneath. Carl tapped the plate.

Come into my office, he said.

Inside was dark and fetid; a small, square room. It looked empty to Lewis, who took a moment to adjust to the change of light. He could just make out the oily black cobwebs hanging from the ceiling, the splotched concrete floor, and a shape low down behind Carl. There was a stench filling the air which made Wayne gag.

Erh! Stinks of cat piss! he said, and Carl shook his head and laughed,

No, my little friend, that's the scent of *pussy*.

The shape Lewis saw revealed itself in the dimness; it was a stained mattress, doubled over. There was nothing remotely electrical in the station, nothing that would kill anyone. Lewis stayed at the open door, breathing through his mouth, while Carl bent down and pulled an aerosol can from behind the mattress. He shook it hard, rattling the bearings inside.

Shut the door, he said to Lewis, who simply waited, looking at him. Carl clattered the can in warning,

Out or in, you. Shut the fucking door.

Lewis took a step back into daylight, pushing the door to. He had a mind to slip the lock over the hasp and trap them both inside. It was always like this with Carl. Lewis considered how it would be to simply leave Wayne and walk away. For starters, his mother would kill him; and even if she didn't, he couldn't live with himself if anything bad happened. He wasn't tempted until he saw Sam Robson crossing the street towards him. The boys nodded at each other, awkward but friendly. Sam said something Lewis didn't quite catch.

What?

Have I missed it? asked Sam, Has the bus gone?

Lewis turned his head and nodded towards the far end of the street.

Looks like it's just coming. You off into town?

Sam shrugged.

Gonna buy a record. You going in?

Lewis gave an exaggerated sigh and gestured to the sub-station.

I'm waiting for Wayne. He's in a meeting.

With Sharkey? said Sam, shaking his head, What's he cooking up this time, glue?

Something out of a can, said Lewis.

Sam put his arm out to signal for the bus to stop, running along the edge of the pavement as the doors swung open.

See ya, he said.

Lewis took a step back and leaned against the wall of the substation. From inside there came a rushing sound, like air escaping from a tyre, and a whooping noise that Lewis knew could only be his brother. He opened the door a crack and peered into the darkness: the atmosphere was thick as frosted glass. Wayne fell out at once, coughing and spitting, tumbling sideways onto the grass. Carl rolled out after him, and they both lay there, in broad sunlight, in view of the houses surrounding them, and the street, and the cars going by, straining their lungs for breath.

Fucking mad, you are! Wayne said, after a minute, You trying to kill me, or what?

Carl lay on his back, his chest heaving.

Not today, spaz-boy. Just thought we'd get a huff or two before . . . setting off.

Lewis stood above them. The fumes coming off them made him lightheaded. He gave Wayne a kick.

Get up, he said, We're going.

We certainly are. We're all going on a summer holiday. No more worries for a week or two. Except not in a bus.

We're going into town, said Lewis, I told Sam we'd meet him in Spillers.

Sam Robson? That dead-head? Yeah, man, said Carl, in a drawling imitation, Cool, ma-aan.

Wayne laughed until he choked, pulling his sweatshirt up over his face and coughing into it. Carl took this as encouragement.

Do as your brother says, he mocked, And run after your boyfriend like a good little spaz.

And you can fuck off, *Fish-stink,* said Lewis, feeling a pulse throb in his head.

Carl stood up, glanced over at Lewis, as if considering a fight, then back to where Wayne was lying.

How does a spaz run home? said Carl, He runs like this!

And did a staggering lollop over the grass, falling down next to Wayne.

Wayne put his arm up and slapped him on the head. They both fell back, laughing hysterically.

Lock it for us, there's a good chap, said Carl, throwing a bunch of keys at Lewis's feet. Lewis didn't move.

Don't call him a spaz, he said, standing over Carl. He would like to aim a kick at that wide mouth, felt a twitching in his knee, an ache to do it. Wayne looked up at his brother.

Come on, he said, appealing to Lewis, You can't abandon us *now.* We *need* you.

For what? said Lewis, kicking at the bunch of keys instead.

Yeah, spazzman, for what? Bad enough having one spazzing spaz, said Carl, before breaking into his hyena laugh.

He looks older, said Wayne, as if it were obvious, He looks old *enough.*

The two boys lying on the ground peered up at Lewis. Carl considered this.

You're right, he said, and turning to Lewis, Your brother needs you, *mate*. To help him with a favour he's got to do. Mate. A little debt he owes me.

Why should I? said Lewis, looking at Wayne.

Why? asked his brother, Why? And then, breaking into song, *Cos it's a nice day to . . . start again!*

Carl let out his high, metallic laugh.

# TWENTY-THREE

They're moving at the speed of light. Lewis in the back seat with his eyes shut and stinking of petrol, Wayne in front, pulling on a cigarette and handing it back to Carl, who angles it in the corner of his mouth, just like his father does, but who doesn't drive like him. Who drives like Ayrton Senna.

They robbed the car from a side-street off Moorland Road, cutting across the park and straight over the football pitch. The hair-coated blankets they'd found in the back of the hatch got ditched in the long grass on the edge of the children's playground, and the thermos was hurled over the fence and onto the bowling green. All the while they laughed, except Lewis, who was scouring for children, park attendants, anyone that Carl would think it might be amusing to run down.

At the garage at the bottom of Newport Road, Lewis—who looked old enough—got out and held the pump and fed it into the hole and pressed the trigger. He didn't know how to make it stop and his hands were shaking, and the petrol spilt all over the tarmac and down his trousers. Any second now and the bald guy they called Fester would be out of the booth and running. Lewis was meant to walk up to the door as if to pay, cut sideways down the alley, and meet them at the corner of the next street. Lewis planned to not get back in the car. But Carl had a plan too, hissing at Lewis to get in before he was done, and revving the engine, and making

Lewis panic so the hose snaked round his leg and he fell onto the back seat with his feet sticking out and the door hanging open like a broken wing. And now they're laughing their heads off up front, laughing because they'd got a full tank in the car and two bottles of Manny's home brew inside them and two more stashed in the footwell, *cooling*.

The world's our fucking oyster! shouts Carl.

Whatever that means, says Wayne, glancing backwards at Lewis, trying to include him. But he's not forgiving either of them and he mutters, not quite under his breath: Means it stinks of fish.

He can hear Wayne singing above the over-revving engine, then whooping as Carl cuts the corner, then singing again. Lewis is no coward but he's just not looking. He's sick with the rear suspension and the petrol vapour coming off him. Every time he opens his eyes, he sees the fat green gonk hanging off the rear-view mirror, twirling round and grinning and making him feel a deep rumbling sickness. Wayne turns to his brother and thumps him on the knee.

I told you! he shouts, over the wail of gears, Goes like shit off a shovel!

The sky whips past, but Lewis still isn't looking.

Let me out, he says, through his fingers.

He leans forward between the front seats and grabs Carl by the shoulder. Carl turns his head, but like the pro he is, he's keeping his eyes on the road.

Not scared, are you, butt? he says, We haven't even started yet.

He takes his hands off the wheel and pulls his jacket off one shoulder, then the other, letting the car veer sideways as he wriggles his arms from his sleeves, waiting for the last second before jerking the car back on course. He tosses the jacket into the back, catching Lewis full in the face. Wayne swigs from the old lemonade bottle and offers it to Lewis.

Like Alka-Seltzer, he says, pointing the neck at him, Go on. It's alright, this.

The liquid is the colour of urine, with a cloudy froth on top. Lewis takes a sip, tasting sweet and bitter, and then another.

*There is nothing fair in this world, and there is nothing safe in this world, and there is nothing sure in this world . . . look for something left in this world . . . START AGAIN!*

His brother sings, rapping on the dash with his fingers. Lewis is pretty sure it's not fair and not safe, and he knows what's going to happen: it's way beyond his control. Carl will crash this car; they will run along the back streets, probably bleeding, maybe with something broken. They'll be cowering in some alleyway behind the bins and whether the police find them there or come for them later, they'll end up in Borstal. Lewis longs to rewind the day, go back to the bus stop and Wayne picking at the flaking paint with his fingernail. Sam would get there before Carl arrived, and the three of them would get on the bus, running up the stairs to get the best seat on the top deck, and in this other version they'd be in town, posing in the record shop. Lewis would buy the Sly and Robbie record he wanted, trying to be cool and restrained as he asked the assistant with the dyed black hair to play it for him. And Wayne would flirt with her, singing out of tune, being his usual nuisance self. But things could still turn out badly: Carl could still show up. No, he'd have to go further back, to when his mother left the house for work. He would wind it back to there, or further, yet further back, unspooling the hours until he found the right place to start time again. As the houses streak away on either side, Lewis knows where he would begin the re-run of this day: he would go after his mother with her cigarettes, and he'd give her a proper hug and she'd say, Get away with you! Go on, and make sure he takes his pills, mind.

Lewis hands the bottle of home brew back to his brother and looks into his eyes: they are too bright, and too shiny, and it's too late now for rewind.

They enter a long back street parallel to the river, lurching up over the pavement and down again, fast and reckless, so Lewis's nausea is turned to fright. Two children playing at the roadside jump off the kerb and into a hedge. Through the back window, Lewis sees their faces, round and wide-eyed with shock. Carl spins them sideways into a tree-lined lane.

Here it is: the long, leafy lane and the sunshine, and the trees flashing by, and the river running in a black spill to the right, and the bridge up ahead and the trees going dark and light and dark and light and dark, and in the front seat Wayne stops singing. Only the sound of the engine now as he jerks forward, arches back, throwing his right arm in the air like a stripper flinging off a glove. His body goes stiff as he jerks again, out of the seat this time, his head hitting the sun-roof with a crack. The bridge is speeding towards them. Lewis bends forward to hold him down, shouting at Carl to stop. Wayne's knuckles hit the dashboard and the windscreen, and the rear-view mirror, whipping the giant gonk from side to side. Carl takes his eyes off the road.

For a few seconds, they're airborne, sailing into the sky, until the same sky turns over and becomes the floor. Then it's night and Wayne's not singing, and there's no noise at all now, and no one else. As they sink upside down into the river, a picture comes unbidden to Lewis, of a giant who came to visit, with green eyes and wild hair. The giant must have picked up the car and slipped it in his pocket. That's all that's happened. But now the giant is on the move, his body rocking from side to side as his huge hobnailed boots negotiate the river path, and even though the pocket is green and made of wool, the car is rocking too, and it's slipping further down to the bottom, where there are bits of fluff and tangled threads and shreds of old tobacco. A shoal of coins zigzags past the window, swimming up and out of sight.

They're not coins, thinks Lewis, They're fish.

He thinks again.

They're not fish, they're bits of glass. We're in the water.

He can't see Wayne; as the car noses the river-bed, bounces, turns sideways, he is thinking of nothing, and hearing nothing but a raucous banging which comes from inside and which he doesn't know is his heart. Behind him, the hatch cracks open: Lewis is sucked from the back seat like pus from a boil. Up and down looks all the same but his body is drawn one way. He sees nothing, then at once a hand looms into his vision; only when he makes to grab it does he realize it's his own. The water is black and then dark blue and shapes appear above him; a cloud of grey tortoises with huge flippers, which become ducks, paddling madly away, and a stream of white foam which looks like sick, coating the top of his head and fizzing through his hair.

When he opens his eyes, he sees shoes and boots with legs sticking out above them, and the wheels of a pushchair with mud in the tracks, and the long bent neck of a swan. Its black eye stares at him. He's tasting iron and petrol and home brew, and he's crying out Wayne.

Here's the one thing that in all the forgetting he could not fail to remember: at the hospital, there was a dead brother and a living one. His mother would see one of them lying on top of the sheet and the other underneath. And when she came and walked round the curtain into his cubicle, she had thought to find Wayne. It was a simple mistake: the voices belonging to the shoes and boots above him had asked him questions, who was he, who should they fetch? Only Lewis had been calling for his twin. He had been crying out Wayne. It was such a simple, innocent mistake; no one could be blamed for it. And even though he could forget nothing from then on, it was a most particular cruelty that he would remember the look on his mother's face when she saw which son was spared.

# TWENTY-FOUR

Make the rain fall and the sun not shine, make that bend in
a leafy lane a straight, clear road. You can't. You can't undo.
Lewis was told it would get better in time. Time is a healer,
people would say, for want of something more honest,
meaning, perhaps, that time equals distance, and things
look less significant when they're further away. But all
that time did for Lewis was to amplify the moment. In his
dreams, the giant—who lifted the car that day and put it in
his pocket—would appear on the bridge, or at the top of
the street, or outside the petrol station, or just at the moment when Wayne takes the stolen cigarettes from his back
pocket. Lewis would hear the giant's footsteps on the stairs
above them. He never saw his face, but over time, it assumed the thunderous countenance typical of his mother's
boyfriends.

In waking life, everything sets him off. A knock on the
door becomes the rap of knuckles on the windscreen; the sight
of a swan gliding on the water makes his bones jar; the smell
of petrol becomes the gag of suffocation. And at the end of
the earth, in a ramshackle guest-house where he knows no
one and owns nothing and wants nothing, and where he is
less than nothing, an innocent painting of a river and a leafy
lane becomes a scene of death.

Lewis pulls the painting off the hook and turns it over on his lap. He fights the urge to smash his fist through it. He takes a deep breath, tells himself it's a scene that was painted a century or more ago. It's not even the real thing; it's a *reproduction* of someone's idea of a river and a bridge. Maybe the place doesn't even exist. So he tells himself: it's a reproduction of a reproduction of an invention, it's entirely blameless, and it's not even real. Another deep breath, and he's counting again: one, Anna, two, Anna.

He must consider her: she is blameless too, in all of this, and his feelings for her *are* real. Lewis is ashamed at this crack that's appeared inside him, this fissure which feels wide enough to put his fist in and which feels like love. He won't gamble with Anna; he will leave her alone.

After Wayne's death, the families had kept Carl and Lewis apart: it was a requirement of the court that the boys would not be allowed to associate—as if Lewis had ever wanted to associate with Carl. And as soon as the inquest was over, Lewis, out on licence, was sent to live with an aunt in Monmouth. Out of trouble's way, his mother had said, meaning out of her sight.

It took twenty years before he felt ready to face her again, although at the time, he couldn't really say why he felt ready. He'd thought it was to help him confront his problem; now, after Anna, he understands: it's because she would never come looking for him. You can't make peace with Christmas cards, and more than anything, he wanted peace. Peace, and presence, and what was left of his family; he wanted his history back. All he'd found was another of her boyfriends. But he'd found Manny too, and finally, even though he wasn't consciously looking, he'd found Carl. A sharp taste fills his mouth. He knew it, as soon as he saw the windfarm; pressing Anna close to him on the sand and seeing the faint pinpricks in the distance. Lewis closes his eyes and sees again the photograph of Sonia on the beach, her arms outstretched and her head thrown back, her dark hair in jagged spikes. He only has to move his thumb away from the edge of the photo to find what was missing: a line of white turbines on the horizon.

Lewis feels Carl near, so near, he can almost smell him: it's not about things anymore, if it ever was. Carl can steal a van, he can steal a bracelet, but he can't steal Lewis's past. He replaces the picture of the river on its hook, and slowly puts on his clothes.

**lagan**: *n.* goods or wreckage lying on the bed of the sea, sometimes marked with a buoy for later retrieval.

# TWENTY-FIVE

Anna and her mother had never been abroad together before, but they had been to the seaside. Anna's memory of it is vivid, how they made sandwiches in the kitchen in the early morning, whispering to each other so as not to wake her father, and how they had to take a train to get there. The station was crowded with families carrying heavy bags of food; the children swinging along with their buckets and spades; one little girl even had an inflatable dolphin. Inflatables were rare in those days. A whole gang of them was going from their street: the Cleys at number six, Ronnie and Tim from next door, and the entire Farrugia family, including their ancient grandmother, whom everyone called Nonna. The Farrugias had brought a suitcase packed with food, and when they weren't all taking turns to carry it, one of them would break away from the main group and run to hold Anna's hand. It was a month before her father died, but Anna wouldn't have known it then. She was very little: six—seven, nearly. She can't recall exactly, but she remembers it was before she had learned to swim. Her mother had given her a rubber ring with yellow stripes, but she still wouldn't let Anna go in the sea. She said it'd be no use in the current, or if a shark came in. Of course, a shark on Brighton Beach would have been her mother's idea of a joke.

Now they sit squashed in their airline seats, and her mother can't stop fussing with the safety belt.

You were eight, I'm telling you, her mother says, How is this supposed to *go*?

Anna leans over and shows her mother how it clips and unclips, how she can pull it to the desired width.

And when do we get a drink?

We haven't taken off yet, Anna says, And I was definitely younger, because I'd just started those swimming lessons at school. Remember?

You were eight, says her mother, finally. Nodding to the bag at Anna's feet, she adds, Give me one of those sweets, love, I've got heartburn bent double like this.

The flight is going to Crete, and it's full. The pilot tells them they are waiting for a couple of people, a last call has gone out, and if they don't appear there'll be a short delay while their bags are removed. He announces this in a reassuring, almost bored tone, but her mother seizes on this fact.

They have to do that, she says, Just in case they've put a bomb on board.

The man in the seat next to Anna gives them a quick glance. She whispers to her mother.

Mum, I've told you. Don't say those things. Don't say bomb on here. They'll throw you off.

*You* just said it, she says, fumbling with the packet of indigestion tablets, Maybe they'll throw *you* off. When do we get a drink?

~

As the plane travels through the air, Anna shuts her eyes and pretends to sleep. She isn't tired, but the sunlight outside the window is too intense, and she's weary of her mother's constant exclamations.

That'll be the Alps, her mother says, wiping her breath from the porthole with her handkerchief.

Anna looks for the hundredth time. It's a cloud.

That'll be them, all right, she says, closing her eyes again. She would like to look at the clouds properly, without her mother wittering at her: she wants to imagine Lewis, sitting cross-legged and smiling in at her, his roll-up dangling from the side of his mouth and his green eyes shining. She finds it frustrating that she can't remember his face, just details: the flecks of hazel in his eyes, the long white scar under his bottom lip; his smell. She's near to it now, there's something about the scent of him, a familiar, long-ago . . .

They say if you look hard enough, exclaims her mother, breaking the spell, You can see all the dead climbers. They just leave them there, you know, in the snow. They're preserved, she adds, in a whisper.

You're confusing it with Everest, sighs Anna.

Don't be ridiculous, we won't be crossing Everest! Your geography's rotten!

The man next to Anna presses the bell above his head. Her mother gives her a nudge.

He's pressed that bell, she says.

When the steward comes, he orders a second drink.

Would you like one? the man asks, in a friendly tone, and Anna accepts for both of them. Her mother looks suspicious, but when the whisky arrives, she smiles and waggles the miniature at him.

Down the hatch! she cries.

The man nods, and gives a wink only Anna can see.

Maybe that'll shut her up, he mutters, leaning back into his seat and smiling in a way that Anna finds extremely offensive. She closes her eyes again, careful not to take up too much of the arm-rests on either side. She dreams of deep water.

~  ~

Anna found it extraordinary that the swimming teacher was also the dinner lady. Her name was Mrs Chambers. She had an old face, and dyed orange hair which looked like fuzzy felt. As Anna and the other children shivered in the shallow end, Mrs Chambers stood at the edge of the pool. She'd still got on the checked overall she wore when she dished out the mash.

Hands on heads, now bend at the knees! All the way down, don't think I can't see you at the back, Philip Cross. All the way down!

Anna's first plunge into the water was shocking. It went straight up her nose, with a stinging black pain, which made her forget not to breathe in, and when she surfaced again, choking, everything was blurred. But she could hear Mrs Chambers's shouts echoing in the vast pool.

Anna Calder, you'll go straight back down! Straight back down!

And Anna went straight back down, but with her hands on her head she still couldn't stop the water from shooting up her nose and swirling in her ears.

Afterwards, in the changing room, she felt blind and sick and partially deaf. Her friend Yvonne was standing on tip-toe, trying to comb her hair in the mirror. Yvonne had managed to get dressed quite easily, but Anna was still struggling with her woollen tights. They didn't seem to fit any more; it was as if her legs had got longer and fatter. She pulled them up as far as they'd go, which left the gusset stretched taut between her knees.

Look at you, said Yvonne, peering at her, Oooh, Count Dracula!

Anna hauled herself up on the ledge and stared into the mirror. Her eyes were full of blood. She'll definitely go blind, she thought. She might even die. In those days, in Anna's world, it was possible for anyone to die, without warning.

~ ~

Anna's mother is delighted with the room and the view over the harbour, but is most impressed by the barking dog. It's chained to a stake in a building plot just beyond the hotel wall, and has been straining at the end of its leash for the last ten minutes, letting out hoarse yelps. Anna had spent hours on the Internet searching for the right hotel: air-conditioned, a room with a view of the harbour, no all-night club below. The one she found looked perfect; a faded, colonial-type place, with a cool garden surrounded by trees. She didn't anticipate barking dogs.

I can ask them for another room, she says, I'm sure they'd be happy to oblige.

Oh you, don't fuss. It's only a dog. Even a dog has to sleep, says her mother.

Anna puts her suitcase on the bed near the window, just the same, and before they go out for dinner, she pulls in the shutters and locks them. It's suddenly quiet enough to hear piped music.

Fancy that! her mother cries, opening the window at the other end of the room and peering over the gardens, They've got a band. Cabbage would've loved that!

~

They're sitting under a café umbrella, looking out at the sunset. Their plan—Anna's plan—is to have a light supper and a good night's sleep. She has the car-hire people coming early in the morning, and is finding the conversation wearing: her mother has remarked fully and loudly on other people's idea of holiday clothes, has listed the various kinds of vessel on the water, and the numerous types of fish lined up along the quayside in their crates of ice, and now she's turned her attention to the menu, which she reads out to Anna, item by item. She pauses just long enough to suck on her drinking straw.

This cocktail tastes a bit odd, she says, taking another experimental sip, It's sort of . . . minty. I said, *it's very minty,* Anna, she says, louder.

That'll be the crème de menthe, mum, I told you you wouldn't like it.

I didn't say I didn't *like* it, only that it tastes minty. Like Bisodol. And don't call me mum.

Sorry. Rita. Have you decided what you want to eat— *Rita*? Anna smiles up at the waiter hovering at the edge of the table.

I'll have him, says her mother, On toast.

Anna feels a crimson flush on her face, but the waiter grins.

I'm afraid I'm off the menu tonight, madam. But maybe tomorrow?

It's a date, says her mother, So tonight I'll settle for the lamb. As long as it's got a bone in it. I've got a little friend, you see.

The waiter nods.

With chips, madam?

Go on then, as it's you. Give me some chips as well.

~

Her mother leans on her arm. They're staring at the water, and at the sky, which has turned from pale blue to a damp, drizzled grey. A wind blows up from nowhere, gusting around the harbour and shivering the lights strung along the waterfront.

I don't feel right, Anna.

How not right? Is it your hip?

Not that. I think that plane has done something funny to my ears. It's like the ground's not steady. Like when you come out of that lift in the shopping centre. You know—wonky.

Anna feels the weight of her mother against her.

Maybe it was that second cocktail, she says, Or the lamb.

Maybe! says her mother, and patting her handbag where she has stashed the bone, No. The lamb was lovely. Didn't that plane make *you* feel ill?

A bit, says Anna, But you know me—any excuse. What did you always say to me? Hypochondria is a real illness?

This makes her mother smile. She shifts her weight, looking about her for a bench to sit on.

Why don't we go back to the hotel? says Anna, And relax in the garden?

Good idea, says her mother, A brandy would settle all that food. Cures all known ailments, she says, Even hypochondria.

~ ~

When Anna got home from the swimming lesson, she showed her mother what had happened to her eyes. She'd been off school too much since her father died, with various ailments that had no specific source. Her mother said they were just worries, but the redness was plain enough to be real, and Anna felt sore when she blinked, as if someone had blown sand in her face.

It's the chlorine they put in the pool, her mother said, tipping Anna's chin up to the light to see better, You must be allergic to it.

I've got something in my ear too, said Anna, trying not to cry, It's all stuffy.

That's just water, said her mother, It'll be gone by tomorrow.

Anna woke in the dark, with a fierce pain in her left ear, as if someone had pushed a knitting needle through to her brain, and was jabbing it back and fore. Her cries woke her mother, who went straight across to Nonna Farrugia. While her mother stood waiting at the gate for the doctor to arrive, Nonna sat with Anna, who was holding a hot water bottle against the side of her head and screaming with delirious abandon. She wanted her father, but she didn't know where he'd gone.

He's gone to heaven to be with the angels, darling, said Nonna, when Anna cried for him. The old woman pulled Anna towards her, held her tight, and cried with her.

Anna cannot recall any more of that night, not the doctor or the trip in his car to the hospital, nor the nurses or the cool pillow, nor her mother, sitting at her side in the half-light. Even though she has been told this story over and again, fever had wiped the memory. But Anna can recall Nonna, her arms around her, the skin on them warm and soft and loose-fitting. And Nonna's extraordinary wailing, as if she could blot out all the pain simply by being that much louder.

~ ~

Wake up, Anna! Wake up!

It's jet black in the room. Anna turns over on her hearing side to find out what the fuss is about.

Anna! Anna, quick!

Her mother is swaying on her bed; but no, now her eyes are growing accustomed to the darkness, Anna sees that the bed is swaying, and above it the chandelier is chattering its glass.

We're having an earthquake, you deaf moo! shouts her mother. She staggers across the floor towards the shutters and hangs on to the hasp like a man at sea. And then it's over. In the distance, a siren goes off.

Right. That's me, her mother says, grappling her way towards the light-switch; the room is filled with sudden, swinging light.

It was only a tremor, mum, says Anna, They have them here, sometimes. I should've mentioned it.

She watches as her mother zips herself into her skirt, and puts her handbag over her shoulder. There's a finality to her actions which makes Anna's bones ache.

What are you doing? she says.

Well, I won't sleep now, will I? What if there's another one? I'm getting my stuff together.

Anna can't argue with this logic. She swings herself over the edge of the bed, and watches as her mother goes into the bathroom. She waits, not quite knowing what to do next. Her mother's voice comes echoing over the partition.

I knew something wasn't right down at the harbour,

Anna. I could feel the ground wobbling. I must be psychic, mustn't I?

Anna stares at the ceiling.

What am I thinking, then? she says, to herself.

In America they have them bags you know, her mother continues, With chocolate in them. For emergencies. They're called . . . emergency bags.

The dog has started barking again. Anna considers the bone in her mother's handbag, but before she can suggest this diversion, there's another shout from the bathroom.

Anna! Come and see this!

Her mother is on her hands and knees on the floor, with her head cocked low. It looks as if she's listening for another tremor. She's staring at the space under the basin.

Well, I never, she says, her face full of wonder.

Anna crouches down next to her, and follows her finger to a line, a large diagonal crack running from the floor tiles to the top edge of the wash-stand.

That wasn't there before, her mother says.

It might have been. We might not have noticed it, mum.

Might not have noticed? It's like Cheddar Gorge. We'll have cockroaches any minute, you'll see. Pass me down that toothpaste.

Anna watches as her mother squirts a steady wodge of Colgate into the crack, smoothing it out with her finger.

What do you think that's going to do? Poison them?

Anna's mother looks up at her and starts to laugh. On her hands and knees, with her head hanging down and her bag half off her shoulder, she laughs until she's winded.

At least if they bite us, they'll have nice fresh breath!

# TWENTY-SIX

The woman at the Information Centre eyes Lewis with suspicion. He has circled the exhibits twice, picked up a stash of leaflets only to discard them again, and he's been scrutinizing the scale models for ten minutes or more. Usually it's local lads who give her trouble, seeing if they can get the blades on the models to move faster, or flicking their chewing gum at them. She watches as Lewis puts his hand up to the blades before she speaks.

Is there anything I can help you with, sir? she says, trying to make her voice at once commanding and friendly, Only, visitors are not allowed to touch the interactives.

Lewis draws his hand back and slides it into his jeans pocket. He turns around, smiling.

No, he says, There's nothing I want.

She waits, unsure of what to say next.

You can take a trip out, you know, to see them close up, she says.

Lewis approaches the desk and leans on the glass counter. He smiles again, showing his teeth as he bends near.

In a boat? he whispers.

That's right. We've got a leaflet somewhere.

No don't bother, he says, But now you mention it, there is something you could do for me.

The woman smiles back. Behind him, a school group is being led round the exhibits by a young man who looks barely old enough to be their teacher: she will have to keep an eye on them, too.

I have a friend who works there—on the project. Only I've lost her number. I wonder, do you know where the employees are billeted?

The woman laughs lightly. She gets all sorts of requests, but this one is new.

I imagine they're *billeted* all over Norfolk, she says, aping his tone, It's quite a large workforce. Have you tried calling their main office?

They don't give out addresses, says Lewis flatly.

The woman shoots him a narrow-eyed look.

Quite so, she says, Well, I've got a leaflet here somewhere listing all the current Velsters projects. That might help. Bear with me.

She turns to fetch him a leaflet off the stand. By the time she's found it, he's gone.

~

It's the last day of October. Despite the constant onshore wind, the temperature outside is mild compared to the air-conditioned chill of the Information Centre. The whiteness of the sun makes everything look fresh. Lewis is growing to like it: the regular buffeting action of the breeze makes him feel as though he is being cleansed, as if it's searching out the dust inside him and blowing it into space. In fact, the whole place is growing on him, so far is it from the cram of London, or the bad taste in his mouth that has become the memory of Wales. He could never understand why people ran away to remote places when the easiest way to lose yourself is in a city. But now, he knows why. It's the *feeling* of being remote, inside, in the bones, that makes it so alluring. He misses Anna: it's been four days since she left, and another three until she's back. He knows his inactivity is linked to her: whatever else he plans—and the plan is only to find Carl—he would like to see her, just once more. He fantasizes about the things he would tell her and how he would hold her, and this detaches him from the other feeling he has, as though he's lost a skin, as though he's been flayed. There's a sharp keyhole of black-ness when he tries to remember the last night he spent in Cardiff, and the recce of the house. Even thinking about it makes the blood beat behind his eyes. He walks along the beach wall, still looking all the while at the thirty wind tur-bines on the horizon, spinning air into heat. He stops to look again: now there are twenty-eight, now twenty-five. He shuts one eye—the one that's throbbing, and counts again: thirty. He feels a dark bloom growing at his temple. He opens his hand and stares into it, seeing the lines blur and merge into one. Lewis can sense, rather than see, a shadow growing over the vision in his left eye, as if someone beside him has put up their own hand to block the light. He feels the panic rising and tries to breathe through it, expanding his chest and ig-noring the catch inside, like a crochet needle hooked between his ribs. A prickle of sweat at his hairline, heat in his armpits. He knows if he looks upwards, he'll see a cloud of black water, the bubbles hissing past him to the surface, a snake of oil smearing his vision.

# TWENTY-SEVEN

The man delivering the hire car is Anna's age, with a neat moustache and delicate hands. Despite the heat of the morning, he's wearing a suit and tie.

Where are you taking us, then? asks Anna's mother, smiling up at him. Her lipstick is perfect today.

He's not taking us anywhere, I'll be driving. Mr—erm—sorry, I didn't catch your name, says Anna, This gentleman's just dropping the car off, mum.

It's Nick, isn't it? her mother says. She gives Anna a quick, disgusted look, Nice to meet you, Nick. You'd be very welcome to come too. *I* won't object. We're going to the *beach*.

In the car, they don't speak. Anna's mother grips the seatbelt every time a vehicle approaches from the opposite direction. Anna can feel the silence like a current in the air: her mother would like to give a running commentary about the state of the roads and the other drivers, and Anna's own struggles with the unfamiliar gearbox. She says nothing until Anna negotiates a tight bend, taking them over the white line in the centre of the carriageway.

You've got to get in more, she snaps, You'll get me killed.

Good, says Anna.

Don't be horrible to your mother.

Well, stop showing me up. Why do you have to flirt with everything in trousers? 'Nice to meet you, Nick! Coming to the beach, Nick?' For God's sake.

Exasperated, her mother shakes her head.

His name *was* Nick, I tell you. I heard him say it. You don't listen, that's your problem. And he was such a pet. If you'd have shown him some encouragement, we'd have a *proper* driver.

I am a proper driver, says Anna.

Her mother stares through the windscreen.

I mean one that can drive, she says.

Anna almost misses the sign for the coast. She turns too quickly, the map and water bottle flying off her mother's lap into the footwell. Her mother bends to retrieve them, still talking.

Just because you don't take an interest—doesn't mean I have to be rude as well. One ignoramus in the family is quite enough, thank you.

Can't hear you, mum, says Anna, through clenched teeth.

You'll have that on your tombstone, I reckon. Can't hear you! Can't hear you!

~

Even though they've made an early start, the beach is busier than Anna would like. A large gathering—a mixture of old and young and male and female—has claimed a space near the rocks. They look like a family group. Further over between the trees and the shoreline is a long row of gleaming bodies lying in the open. Her mother makes to approach them, but Anna doesn't want to get too near, and puts her bag down on the first patch of rough sand they come to. There's a smell of thyme, and roasting meat from the café halfway up the beach. Anna rolls out a beach towel for her mother, and one for herself, and then pauses.

We could go up to the café, mum, if you like, she says, trying to make peace, You could have a cold beer.

Why don't we sit up there, says her mother, pointing to where the family group is, And make camp first.

Seeing Anna's face set, she tries another tack.

There'll be a bit more shade for you.

I'll be all right, here, mum. I just thought it would be nice to get a drink, maybe a sandwich.

*They* won't mind. We won't be invading their space, her mother says, moving towards them.

Anna pulls up the towels and trudges after her. They pass the family, Anna's mother waving and shouting out a cheery *kalimera!* and Anna follows behind, crushed with shame as the group stop what they're doing to stare at them. They settle in the shade. The boulders below them are huge and foam-flecked, with small spits of sand in between. Two rock pools, deep and clear, stare up at the sky. The waves cut a churning path through the rocks, and the tide washing in and out is a noise that's familiar to Anna: it's the sound she hears in her head at night, in the darkness.

Didn't know you could speak the language, Anna mutters, moving their bags slightly further away from the family.

The hotel lady taught it to me this morning. At breakfast. Which was very nice. You wouldn't want a sandwich now if you'd had some breakfast. It was boiled egg, and toast and honey. I can still learn things, you know. I'm not senile.

Her mother unbuttons her blouse, exposing her camisole and the crêpey skin of her throat. Underneath, she wears a one-piece swimsuit in royal blue. Her hair stands on end, feathery in the dappled light. She doesn't stop chattering as she pulls the camisole up over her head.

The honey's lovely, isn't it? I think it must be local. Now, Cabbage, he loves his honey. Bran, and sliced apple, and sultanas, and yoghurt, all with honey on the top. I don't know where you put it all, I tell him, Mr Hollow Legs! We'll get some to take back.

Anna flips the lid on the sun-cream and sniffs it, passing it to her mother, who is smoothing her hair down with her hands.

We've only just got here, she says, trying not to look at her mother's head, at the pinkness of her scalp.

I know. I'm not senile.

You've already said that, says Anna, in a spiteful tone, The care homes are full of old people, dribbling and chanting, *I'm not senile, I'm not senile!*

I don't know why you're so nasty to me. You've been in a bad mood since we left England.

Yes. And d'you know why? It's been Cabbage this, Cabbage that, even before we got on the plane. If you miss him so much, why don't you send him a postcard?

Her mother rummages about in her handbag, peering into the depths and banging the sides together. Specks of dust glitter the air.

Ah, she cries, finding the phone, which she tosses onto the towel spread out between them. Anna stares at it. It's thick as an ingot, covered in plastic leopardskin print. She pulls a face.

Whose is that?

It's mine, says her mother, Well, no, it's Cabb— . . . it belongs to a *friend.*

I thought you said no phones, says Anna, the words coming hard from her mouth, In fact, I distinctly *heard* you say you didn't want me to bring my phone. No phones, you said, no phones, no sketchbooks, no worries: we're going to have a proper holiday.

It's for emergencies. Anyway, I can't get the bugger to work. International roaming, she adds.

So? says Anna.

Doesn't roam.

Anna picks it up and presses the buttons. She puts it to her ear.

Hi, Brendan, she says, after a pause, Just letting you know we got here safely and we're having a *lovely* time. Wish you were here, et cetera. I'll call you when we get back. From *my* mobile.

She throws the phone down, staring hard at her mother. Now, would you like me to call anyone for you?

Her mother sniffs the air.

If you show me how, I might do it later.

Suit yourself, says Anna, But you'll only forget.

Anna's mother shoots her a hurt look. She turns to stare at the view, whistling to herself, while Anna straightens out the towels again, arranging the bags behind her. She leans against the rock, opening her paperback and breaking the spine with a swift crack. She's on page five when her mother bends across, gesturing with her arm for her handbag, which she finally grabs by the strap, lifting it across Anna's body. A cascade of sand sprays Anna's shoulder. She stares in fury over the top of her book as her mother rummages again, mumbling to herself. Out of the bag, she takes a compact. With a trembling hand, she reapplies her lipstick.

What are you doing *that* for? cries Anna, Who are you hoping to impress? The fish?

I've worn it all my life, says her mother, Why should I stop now?

Because no one's looking.

*I'm* looking, she says, too quietly for Anna, who has turned over onto her side.

They stay like this all morning, under the overhanging rock, the woman in her blue swimsuit and pink lipstick, gazing at the sea, and her daughter, long and narrow beside her, reading her book with one arm crooked over her head.

~

When Anna wakes, her mother's gone. She sits up straight, shading her hand over her eyes, and searches the sand, and the boulders, and the sea below. She climbs up onto a jutting slab of rock, just in time to catch sight of a slip of colour moving between the boulders and into one of the rock pools beyond. She yells, then runs, scrabbling down the steep slope until she's on the sand and shouting.

What the hell are you doing?

I'm having a stroll, says her mother, What does it look like?

How did you get down?

Her mother wades back into the shallows, her face creased and sweaty.

One of those young boys gave me a hand. They're not Greek, you know. They're German. But they're ever so nice.

She bends slightly to one side, bouncing on her left leg, and then does the same with the other side, as if she's warming up for a sprint.

My hip's much better, she says, Feels easier. Must be the weather.

Coiled over her shoulder is a length of pale green rope. She pats it fondly.

I saw this, and I thought, that's a very unusual colour for seaweed, but look—it's fisherman's rope! I followed it all the way out. It must be twenty foot long.

Anna can't trust herself to speak. She looks at the rope, and her mother's hands, turning it over as she admires her find.

Can we take it back as a souvenir, Anna? she asks, It's such a pretty colour.

Let's go back up, Anna says quietly.

Her mother looks out over the pool, her eyes following the marks in the sand where she has dragged her find.

I wouldn't mind a dip. I'm feeling a bit hot.

But you can't swim, mum.

No, but you can, nearly. You could float me.

Anna doesn't understand her at first, but then her mother ties one end of the rope around her waist and passes the other to Anna. Feeding the line out behind her, she wades into the pool.

You just lean against that slab, there, she shouts, And hold on your end, and I'll have a little paddle.

Anna ties the rope around her own waist and catches the end tight in her fist. She watches as her mother spreads her limbs, dipping up and down like a starfish on the surface of the water.

# TWENTY-EIGHT

Lewis is shaving when he hears the knock on the door. He calls from the bathroom, but is surprised to find Marta already in the room, putting another tray down next to the one on the table. He wipes off the residue of foam with the palm of his hand.

Good afternoon, Mr Caine, she says, turning, I hope you don't mind, but I've brought you some lunch.

He's conscious of the enforced closeness of them both, and of the small white towel he's wearing around his waist. The sight of the trays cluttering the table, the smell of fried food, renders him mute. Marta straightens the edge of duvet, smoothing it as she ducks past him.

Mrs Calder and her daughter will be returning at the weekend, she says, So you will tell me—or Mr Savoy—if there's anything else you need.

She turns back to the door, falters, and then decides to say her piece.

I notice you didn't come down yesterday. If you prefer your meals up here, do let me know. And this evening? You'll join us, I hope?

Her voice is light, appealing, and her manner is familiar. But looking at her face, Lewis sees she isn't flirting with him.

Dinner parties aren't really my thing, he says.

The corners of her mouth twitch. She shrugs again.

Of course, she says, Whatever you wish. By the way, it's usual for me to clean the rooms up here—change the beds and so on—on Fridays.

Lewis looks about him, and down at himself, his bare feet on the rug. The room looked fine before she mentioned it, but now he imagines bolts of dust rolling under the bed, particles swimming in the air, and him, breathing in the slough of someone else's skin.

You couldn't do it today, could you? he says, lifting himself onto the balls of his feet.

Marta smiles at this.

What's funny? he says.

She's still smiling, but more uncertain now she's heard his tone. She puts her hand on the edge of the door.

Forgive me, you're not dressed. Today *is* Friday, Mr Caine.

When she's gone, he goes back into the bathroom. A scurf of foam sits along the length of his jawline. He splashes water on his skin. His heart is racing, and he breathes out slowly, counting. In the mirror. He sees how tense his face is—how *shifty*.

Relax, he says to himself, baring his teeth over the word, It's only a day. You've only lost one day.

# TWENTY-NINE

Anna looks again at her watch. Her mother has been in the bathroom for over an hour. At this rate, they'll be eating at midnight. She stares out over the balcony at the last smudge of sunset on the sea. Down in the building plot, she can just make out a corrugated iron arc, with the back half of the dog sticking out of it. It has been quiet since her mother started feeding it; Anna suspects it's got a stomach ache.

Are you alright in there, mum? she calls. She thinks she can hear noises, but it could simply be a pocket of sound: waves crashing on the rocks, resonating inside her head.

I'm nearly—, her mother falters, I'm just coming.

When she opens the door, Anna sees at once what the matter is: her mother's face is as shiny as a Maundy penny. She's put white highlighter under her eyes, panda-fashion, and has scored two long brown furrows to mark the place where her eyebrows used to be. But there's no lipstick; she's wiping her mouth with a tissue.

Can you do it for me, love? she says, holding out the tube of lipstick for Anna, Only, I'm feeling a bit gippy.

She sits on the edge of the bed and closes her eyes. Standing over her, Anna has to compose herself before she dares put the colour on her mother's mouth. She takes the tissue out of her fist and unfurls it.

Shall we just take a bit of this off? That bathroom light,

it's deceptive, she says, examining the slick of highlighter across her mother's cheekbones, Was it the fish you ate for lunch, d'you think?

It's those glasses, says her mother.

Anna concentrates, licking the tissue and dabbing at the make-up.

What is? she asks, peering into her mother's face.

Those glasses! says her mother, opening her eyes and blinking at her, Can't get your make-up on when they're on, can't see to put it on when they're off.

I think I follow you, says Anna, her tongue on her lip, But this isn't eyeshadow, is it, mum? What is it?

Brighteyes, says her mother, Cabbage got it for me, off the net. It's like Tippex, she grins, Obliterates everything. Makes me look about eighteen.

In your dreams, says Anna, Now, come on, pucker up.

Her mother closes her eyes again and makes a moue, before breaking into a smile.

I used to do this for *you,* when you were small.

Yes, mum, keep still.

Her mother smiles wider. Anna takes a step back, waits.

You were a right little nag, she says, 'Now do me! Now do me!' And whatever it was—lipstick, eyeliner, nail varnish—you had to have some too. Old Mrs Farrugia was appalled. She'll be trouble when she's older, she used to say. But you just wanted to be like me.

She could talk, says Anna, the lipstick poised between her fingers like a stick of chalk, Old Nonna, what did she look like?

That hair, nods her mother, Black as the ace of spades, and how old was she?

Seventy? guesses Anna.

It was boot polish, her mother says, pulling a grim face, That's why she wouldn't go out in the rain.

And *her* lipstick, chimes Anna,

Was the colour of pig's blood! Finishes her mother, and they both laugh at the memory.

Whereas yours, Anna says, gesturing her to close her mouth, Is as pink as a seashell.

It's called Crystal Coral. I won't tell you who chose it for me. It'll only put you in a mood.

You'll be wearing Crystal Coral on your nose if you don't shut up, says Anna.

That's what he says when he does it for me, says her mother, behaving now and offering up her face so that Anna can put a sweep of colour on both lips. Anna dabs off the excess with the tissue and stands back to examine her handiwork. Her mother presses her lips together with a quick squeaking noise.

We need our men friends, don't we, for more important things than sex.

Seeing Anna blink at what she's just heard, she rushes on,

Not that we *have* sex, you understand. I closed that gate, or door, or however it is you say it, when your father died.

Anna is looking at her mother but her mind is moving backwards. She's thinking of a closed door, and how, suddenly, and with no effort, there's one opening now. It will allow her to ask important things, it will allow her—if she's careful—back to the time before it was closed. Her mother has moved on, heaving herself off the bed and bending over the side. She's still talking, slightly embarrassed, and oblivious to the way Anna is standing still, hardly breathing.

But you see, Cabbage, now, he's good at make-up, her mother says, scrabbling under the bed and pulling out her sandals, He's got the theatrical backdrop.

Background, says Anna, tuning in again to what her mother has been saying.

That's what I said, deafy, she scolds, and then, in a put-on, creaky old voice, she cries, Isn't it windy? No, dear, I think it's Thursday.

So am I, laughs Anna, adding the punchline, Let's go and have a cup of tea.

Her mother swings her handbag over her shoulder.

Did someone say G&T? she says.

~ ~

Anna's deafness didn't go away when the infection cleared up. Her mother took her to the clinic. They were used to the mother and daughter by now, and kind, because they knew about their grief, how it had made them both ill in different ways. After the doctor had put the instrument back in its box, he turned to Anna's mother.

There's some scarring, but there shouldn't be any lasting effect. People with perforated eardrums can hear perfectly well, you know.

At her mother's insistence they were referred to an ENT clinic, to see a specialist. She attached Anna to a machine, and sat close, holding a pair of headphones.

When you put these on, you'll hear some noises. Just press that button as soon as you hear them, okay?

Anna did as she was told. She pressed the button when she heard a noise, and, unsure of herself, she pressed when she didn't. Sometimes the noises seem to meld into each other; they travelled over the top of her head in a swirling loop, and under her jaw like a chin-strap. It was quite monotonous until one particular noise made her straighten up with shock: someone was calling her name.

Afterwards, she waited while the doctor studied another machine. She was saying something: Anna could see her lips moving.

Can't hear you, she cried, pulling off the headphones. Anna's mother tutted at her daughter.

Of course you can't, with those things on, she said.

The doctor was talking about glue and grommets, and showed them a huge plastic model of the ear. When Anna got bored trying to follow their conversation, she played with the pieces, which fitted together like a jigsaw.

There's perhaps a very slight loss in the left ear, the doctor said, looking from mother to daughter, But it's not unusual at this age, especially after an infection. We'll just monitor it for a while.

Anna's mother was pleased with the news. As a treat, they went into the Sarsaparilla Bar on the high street. Anna's mother ordered a coffee, and the man came from behind the counter and crouched down and said to Anna,

Hello, little one. I'm Sammy.

He put his hand out to shake hers. Anna pushed her hands deep into her pockets, which made her mother laugh. Sammy laughed too, staring up at her mother and shaking his head. He looked like one of the men in the photographs on the wall behind him; they all had slicked hair and wide white grins. Sammy said they were actors, and her mother went across to look at the signatures on the photographs, exclaiming whenever she saw one she recognized. Watching how easily impressed she was made Anna feel even more uneasy: she hoped Sammy wasn't an actor.

Even though there was music playing and her mother and Sammy were talking and laughing, Anna blocked them out. She listened purely to the noises inside her head: soft scratches, like a mouse in the skirting, and faint bleeps, and echoes. She wanted to tell her mother that she could still hear them, could still hear her name being called. She watched her carefully: her mother had pulled her headscarf down around her neck, her hair burnished auburn under the spotlights. Her lipstick on the edge of the cup formed a blurred pink bow. When Sammy brought her another coffee, he slid onto the vacant stool next to Anna and did his smile. He had a thin stick between his teeth, which he moved from one side of his mouth to the other. Anna sidled off her stool.

I need to pee, she said, looking around her.

When she came back up the stairs, her mother was waiting by the door with her headscarf in her hands.

See you soon, I hope, Sammy shouted from behind the counter, which made her mother turn round and wave at him.

They went to the Sarsaparilla Bar after each appointment at the clinic. It had become a regular event. Anna had dandelion and burdock and her mother had coffee and a conversation with Sammy. Once the usual preliminaries were over—Sammy asking if there was any improvement, and offering commiserations—he always did the same thing: he sat close to Anna and conducted his own experiments, talking behind his hand, or pulling his sweater up over his face and whispering into his chest. Anna had to guess what he was saying, and even though he was funny, speaking like Donald Duck or mumbling rude words, she dared not laugh. She understood how she was caught; if she laughed, they would know she could hear him, and he would be her new father; and she'd never go back to the clinic. Anna couldn't allow that to happen, not now that she knew. At first, she couldn't identify the voice calling her, so she tried to ignore it. But gradually, it took on a familiar tone. The pattern was always the same: it would start with just the bleeps and taps, until she could hear a faint whisper just behind them, getting closer, closer in her ear. It was her father's voice. He would call her through the machine: Anna, Anna, gentle but clear, until the voice faded, and all that was left was an echo, the ghost of him in her ears. What Anna wanted was a way to answer him, but she didn't know how. She thought he might be lost. Or that she was lost, and he was searching for her.

There's no discernible damage, said the doctor, at their next visit, And the tests are—she searched for the word—Unambiguous. As far as they can be.

Anna sat quietly with the headphones round her neck. The sun shone like gloss on the window.

So what do we do now? asked Anna's mother. She was wearing a black coat this time, and held a black headscarf in her hands.

We can continue to monitor the situation, said the doctor, With conversion deafness—

Anna's mother interrupted,

With what, did you say?

Conversion deafness—it's possibly—um, there's no physical cause, at least none that we can find.

She paused, looked steadily at Anna's mother,

I can refer you to a counsellor, someone who can help you with your loss.

It's not me who's deaf, said Anna's mother, flipping the headscarf over her hair and tying it tight under her chin, Thank you for your time, doctor.

~

Her mother was wearing her best black because it had been a whole year since Anna's father died. After the clinic, instead of going to the Sarsaparilla Bar, they went to visit his grave. Anna wanted to wear black as well, but she didn't have any black. She wore her school uniform, which was grey, with a white blouse, and they bought a bunch of yellow flowers in paper wrapping from a stall outside the cemetery. They spent a long time walking the path between the graves, so in the end, Anna thought her father might really be lost, the way her mother kept saying his name, and wandering from place to place, and turning back on herself. When they'd walked nearly the whole way round, her mother let out a yelp and fell to her knees. She put the flowers on a flat stone; Anna understood that her father was beneath it.

We'll get a headstone, she said to Anna, And put some words on it. That'll make us both feel better. Better than any counsellor.

Is it a headstone because it's on his head? asked Anna, trying not to cry.

No, pet, his head will be fine. It's so we can find him again, when we next come to visit.

Will Sammy be coming too? Asked Anna, staring at the splash of colour marking the grave.

Who? said her mother, and taking a sharp breath, No. No Sammy. You must understand this, Anna. There'll be no more doctors, and—listen to me—definitely no Sammy.

# THIRTY

Lewis sits on the bottom step of the Nelson memorial. It has been cordoned off with red and white tape, which flutters with the rhythm of a kite on a line. It reminds him of a crime scene, but the notice printed on an adjoining piece of hardboard announces a restoration project, and the name of the firm. There's the gusting wind again at his back, blowing off the sea. He smokes a cigarette, cupping his hand around the tip to make it last. He keeps the guest-house in full view, afraid that were he to shut his eyes, it might simply vanish. He fixes on his window at the top. If Marta took a look out through the nets, she would see him sitting there, like a dog waiting to be let back in. To the casual eye, he would appear fairly relaxed. In fact, his blood is so quick with excitement that he can feel himself shaking. And it's all down to Marta and one word.

She was standing in the hallway, talking in a foreign language on the telephone, when he came down the stairs. He was just about to pass her when she caught his eye, and put her finger in the air to indicate she wanted to speak to him.

Mr Caine, she breathed, flushed from her goodbyes to whoever was on the other end of the line, Are you going out? I could make up your room?

He thanked her and opened the front door.

And dinner? she asked, bending round him to catch his eye, Only my son Kristian will be joining us tonight—he's an engineer just up the road here, you know, on the Velsters project, and he finds Mr Savoy a little—here she dropped her voice and tried not to smile—A little concentrated?

You'd like me to dilute, said Lewis. He could feel his heart racing beneath his jacket, felt the words thicken on his tongue, but he smiled, as casually and unshiftily as he could, before skipping down the steps.

And he is still strangely elated. He'll wait on the steps, and when he's given Marta enough time to do his room, he'll wander back in. He'll be in a clean room, with a definite way forward. In his mind, the evening is shaped as a Venn diagram, one overlapping circle is the Velsters project, the other is Sonia; in the centre, just where he wants him, is Carl.

## THIRTY-ONE

It's hot inside the restaurant, and perilously dark, each table lit by a tealight in a shallow bowl. Seated behind the plate-glass window, Anna and her mother share the view of the harbour, a petrol blue sky gradually turning navy. They watch as people drift along the promenade. Anna's mother makes wry comments about the clothes, the hairstyles, the fake tans on show. The maître d' stands outside, trying to tempt them in to eat; it's late season, every potential punter is treated to an abundant and showy welcome. Anna's mother is fascinated by the goings-on; as they wait for the drinks to arrive, she observes everyone closely.

The evening has already taken flight; a party of lobster-coloured tourists across the aisle talk loudly over each other, posing for pictures and clinking glasses together. Before she's even tasted her drink, Anna is asked to take a group photo-graph. Her mother is up from her seat immediately. She yells instructions at them, organizing the party into a grinning semi-circle. Above the din, Anna tries to make out what she's shouting. It sounds like 'say fantastic,' but there's a roar of laughter, which makes Anna think it must be something rude. Her mother slumps back in her seat, steadying herself by grip-ping the edge of the table.

Okay, David Bailey, here's your raki, says Anna, pushing a sweating glass towards her.

It'll be all a blur, she says, nodding her head over to the group, Never mind. They won't know that 'til they get home.

Well, they look fairly tanked up, agrees Anna.

Her mother bends forward, so the gold chains around her neck swing in the candlelight.

No, no, she whispers, Look at me. Talk about virgin on her wedding night!

She stretches her arms out over the cloth. Her hands quiver like autumn leaves.

Haven't you got tablets for that? asks Anna, staring at the long fingers, at the dress-rings catching the light. Her mother wrinkles her nose.

Can't have both, she says, clasping her tumbler, And I know which one makes me feel better. Chin chin.

Anna raises her glass, and as they drink, they hold each other's gaze. Now is the time, she tells herself, Now is a good time.

Whatever happened to the tourmaline? she asks, stroking her mother's fingers, I used to love that ring when I was little.

Her mother studies her hands.

Oh, now that was the only real one of the lot of them, she says, I've left it safe at home. But the rest were just glass, you know. Funny how if you're told something's true you'll believe it, even when it isn't.

Dad told you?

He was ever so good at putting on a show, she says, smiling, We both were. He always wanted to be an actor, you know.

She leans close, her voice confidential,

But he was never quite good enough. Never *top-drawer*. And he said I held him back.

Anna rushes to her defence.

That's not true! You had a lot to put up with, she says.

Her mother bats a hand in her direction.

Oh. You mean the flirtations. That wasn't anything, dear, believe me. It's all different now, of course. Back then, you were in it 'til death do us part. Nowadays, people get divorced if they don't like the same brand of coffee.

So you knew? says Anna, shocked by her mother's candour.

Her mother drains her glass, holding it out to Anna for a refill. She gives her a sceptical look.

In those days, they called it 'free love'. But you see, love is the opposite of freedom. Everyone knows that. We had terrible fights about it; he wanted free love for himself—but I had to pay.

Anna is dumbfounded. She was hoping for a certain intimacy, but she hadn't bargained on this.

You had rows? she says, shaking her head, But I never heard you.

Anna, you never hear anything. You were deaf before you went deaf. You'll find out one day; it's a tricky old thing, love.

But surely it doesn't have to be such a—Anna searches for the word—Such a sacrifice?

Her mother hoots with laughter. When she sees Anna's puzzled face, she leans across the table and grips her fingers. She holds on tight.

Your chap, she says, out of the blue, Now, take him, for example.

Anna stiffens at the change of tack.

What chap? she says.

Your Mr Caine.

His name's Lewis.

Her mother's face lights up, delighted.

Lewis, she says, What a lovely name. So. Do you think your Lewis is going to be easy to love?

Anna fidgets with her drink, sipping the raki, feeling the cool burn of spirit in her throat and the warmth of her mother's grasp. She wants to be sure of her voice before she answers.

We hardly know each other, mum. I wouldn't call it love.

You might not call it that, says her mother, But it's as plain as Julie Andrews to everyone else. And you don't *need* knowledge to fall in love, my girl. In fact, that's the last thing you need. By the time you'd got to know all about him, you'd be put off for life. That's your trouble, she says, with a satisfied pursing of her lips, You get to know your chaps too well before deciding to fall in love with them, and then, of course, you can't. It's called 'falling' for a reason, Anna. Not *jumping* in love, or *sliding* in love, or waking up one morning and *deciding* in love. Falling. That's what it is because that's how it feels. You slip off the edge. You fall.

The waiter sets a bowl of bread on the table and takes their orders. Without prompting, he brings Anna a bottle of white wine and pours a measure into a fresh glass.

On the house, tonight, he says, As it's the last time I serve you.

For now, says her mother, with a pantomime wink, Unless you want to come back with us?

The waiter smiles broadly and nods his head.

Of course, he says, moving to clear the next table, It would be an honour.

Anna takes a deep slug of wine. Tonight, her mother can flirt all she likes.

I can't take too much of that stuff, she says, waving at the bottle of spirit, It's like fire.

You can get used to anything, says her mother.

Are you talking about the raki, or dad? asks Anna, only half-serious.

Her mother's face takes on a distant, troubled look.

What's that joke, Anna, about the man banging his head against the wall?

Are you feeling alright, mum? she asks, noticing how wide her mother's eyes look behind her glasses, You're not about to have one of your spells?

They are not spells, Anna; they're just my brain having a rest!

The way she says it makes them both laugh.

Like a little holiday from yourself, Anna says, joining in.

That's right, a respite from the rest of me. God knows where I go, but I don't mind the journey as long as I come back.

She tips the last of the raki into her glass and makes a signal to the waiter to fetch another one.

These little bottles, she says, They don't touch the sides, do they?

~   ~   ~

Over a thousand miles away, Lewis has showered and shaved, he's wearing a clean white shirt and his best jeans. He stands on the landing, listening: the quick bright chime of glasses, followed by sounds of laughter, drift up from below.

He tracks the noise as he takes the stairs. They are sitting at the table, three of them reflected into six by the picture window; and the glow coming off their bodies, the heat they generate in the small corner, makes his chest feel tight. Vernon Savoy is wearing a purple waistcoat and a polka-dot bow tie, and what appears to be a pair of Oxford bags; a bucket of champagne is perched at his elbow. Marta looks like summer in a pale yellow dress. She has made an effort; the table is laid formally, with a white cloth and silverware, giving the municipal dining-room an atmosphere of intimacy. Despite this, Lewis knows it will be difficult to be civil; the clutter of the group, huddled together in one corner as if under siege, makes Lewis long for emptiness. Marta stands up when she sees him, to make her introductions. Her son looks younger than Lewis imagined, and when he in turn gets up to shake his hand, Lewis notes the slightness of his build. Kristian's collarless shirt and the bangle on his wrist make him look girlish. But he has Marta's tough, open features, and her accent.

Pleased to meet you, he says to Lewis, As you can see, we're having a small celebration.

Lewis sits in the vacant place opposite Vernon and Kristian, stretching over to take the champagne from the bucket and then pushing his chair back from the table-edge to give himself more space. He fills his glass, and seeing Vernon's eyebrows rise at the near-empty flutes on the table, tops them up.

Sorry, he says, I'm forgetting my manners. What's the occasion?

Vernon lets out a titter,

It's a wonderful toast, he says, catching Lewis's eye, Highly unusual. To Scrooby-Doo!

He raises his glass and drains it, as does Lewis. The champagne is arid on the back of his throat. He resists the urge to cough. Marta and Kristian exchange a meaningful look over the rims of their glasses, before Kristian interrupts.

Actually, Vernon, it's Scroby, he says, and turning to explain to Lewis, As in Scroby Sands.

Sorry, man, I'm no wiser. Maybe another one of these will make it clear.

This time, he hands his glass to Vernon, who pours in the last of the champagne.

It doesn't go far, sighs Vernon, heaving himself up from his seat, I'll just pop and get another one.

Kristian hunches his shoulders, as if he's about to reveal a secret. His words are slow and precise.

We have completed the project, he says, The systems are up and running.

Marta joins in, unable to keep the boast from her voice,

Kristian is one of the project engineers, she says, So it's a good day for him. A good day for the planet!

I'll drink to that, says Lewis, just as Vernon returns with a fresh bottle of champagne.

So will I, he says, I'll drink to that! What is it we're toasting again?

Ecology, says Lewis, looking steadily at Kristian, Tell me more about Velsters. What sort of team have you got there?

Kristian talks while Marta goes to check on the food. Already bored by the topic, Vernon makes his excuses and trundles out behind her. Lewis can hear his plummy tones, punctuated by quick snorts of laughter, echoing in the kitchen. Marta's voice is too low to carry. Kristian is glad to be asked about his work; he has an evangelical fervor about wind technology that Lewis finds charming, but ultimately dull. He's not interested in renewable energy, alternative power. If anything, he's slightly averse to thinking about it; he's reminded of Miss Hepple and her hippie clothes, of her 2CV. On the back window was a peeling sticker; a sunshine face with Nuclear Power? No Thanks! written round it in a circle. Half-listening to Kristian's descriptions, he sees the turbines now not as beautiful sea creatures, but as brutish things, like the chimneys of a power station. But he lets the young man talk, grateful for the breathing space it allows him. He is waiting for a window.

So the work is finished now? says Lewis, when Kristian finally pauses.

Well, really, it has only just begun. Although—here he lowers his voice, eyes sideways at the door—It may be that, personally, *my* work here is done. I will be needed on another project. Just don't tell my mother.

And the rest of the team, says Lewis, moving forward an inch, What about them?

Kristian shrugs, turns down the corners of his mouth. Lewis wills him to say a name.

The analysts, the operations people—all the people who maintain the site—they will have work to do, of course.

He isn't just going to say a name out of the blue. Kristian won't say Sonia's name. Lewis slumps back in his seat, just as Marta and Vernon arrive with the food. He feels exhausted. He has learned more about wind-farms than he has ever expected or wanted to, and nothing about Sonia. The hopelessness of it overwhelms him. While the others spear their forks into potatoes, pour sauce, pass each other salt and pepper, Lewis bends his head and shovels in the food. He's almost filtered out the conversation when Kristian leans in across the table.

I'm saying, Mr Caine, you can take a boat out to the site,

if you'd like to see the turbines up close. I could accompany you.

Lewis shrugs.

Boats aren't my thing, he says, sucking his teeth. Realizing how abrupt this sounds, he softens, Thanks, I would like to see them up close. I'm just not keen on the water.

Kristian grins.

So many people who don't like the water are living here! It's amazing, yeah? My friend Sonia, she won't take a boat trip, but she'll fly in a helicopter, for sure. I prefer to take my chance on the sea. The other day—

Where does she take a helicopter, interrupts Lewis, feeling a burn in his throat, At Scroby?

No, she's at Winterton, at the lodge there. There is a base, you know, for sea rescue, and some private charters. But she wants to take some souvenirs—some pictures—of the wind installation at Somerton, says Kristian, It has a great name: Blood Hill!

Everyone laughs at this except Lewis, who shoots Kristian a puzzled look. He can't tell if it's the way he talks or the champagne, but he's struggling to follow him.

Your friend's working at the helicopter base? he asks, trying to keep the intent out of his voice.

Ah! You'd like a helicopter ride, says Kristian, Perhaps I could arrange it.

Lewis turns the heat of his gaze onto his plate. He'll just have to be direct.

So Sonia, he says, She's there now, at this Winter place?

Winterton, yes, for a few days, I think, to look at Blood Hill. It is the first installation we make; smaller, but very effective. They use a system—

Bored by the conversation, Vernon raises his glass,

Somerton, Winterton, how fabulous, he cries, Now I'll drink to that!

Blood Hill, says Lewis, in his head, For fuck's sake. I'll drink to *that*.

# THIRTY-TWO

The wind barrels around the side of the hotel: rising from her deep, wine-drenched sleep, Anna dreams of being on a ship. It is not an unpleasant dream, and she's had it before: she is aware of the exact location of the lifeboats, has worked out her exit strategy, and she's wearing her rubber ring. It's just that, this time, she can't find her mother. She's looked in the cabin and the bar, and is making her way up to the top sun-deck when she hears, quite distinctly, her father's voice.

Anna, he calls, Anna.

She follows the sound up to the deck and through a throng of people all gasping with amazement. In front of an ordinary school chalk-board, her mother is giving a lecture. She has drawn a great many pictures on the board, and her hands are white with dust. She's throwing aniseed twists into the crowd.

Look at the lustre, at those facets! she cries.

Anna wants to ask her mother where her dad is, but she can't make her voice heard above the din. Without warning, Nonna appears and puts her arms round her. Anna smells garlic and 4711 cologne.

He's down there, Nonna says, pointing at a dot in the sea, Go on, child, jump!

Anna squints at the figure in the water; the waves are a tripe-grey, rolling mass.

Just do as she says, dear, and dive in, urges her mother, taking Anna's elbow and leading her to the guard-rail, You've got nothing to fear. We've all *been* there, you know.

Anna stares at the figure, nearer now, and sees it's not her father at all. She leans further over, to get a better look. The face is familiar. She leans further still, further and further, and feels the rail slide away from her grip as she tips into space. Now she's tumbling, past the lower deck and the aerobics class in mid-jump, past the duty officer sneaking a sly cigarette, past the porthole where Vernon's round face stares out at her. She closes her eyes and waits to smash into the sea.

~

The morning sky through the half-open shutters is the colour of raw dough. Anna turns over, sees her mother's bed is empty. With a dry mouth and a banging head, she recalls the previous night. They'd talked, and drank, well into the early hours; they'd discussed love and men and sex like two old friends. She can't recall exactly what was said, but her nausea is mingled with shame: she remembers telling her mother, to wails of laughter and the occasional, intense silence, about Roman and all the others—even the married one. And she'd cadged endless cigarettes from the waiter. Anna feels furious with herself: now, everything she said will be hurled back at her. Her mother will just be waiting for the most inappropriate moment.

Bugger it, she says, pulling on her clothes, She was probably too pissed to remember, anyway.

Anna passes through the foyer and out round the back of the hotel. She finds her mother crouching down at the far end of the yard; in her arms, the big round head of the dog.

What are you doing? she says. She stands over them, her hands on her hips.

And a very good *kalimera* to you too, says her mother, I was just saying *yassou* to Geoffrey here. I shall so miss him.

Geoffrey?

Her mother grins up at her,

An old, very old boyfriend, she says, turning to the dog, But *very* handsome. I told you about him last night, remember?

She stands up, and the dog, freed from the embrace, slumps down on the ground at her feet.

He's going to miss me too, she says, That's plain enough.

We should get going, says Anna, We've got to be at the airport in an hour.

I know, I know, says her mother, waving her away, Don't get your thong in a twist.

Anna follows her mother back through the foyer, fuming.

I do not wear a thong, she says, so loudly that the woman at reception raises her head, I do not even *own* a thong.

Her mother sniffs,

That's not what you told me last night, she says.

Anna refuses to answer. It will be an easier journey back if she doesn't respond to her taunts. Her mother repeatedly prods the lift button.

The light's on, mum, says Anna, pointing at the lit-up arrow.

But no one's home, says her mother, Got out the wrong side of bed, did you?

I had a bad dream. We were on some kind of ship, and you were giving a lecture and I fell in the sea.

Her mother laughs, warming to the story.

Trust you to wreck my cruise of a lifetime, she says, nudging Anna to show she's joking, So that's why you're so cross. I dreamed once that your father ran away with Hattie Jacques. It took me a week to forgive him. Sophia Loren, now, that I could understand. But Hattie Jacques!

Dad was in the dream too. He was swimming in the sea.

Her mother looks up at her, round-eyed.

Can't have been him, she says, He loathed swimming.

Anna feels her headache scythe across the back of her eyes.
It was *my* dream, mum, I think I'd know.

Wonder what it means, her mother says, archly.

It means I had too much wine, says Anna.

Your father hated the water. It was as much as he could
do to take his socks off and paddle afterwards. But you'd
know that.

Anna thinks she's misheard.

After what? she says, confused.

After that time in Cornwall, says her mother emphati-
cally, as if Anna's a simpleton, When he nearly drowned.
He'd got an ant bite on his elbow and went in the sea to
cool it off.

She presses the button again. From far above comes the
sound of doors sliding shut, and the steady grumble of a
motor.

I don't remember it, says Anna, How old was I?

Her mother inspects herself from all angles in the mirrored
walls of the lift.

You? You weren't even born, silly, she scoffs, It was on
our first anniversary.

Then how could I remember? says Anna, through gritted
teeth.

I didn't say you'd remember. I said you'd *know*. Do
keep up.

Anna follows her down the cool marbled corridor. Now
there'll be a fuss with the key, as there has been every day of
the holiday.

And how would I know? says Anna, staring holes into the
back of her mother's head.

Because you've inherited the same fear, obviously. I've
been observing you—you sit so far back from the sea, you
might as well stay in the hotel. Here, I can't get this key to
work.

I've left it open, says Anna, turning the handle.

And you a city-dweller, says her mother, disappearing into the darkened room. She opens the shutters at the far window to let in an even pool of light, and turns to her daughter,

So, if it wasn't your father swimming in your dream, who was it?

# THIRTY-THREE

The light over the east coast is soft and grey. There's no wind, and the stillness of the day is broken only by the liquid trill of a blackbird, and the random cries of the gulls as they fall and rise over the sea.

Anna's room is not what Lewis expects: it's a scene of devastation. The wardrobe doors are hanging open, the clothes spilling out all over the floor; there's a slump of books across the bed and a nest of dirty cups on the bedside table. The walls are covered with sketches and Polaroids, all showing the same scene: the wind-farm, both imagined and real. Thick rolls of paper have been wedged with a steam iron against the back of the desk, and the desk itself is littered with an assortment of charcoal stubs and scrunches of balled-up paper. He unfurls one, holds it one way, then another, then turns it upside down and takes it to the window. It looks like a seascape, but he can't be sure. Perhaps it's a skyscape. He thinks it's very beautiful. Tempted to flatten it, he considers the iron—whether that would do the trick. There isn't time. Turning the sketch face down onto the blotter, he presses out the creases as best he can, then rolls the paper into a tube and slips it in his jacket pocket.

He has a gift he'd like to leave her, but he can't think of where to put it in all the mess. He doesn't consider that Anna would know exactly where everything is. Deciding that she'll find it eventually, he takes the book of poems and leaves it open on the bed, using the box of matches he stole from her to wedge the page. A last look at the room; nestled among the bedclothes and the spilling books, and looking completely at home, is his love-song to her.

*A Woman to a Man*

*To own nothing, but to be—*
*like the vagrant wind that bears*
*faintest fragrance of the sea*
*or, in anger, lifts and tears*
*yet hoards no property;*

*I praise that state of mind:*
*wind, music, and you, are such.*
*All the visible you find*
*(the invisible you touch)*
*alter, and leave behind.*

*To pure being you devote*
*all your days. You are your eyes,*
*seemingly near but remote.*
*Gone now, the sense of surprise,*
*like a dying musical note.*

*Like fragrance, you left no trace,*
*like anger, you came my way,*
*like music, you filled the space*
*(by going, the more you stay).*
*Departures were in your face.*

Anna reads the poem twice, the little book trembling in her hands. He's left no note, no sign, nothing except this and an empty match-box. She buries her face between the pages to find the smell of him; leather, cedar, sea-salt. She could wail with the pain in her. Marta said she had heard the front door closing just before lunchtime. Thinking it was Anna and her mother returning home, she'd gone out into the hall to greet them, only to find a heap of notes and small coins on the table. Who else could it be? Marta said, with a sad smile— and not waiting for a reply, added—It could be no one.

Marta's calling her now, from the floor above. Anna shouldn't be angry with her, but she feels it anyway, feels a growing frustration with everyone here—Vernon and her mother, cosying up in the lounge, and Marta, clean, efficient Marta with her bright, artless tones, shouting at her. Anna listens more closely: the tone isn't bright—there's an edge of panic there. Anna takes the stairs two at a time, swinging round the door-frame of Lewis's room. Marta is standing at the window, holding up the net curtain.

I didn't hear anything, she says, as if to apologize, Not a sound.

The room is bare, much as Anna remembers it from her first night at the house. But the window is clear in the middle, as if a cloth has been wiped over the glass. Closer, Anna feels the faint waft of sea-wind on her face.

He smashed it? says Anna.

And this one, says Marta, holding up the net at the second pane, And look here.

She turns to the little table; the tray and the tea-things are covered in shattered glass. Hanging lopsided on the wall is the picture of the river, a diamond smash at its centre. Anna lifts it up to the light. There are fragments of glass stuck around the edges of the frame, and on them, on the picture itself, a thousand dots of dried brown blood.

Is this all the damage? asks Anna, composing her face.

All I can see, says Marta, There's nothing in the bathroom.

Anna closes the door and sits on the edge of the bed. Marta stays at the broken window, as if on watch.

Did you see him at all yesterday? She asks.

Marta's face looks pale blue in the window-light.

Yes. In fact, he had dinner with us. He was quite sociable. Kristian rather liked him.

Your son was here? asks Anna

Yes, and Mr Cabbage—Mr Savoy. It was a merry crowd. We had a pleasant evening.

And did he mention anything about leaving?

Anna hears the tone of her own voice, like an inquisitor. Marta shrugs, but her off-hand manner is unconvincing.

He was interested in a place Kristian mentioned. Along the coast here.

Where along the coast?

Marta doesn't answer at first. She sighs. She looks out of the window; she looks anywhere but directly at Anna. Eventually, she sits down next to her on the bed and stares at the floor.

Anna, don't go after this man. He is—look about you—this is a troubled man, a lot of damage inside him. He's dangerous to love.

Anna's heart is banging so loud she's sure Marta can hear it.

Don't tell them two downstairs about this, she says, Just tell them I've gone out for a while. Now, Marta. What place on the coast?

## THIRTY-FOUR

The walking's not so bad, given that Lewis's usual mode of transport is a van. And his feet aren't giving him any trouble, although, as he's trying to stay mainly out of sight—keeping wherever possible to the beach—he has to stop now and then and tip out the sand accumulating in his boots.

Within a mile of starting he came across a man sea-fishing, a black-cut figure against the backdrop of the waves. They were the only two people on the sand. As Lewis approached, walking a curve around the umbrella and boxes set up on the tide-line, the man turned his head to greet him, just the briefest of acknowledgements, and then continued his long stare over the north sea.

Sea on the right and sandy cliff-face on the left is all that greets Lewis after Caister. Occasionally, the cliffs above him have crumbled like sponge cake onto the beach, leaving big-mouthed gaps which reveal a caravan park, the red-tiled roof of a last house, sometimes just another piece of sky.

He managed to find out from Kristian how far he has to travel—eight or ten miles, he'd said, depending on the route. He has a fizzing sensation in his chest that is close to happiness. As soon as he was out of sight of the main road, Lewis found a wheelie bin, and opened the lid. He did an inventory one more time, listing under his breath:

Fleece jeans shirts socks pants washbag book of poems—
no, no poems—knife beans pouch—and chain. No chain.

He took the black pouch out of his kitbag, considered
for a moment, then put it in his pocket: that was all he
wanted. He threw his kitbag into the bin and walked away.
Now, with nothing to carry but himself, he feels light as
the light above him. As he walks further north, the sky turns
itself inside out, so the bag of cloud hanging over Yarmouth
becomes a silver bowl. He has left every penny he had at
the guest-house, but he's hungry and thirsty now. He turns
off the beach at the next gap in the dunes, climbing up the
rough grass path, and sees the start of a road. At the end of
a narrow terrace, just when he's beginning to think there's
nothing to be had, he sees a sign: the California Inn is open
for business.

~ ~ ~

Anna throws her head back and has a scream. When she's
finished screaming, she hammers her fist repeatedly on the
steering wheel, as if that would do the trick. All it does is
sound the horn, which brings Vernon running down the
passageway at the side of the house. He leans his hands on
the garden wall, takes a deep breath, and launches: which is
how Anna notices him, falling like Humpty Dumpty on the
grass verge.

Go away! she cries, For Christ's sake!

Vernon limps over and pulls open the passenger door. He's
smiling but he looks pained.

Are you having trouble? he asks, Only, I could hear that
horn in the lounge.

Anna gives him a withering glance.

What do you think? she says.

Vernon considers.

Well, if the horn's working, it's probably not your bat-
tery. Pop her lid open, and I'll have a little peek.

It's the neighbourhood, Vernon, she says, trying to keep her voice level, Or haven't you noticed?

She points towards his door. At first, he doesn't understand, but then he inspects the tyres, walking right round the car, shaking his head and tutting. She winds down her window.

All flat, he says, The little bastards.

And they've stolen my badge, Anna says, feeling the tears behind her eyes, Brendan got me that not two weeks ago.

You could always go in my car, says Vernon, If it's so very urgent.

Your car? says Anna, stupidly, You've got a car?

Vernon is almost apologetic.

She doesn't go out very often so I keep her locked up safe. Should you like to inspect her first?

~   ~   ~

Lewis orders a pint of bitter and a cheese baguette. He's the only customer in the pub, but he stays at the bar. The girl serving him has a child-like, soft look about her: Lewis wonders if she's even old enough to be serving drinks. While he gulps his beer, she disappears out of sight. From the adjoining room, music starts to play, the unmistakable roll and fanfare of electronic noise. Lewis is thinking of finishing his drink, pocketing his baguette, and walking—what would she do, this teenager, chase him down the road? But instead, he follows the sound round the corner. The girl is playing on a games machine, stabbing her finger at the screen.

Any good? he asks, leaning against the side of the box.

Reflected in her face are sharp squares of coloured light. She doesn't take her eyes off the game, but she shakes her head. Lewis moves behind her to get a better view. It's a pub quiz machine, one of the ones Lewis is familiar with; has, in fact, been barred from playing.

Karl Marx, he says, and she hits the screen.

1939.

Rome—no, Florence. Quick!

Her fingers hover over the glass as the seconds tick down to the next round.

What category? she says, looking up at him.

He chooses film. In the next category, he chooses pop music. When they get to the £20 question, the screen freezes.

Aw, she says.

Lewis wanders back to the bar and finishes his sandwich.

Has it done that before? he asks, as she sidles round the counter.

I don't think it's ever got that far before, she says, eyeing him with interest.

It's probably fixed, he says, pushing the empty plate away, Is there a bank round here?

The girl puts her head on one side. She looks like she's heard this story before, but she surprises him with her answer.

The post office will cash you a cheque, she says, bright with her idea, They're always doing it for me. Or further up the road there's a Budgen, you can get cash-back.

Lewis drains his glass and winks at her.

See you in ten minutes, he says.

## THIRTY-FIVE

Vernon helps Anna adjust the front seat and the wing mirrors, all the while giving instructions.

She pulls a bit to the left, he says, handing her the key, And she's a bit draughty; I've been meaning to get that window replaced, but parts are a devil to find.

I'll be fine, Vernon, thank you, says Anna, impatient to be gone.

He fiddles with the blanket on the back seat, then searches in the glove-box.

I normally keep a nip in here, for emergencies . . . ah, here it is, he says, shaking the flask, Winter warmer!

Vernon, really, I'll be alright.

The engine starts with a shudder, then settles into a coughing rumble. Over the din, Anna thanks him again. Vernon leans through the window and startles her by placing a kiss on top of her head.

You take care, he says, waving her away.

~ ~ ~

From the helicopter, the damage is clear. All along the coastline from north to south, the land is crumbling into the sea. At Happisburgh, the pilot points out the church, the bungalows edging towards destruction, the bed and breakfast house with its garden halfway down the cliff. Sonia leans into her window, shading her eyes from the sun cutting across the cockpit. At this angle, the newly exposed cliff-face looks like a weeping wound, bleeding for miles above the sand. The helicopter rises up and out, over the sea above Horsey, so that the view Sonia has now is like a lost picture of England: the rust and red of the nature reserve rolls away to a wide expanse of green and ochre land. A windmill stands proud above a cut of black water.

It's fantastic, she says, and Alec nods.

It's pretty good, he says, You never get tired of it.

They head inland, flying a wide circle around the wind-farm. On the road into Winterton there's a queue of traffic, tailing half a mile back and disappearing round a sharp bend. At the front is a pale blue convertible. Sonia can't hear the car horns, but she can see the driver making gestures with her arm, instructing the vehicles to overtake. Closer, the wind turbines on Blood Hill form a sleek avenue. Sonia takes photographs from various angles before they arc back out over the village, the painted cottages as small and square as dolly mixtures. Passing directly above Winterton Lodge, Sonia picks out the roof of her Suzuki and that of a dirty white van, before the pilot resumes his course and heads out over the sea. In the distance, the rotors at Scroby wind-farm flicker like candles on a cake.

Fancy a drink back at base? asks Alec.

Sonia puts her thumbs up, grinning with glee. They don't speak again until the landing pad is directly below them and they're touching down. Sonia feels so elated, and so deaf, the tune her mobile plays is like a distant song.

~

Inside the van, a conversation is taking place. Amongst the empty beer cans, crisp packets, sandwich cartons, Rizla papers, and rolls of cling-film that litter the passenger side, Manny tries to find a place to put his feet. He's had to take a coach, two trains, and then another agonizing bus crawl to get this far, and now Sonia's giving him earache. He passes the mobile back to Carl, who is making a cigarette. He jams the phone under his chin.

Okay, girl, see you later, he says, Yeah, I will. I said I will—

Carl glances over to his father,

—No, he's alright. I'll bring him over. Yeah, I'll tell him. Haha, you n'all.

As soon as he ends the call, the phone rings again. Carl says two words which are lost on Manny, and hits the button. The phone rings again.

Will you switch that bugger off, for Christ's sake! shouts Manny, trying to grab it, We've got a problem here, in case you'd forgotten.

I don't see a problem, says Carl, licking the paper edge of his roll-up, We'll go and meet Sonia and then you can take the shitting van, I'm done with it anyway. Give us your return ticket and we'll call it swaps.

You can buy your own bloody ticket! And what d'you think I'm going to do with this? says Manny, banging his hand on the dashboard. The glove-box falls open, causing a sheaf of polythene bags to spill out into his lap.

Give it to back to your friend, says Carl, scooping up the bags and shoving them down the side pocket, Wondered where they'd got to.

He doesn't want it. He wants his brother's bracelet, Manny says. And, oh yeah, I nearly forgot: he wants to kill you.

He'll have to join the queue, says Carl, filling the van with thick, sweet smoke, And dad, let me tell you, it's one hell of a queue.

Manny puts his feet down in the debris and springs open the passenger door.

Come on, I'm not sitting here waiting.

Carl jumps out beside him, trying to keep pace as Manny heads towards the lodge.

What you gonna do? Book yourself in for the night?

I'm going to keep one step ahead, laddo. That's what I'm going to do.

~ ~ ~

Lewis is sitting on the sand, his back against a rusted jag of sea defence. From far off, the groyne looked like a medieval pew—he can't remember the name for the thing he's thinking of—but he knows it'll come back, as everything, eventually, comes back. He's been staring at the ocean for hours now. He's watched the sun, casting a wide net of sparks on the sea, watched it slide across the sky, over his head, and behind him. He's watched the dog walkers, and the birds, but mainly he's kept his eyes on the horizon. The sky now has gone the colour of ice; the sea is tinfoil. When he met the man fishing a few hours earlier, Lewis wondered how he could possibly spend the day staring out like this and not go mad. Now he's beginning to understand: it's the opposite of mad. His hand is sore; the knuckles are busted and there's a star-shaped gash in the centre of his palm. He licks at it, tasting salt, longing for Anna.

Behind him, a notice says Danger! Buried Ironworks. To his left, another notice is pinned to a post warning dog owners that little terns are nesting. A lone seal breaks the surface of the water, his big head bobbing like a black dog, waiting for a stick to be thrown. The seal goes under again, only to emerge a few metres further south, still staring at Lewis with shining eyes. Behind the seal, Lewis sees the wind-farm out at Scroby sands. The turbines are no more than tiny, glittering specks. He puts up his finger and thumb and pinches one between them. Even at this distance, there's no escaping what he feels; Anna is in everything he sees.

Above him, the putter of a helicopter. He's counted three so far today. Shielding his eyes, he catches sight of a figure waving from a window. Lewis waves back, drops his arm.

His hand is really sore. He should bathe it. He's heard that seawater is good for wounds.

~ ~ ~

The landlord at the Fisherman's Return said the lodge was easy to find—a five-minute walk—but Anna's already lost her way. She took the back lane, but when it forked she couldn't remember if he said left or right. The only house in sight is a clapboard cottage on a spit of higher ground. In the front garden, a To Let sign has sagged sideways across the path, the estate agent's details weathered to almost nothing. Anna stands at the garden wall and looks back down the street to the fork in the road. Running up the middle is a footpath leading to the dunes, and on the right-hand side is a white building, almost invisible against the sky. It's not what Anna expects a lodge to look like, but as she gets close, she sees a brass plaque on the front wall bearing its name. Below the plaque is a board with a handwritten list of dates and measurements, and pinned to one side are various photographs of a garden with a shed, a garden without a shed, and a piece of ragged grass with a criss-cross of tape spun around it. Anna takes a few seconds to realize that these pictures are of the same view, photographed over a period of months.

Inside, the reception is deserted except for a parrot in an ornate bronze bird-cage. As soon as it sees her, it starts to whistle and chatter, which brings a woman out of a darkened corner of the foyer.

Talk about Piccadilly Circus, she mutters, folding her newspaper as she moves behind the desk.

My mother would love him, Anna says, She's crazy about birds.

Don't let him hear you call him that, says the woman, with a quick smile, He thinks he's human. Don't you, Gardner? Now, is it a single room you're looking for, or a double?

Actually, I'm looking for a person, says Anna, A man, tall,

dark-skinned. He's got a scar here, she says, running her finger across her chin.

The woman gives her a weary look.

There's no one of that description *staying* here, she says, But I'll tell you what I told the other two who came asking: we're a guest-house, not an information service.

So he was here? says Anna, making sure she heard the hint.

About an hour ago. You could try the pub, or the beach, says the woman, If he's planning on staying, there's nowhere else for him to go.

Anna thanks her and turns away. She gets as far as the door before she stops. The woman is passing behind her, back into the far corner of the room, where a fire burns low in the hearth.

The other two, Anna calls, You said there were another two?

The woman shrugs; she's lost interest in Anna now.

Two men, an old chap and a younger fella. You've just missed them.

Out in the chill air, Anna only half notices the Suzuki with the personalized plate, and the van parked next to it.

She walks the middle of the fork, keeping her eyes on the track, the path growing steadily more hazardous, until she runs out of ground. Now she knows where she is: she's on the edge of a cliff. It's not so far down, maybe thirty feet, and there's a channel cut into the side of the bank. Far out on the horizon, Anna recognizes Scroby wind-farm, dazzling stripes of light in the setting sun; below her is a ribbon of purple sand. She takes the path down carefully, losing her footing and scrambling the last few metres onto the beach. The waves make a raw, gravelling sound as they wash on and off the pebbles at the tide-line. In the distance, two black-cut figures are walking the water's edge, and a third dashes into the sea, following a retreating wave. Anna watches as he bends over double, then starts back, shaking the water off his hands in diamond drops. It can't be him, chasing the surf like a child at play. She stares hard as the man lifts his jacket off the sand and strides along the shoreline. It *is* him: Anna starts to run.

~

Lewis knows the voice calling at his back; he stands perfectly still for a second: he must not be dreaming this. Spinning on his heel, he swerves past Manny and lands a blow directly on the chin of the other man. Carl drops like a stone, more from shock than the force of it, but Lewis isn't going to stop. He shrugs Manny off his back, launching him onto the wet sand, and hammers at Carl's head. On his knees, Carl makes to crawl away, but Lewis hasn't finished with him yet: gripping him in a headlock, he drags him towards the sea, the heels of Carl's boots marking a frantic pattern on the sand. With his cargo wedged under his arm, Lewis strides long and easy into the waves. Manny yells at him to stop, but Lewis hears nothing except the sound of the sea, a fantastic silver noise which he's been hearing all day. It's deeper inside him now than his own heartbeat. He forces Carl under the water, plunging his head down as the tide retreats, grinding his face against the wet sand and stones and screaming at the top of his voice.

How does it feel to drown, cunt? Feel nice, cunt?

Carl is screaming and Manny is screaming, but Lewis hears only the wish-sigh of the waves as they take him, drag them both, further away from the land.

From the corner of his eye, Manny sees a woman in a windcheater running on the sand: she spears herself into the waves, diving headlong as the water surges over the top of her head. For a black minute, he can only see the ocean; he can only hear the ocean. More black minutes as the light dies completely behind the dunes. Only the white tips of the waves are visible as they suck at the sand; then, on the horizon, a thin sliver of moon lifts itself out of the sea. Fixed directly beneath it are two heads, gleaming in the half-light.

Manny's crying a prayer: Please God don't let them drown, Please God, please God, moving into the waves, his body jarring with the sudden cold. He wades out to meet them; between the two figures, the girl is slumped like a doll. Manny grabs Anna's waist and as he does so Carl lets go, buckling onto the sand. Lewis kneels down in the darkness and wraps his arms around her.

# THIRTY-SIX

The voices must be in her head; she's left the radio on again, and the presenter is talking about the threat of London flooding. Two of the men on the panel are having a fierce debate.

You could have drowned him, says the one who calls himself Manny.

Another voice, filling her ear full of static, shouts, Wrong! I *would* have drowned him.

Who's drowned? Anna asks, Am I drowned?

There's a third voice, now, farther off, as if on a distant telephone line.

No one drowned anyone, okay? I take it back. It weren't your fault. You can't take a joke, see? It was just a joke.

Am I laughing, twat? Am I?

Anna feels her body being carried by the water. She's moving through a cold blue space, through wave after wave of noise.

But he's got your van here, so there's no harm done.

For the last—fucking—time, it's not my van. This is *not* about a stinking van!

Then there's no harm done, repeats the Manny voice.

Anna's trying to follow the argument but her good ear is full of liquid. She turns her head towards the sounds, hears crackling and white noise.

No one's drowned, thank God, says Manny.

My brother drowned.

And we all wish he hadn't. But no one's to blame, son. It stops here.

Anna doesn't know who she is, but she knows where: her bed is floating out on the ocean. She has to drink the sea to save London, it tastes mint and sharp, like pastis and lemon, and she can do this easily. But then she has to eat the moon. Above her, she sees it, sitting in the sky like a slice of boiled egg. The taste of it makes her sick, and all the water she has swallowed comes back up again in a hot salt rush. She turns her head, spitting scales of light onto the sand.

We need an ambulance, the man on the phone line says.

She'll be alright, says Lewis, You'll be alright, Anna, just take a breath, that's it, and another one. You're going to be all right.

~

It took Lewis all day to walk from Yarmouth to Winterton, but it will take him just half an hour to drive back. Anna remains silent, curling herself up in the passenger seat, Vernon's blanket pulled tight around her. It's as much as she can do to stop her teeth chattering. She has never been so cold before. In the glare of the oncoming headlights, Lewis steals a glance at her face: he's caught again, with an even deeper anguish than the first time, by the black shadows under her eyes, the way her mouth turns down at the corners.

I'm sorry, he says, Anna, I'm really sorry.

She doesn't reply to this; she can't hear anything over the sound of the engine and the wind gusting through the broken quarter window behind her. They turn off the main road out of Somerton, passing the turbines on Blood Hill, and straight into a hairpin bend. Lewis feels rather than sees the curve the road takes; he accelerates into the first corner, but isn't ready for the second. As he pulls on the steering wheel, the car shudders, rocking up onto two wheels and skimming the verge, so Lewis feels a flare of terror run through him.

Then it's over; they're safe again. He looks across to Anna, smiling with relief, and so he doesn't notice the wooden warning sign at the side of the road. He clips it with his front wheel, sends it flipping over the top of the car and beyond, sailing into a field. They hit the mud slick ten seconds later, spinning like skaters on ice.

~ ~

He shouldn't have pulled that stunt. But he was sick to the bones, of Carl, but of himself especially, for agreeing to be in Carl's company. They'd gone to recce the house in his van, Carl up front, unable to stop bragging to Barrett: *his* van when he got it would be twice the size; this old heap of metal was only to be expected, seeing as it belonged to Lewis; and he was only letting him in on the job in the first place because Manny had begged him.

Lewis could bear all of this, silently watching the road, not paying attention to Carl, who was rummaging around in the footwell, pinging what sounded like small stones at Barrett, who was telling him to fuck off you child, for fuck's sake. He was concentrating, trying to ignore the throbbing pain behind his eye. But then Carl did something Lewis couldn't bear: he started rewriting history.

Just like old times, mate, innit? Carl grinned, licking his lips, We used to go cruising, Gaz. Me and him and his brother. What was he called, again, your brother?

Shut up, said Lewis, his eyes on the road.

Carl turned round to Barrett, who had composed his face into a frown.

Wayne, he was called, answered Barrett, I've heard about it from your mam.

He rested his hand on Lewis's shoulder,

Bad business, that.

That's right, said Carl, But Wayne, now he wasn't a very good passenger, was he?

I said, shut up, said Lewis.

So we got this car, right, Gaz, and we're steaming, and Wayne, Wayne, he goes apeshit, goes la-la on us, and next thing you know, he tips us in the river.

It was you, said Lewis, looking for the first time at Carl.

Me? Me? C'mon, butt, that's not how it was!

As if to distance himself, Barrett leaned back into the interior of the van and let out a sigh.

Give it a rest, Carl.

Carl wasn't listening.

It was your spaz of a brother doing his dancing, he said, turning round to Barrett to demonstrate, flailing his arms in the air, And suddenly, Gaz, I'm not kidding, the whole world goes mental!

Like this, you mean? shouted Lewis, flicking off the headlights and accelerating into the trees. Through the darkness, scything through a gap in the bushes and further into the black, he thought to murder the three of them. The realization filled him with bliss: here we are again. Time has been unravelled. Only now I'm driving. And this time, we'll stay down.

Lewis pressed the pedal to the floor and jolted the van over a steep bank of earth. Directly below, a wide, shining heart-shape appeared in his vision. The second before they dropped into the black, Lewis saw that the heart was no vision; the heart was a lake. It was a reflex—not a thought or a wish—that made his foot hit the brake. It was the same reflex, twenty years earlier, which made him turn and batter the window behind his head, made him push himself up from the darkness, not caring that Wayne was still underwater, not caring about anything except getting air in his lungs and seeing the daylight break above his head.

It took them an hour to free the van from the sinking mud; by which time, Carl had recovered enough colour in his face to laugh about it.

Jokes a joke, mate, but that's going a bit far, he said, Thought we were on for another log flume.

The following morning, Lewis remembered nothing of the night before; not the recce of the house, nor the wild drive through the trees, nor Carl on the journey back, sitting where Barrett had sat, silently smoking one cigarette after another. Lewis had tried to check his kitbag the next day, as he always did, as he had to do. But his hangover was mighty, and Manny was talking at him, nagging Lewis about the mud on his boots and how he shouldn't get it on the carpet. At the time, Lewis didn't consider why his boots would be so muddy: it was as if he couldn't even see them, as if Manny had been talking to someone else entirely. Try as hard as he might, Lewis couldn't put himself in the memory at all.

But now here he is with Anna, and the empty space which had been moving around inside his head, and which he had begun to think of as a fog, is clearing. It wasn't the recce he needed to blank out, it was the memory it brought to the surface. It was remembering the crash; remembering how he had left his brother, remembering the relief at rising through the cold water, the ecstasy of breathing air, and seeing daylight and trees and people after the chill black suck of the river. Remembering how he had left his brother, and not caring, because he was alive, he was breathing air. Lewis wills the whiteness to expand again and cover this memory. He would prefer any void to this; he would like bury the moment for good. The idea that everything will be unearthed terrifies him.

~   ~

Anna's head is bent to her chest; she is very still. Lewis stretches over and rests his hand on her hair.

Marta was right, she says, her voice very small, You're too dangerous to love.

Feeling about in the glove compartment, she draws out Vernon's flask, unscrewing the top with shaking fingers. It's neat whisky, and she gulps it quickly, her eyes watering at the sting and at the confession she's just made. She daren't look at Lewis now, but when she's had enough, she passes the flask to him. He takes one sip, then another, longer pull on the neck, and passes it back. He's not sure he heard her properly; he's not sure of anything except that he loves her back, and dangerous or not, he ought to tell her.

Who were those people on the beach? she asks, finally turning her gaze on him. The engine coughs into life as Lewis turns the key; they crawl now along the deserted road.

They were part of the problem, he says, I don't really want to discuss it.

She keeps her eyes fixed on his profile, persistent.

And you still have this problem?

Lewis laughs, but it's a bitter sound.

Take your pick, he says, I have problems cubed.

Give me one, she says, holding out her palm in front of him.

He drops his speed as he approaches the town centre. He knows his time with her is nearly up.

I have these migraines—I don't know what they are. Absences. Just don't ask, okay?

Anna glares out through the windscreen.

I think I'm owed an explanation, she says. She's about to add, If we've got a future together, but he's too quick for her, his voice rising up like a slap.

No, you're not, he says, I didn't ask you to get involved, right? So back off. No one asked you to butt in.

You'd have drowned that man, she says.

Just when she thinks he isn't going to speak again, he takes a deep breath.

Yes. I would have drowned him.

Then I can't help you, she says.

He slows up in front of the guest-house. All the lights are on, and Vernon, like a worried father, is at the window, holding the net curtains above his head.

I know you can't, he says, pulling into the kerb.

~

Anna's mother stands in the doorway of the Nelson Suite in her old dressing-gown, a towelling turban wrapped round her head. She smells of bath salts and safety and Anna cries out when she sees her. As the mother holds her daughter, stroking her damp hair, pulling her closer, she stares at Lewis. She takes in his wet clothes and the greyness of his face as she feels her daughter shivering through the blanket. A rage, fine and sharp, courses through her.

Marta, she calls, Go and run a bath for Anna, and get her a hot drink. And you—she fixes on Lewis—You come with me.

~

Anna peels off her clothes and abandons them in a heap on the floor. They are stiff and streaked with salt marks. Her skin feels sore all over; the creases of her elbows, the back of her knees; she has bruises on her feet and scores of tiny scratches on her hands. In the mirror, her skin's mottled pink and blue with the cold. She rummages on the floor of the wardrobe for her towelling robe, and hears Marta calling her from the bathroom down the hall. She waits, staring at the dark wood at the back of the wardrobe, willing Marta to call again. When she does, Anna shakes her head in wonder.

~

I've never trusted him, says Vernon, standing in the window and looking out at his car, From the moment I set eyes on him, what did I say to you, Rita?

He turns to face the room. Lewis is leaning against the edge of the table, arms folded, staring into the flames of the gas fire. Anna's mother is sitting in her chair, her eyes fixed on Lewis.

Yes, Cabbage, thank you for that. But as Mr Caine—
Mr *Lewis*—has just been telling us, it does no good to drag
up the past. In fact, it only does harm.

Lewis nods. He's about to say something more when she
cuts him short.

You'll forgive me for speaking plain, Mr Lewis, but we
won't be able to offer you accommodation tonight. I'm sure
you understand me.

I'd like to see Anna before I go, he says.

Anna's mother gets up from her chair and moves to the
side-board. There are several bottles of spirits on a tray, and
two bottles of raki, one wrapped in tissue paper and the other
freshly opened. She pours herself a careful measure before she
replies.

What's the first thing I notice, Cabbage, about a man?

Not quite knowing where this is leading, Vernon takes a
guess.

Um. His eyes?

She passes Vernon a glass full to the brim, and holds out a
smaller measure to Lewis. Just as he's about to take it from
her, she catches his wrist.

His hands, Cabbage, I always notice a man's hands. And I
noticed yours when you arrived, Mr Lewis. Yours are very
strong, aren't they, and such long fingers. Artistic.

As she speaks, Lewis stares at her own fingers on his wrist,
the skin tanned dark as leather.

But those knuckles, she says, Smashed up when you got
here, and now look—smashed again. Not even time to heal
properly.

She lets go of him and offers him the glass of raki.

I'd say, Mr Lewis, that you've got a lot of things to sort
out in your *own* life before you even think of sharing it with
someone. Especially if that someone is my girl.

I've said I'm sorry to have troubled you, Lewis says,
I've tried to explain. But I need to see her. I have to say
something.

That's all very well, says Anna's mother, But I don't think she needs to hear it. Have I made myself plain?

Lewis tips his head back and swallows his raki. He places the glass on the table.

Thank you for the drink, he says, walking to the door.

**interference**: *n.* 1 the act of interfering. 2 electrical or acoustic activity that can disrupt communication. 3 the overlapping effect which occurs when two or more waves pass through the same space.

The snow when it comes is rare: like stage-snow, or a Hollywood idea of snow, it falls thick and steady in fat, twirling flakes. Soon, it coats the rooftops and the gum-spotted pavements, and the trees and the hedges; it covers the cars on the street and obliterates the signs and cones and the double yellow lines that girdle the city. The sound in Anna's garden is of nothing. No distant trains, no traffic; even the birds have been silenced by this strange event. She clears a patch of wet snow off the bird-table and pours out a mound of seed. At the far end of the garden, beyond the brambles, the silver sky is darkening like a bruise. She calls Brendan out to see.

And? he says, when she points up in the air.

It's sort of that colour, but lighter, obviously, she says, See? Between the houses over there. It *could* be that colour.

Inside, the far wall of the kitchen is a patchwork of hues; each large painted square has a note, written in pencil, at the bottom.

Bone white, reads Brendan, Drab—certainly is—Clunch, he says, Always a favourite.

Anna stands back to look at the swatches, her eyes flicking to the window and back, as if to make a comparison.

I'll never get it, she says, It's ungettable.

Brendan prises the lid off a match-pot and sniffs it.

Let's start again, he says, You said it was blue, right?

I said it was liquid. I said it was the colour of water.

Brendan dips the corner of a sponge into the match-pot and starts another square on the wall, roughing out an outline and filling in. He stands back.

Eau-de-nil, he says, How's that?

Anna considers, delves into her toolbox, and brings out a tube of glitter. She shakes it, opens the lid, and tips it into her hand.

More like this, she says, casting a cloud of sparkling dust over the surface of the patch. Most of it goes on the floor. After a minute, Brendan goes up close and blows on it. He retreats, rubbing his eye.

Anna, we have to go and see this light together, he says, Before you do something that leaves me permanently blind. Shall we? Shall we go?

In case you hadn't noticed, B, it's snowing, she says, And this is London. Hardly the best time to brave the gridlock.

He moves to the sink and washes his eye under the tap.

Exactly. This is London, he says, squinting up at her, Nothing settles for very long here—not pigeons, not people, and definitely not snow. Or hadn't *you* noticed?

~

After much heated squabbling about the quickest, best, most direct route out of London, Anna and Brendan fall into numb silence once they reach the motorway, as if they'd left their voices hanging in the chill air of the Blackwall Tunnel. They keep the radio on for traffic warnings, but as Anna branches off towards Norwich, Brendan slots a disc into the stereo. A sound of angels fills the space.

What's this? she asks, taking a sidelong look at the case in Brendan's lap. He lifts it up to the windscreen, reading from the sulphurous light cast by sodium on snow.

Spem in Alium, he says, Sounds like a biology textbook.

Sounds like heaven, she says, peering out through the flakes spiralling in and away from her windscreen, It's perfect.

It was your Christmas present, he says.

Anna blinks, letting the voices surround her.

But you bought me that bird-table, she says.

Brendan settles back against the head-rest and stares through the windscreen.

It was your Christmas present to me, he says.

They lapse into another long silence. At one time, Anna would have joked about her great taste, or how thoughtful she was, but now she feels the reminder like a sting: she'd hadn't bought anyone anything for Christmas; she hadn't even sent any cards. When she thinks of the past two months, she sees it like a hole burnt in paper, the flames licking around the newsprint, shrivelling it to black ash. Her mother and Vernon wanted her to stay and have Christmas with them; Brendan wanted her to go with him to Devon to see his family; but Anna wanted to be in her own bed, under the duvet. On Christmas morning, after a night of vivid dreaming, she set to work. First she took down all the pictures and photographs from the walls, then she mixed some colours. The paint from an old tin of white emulsion she used as a base, adding small drops of acrylic to the mix. This, at least, was something she could do to take her mind off the noise. It had lived inside her head ever since that night on the beach: not at all like the blimps and squeaks and poundings of the tinnitus she'd grown used to. Her doctor could only say that the ear was a mysterious organ, asked her to walk a straight line, then prescribed some tablets in lieu of an appointment with a specialist. She wasn't able to drink alcohol with the pills, so she threw them away. Anna had decided it was the noise of the sea: in the darkness, at night, she would see the colour of the sound, was actually able to walk through it. Inside, was an unearthly light. It was this she wanted as she mixed paint, furious that she couldn't find the exact shade. When Brendan returned from Devon, she'd told him about it.

It'll be that post-traumatic China syndrome, he said, with his unerring capacity for muddying the water, You've lost some vital inner ching and the sound light business is a sign. I watched a programme on it once. All we need to do is some inversion therapy, help you get your Shakiras back.

Despite his diagnosis, Anna was glad for them to set about the search together; the idea was to paint the whole flat in the colour of her vision. He brought her match-pots and swatches and blocks of crystal quartz, happy for her to be out from under the duvet. And now he was going with her to the edge of the country, to find a piece of light. If she valued his friendship at all, she had a poor way of showing it. At the very least, she could have bought him a Christmas present.

I'm so sorry, Brendan, she says now, I've been rotten.

That's right, you have, he says, And not just to me. Are we expected, he asks, At your mum's?

I thought we'd do a detour first, she says, There's something I want to check out.

Great. Keep me informed, won't you?

Brendan leans forward and wipes the condensation off the windscreen with his sleeve.

Anna, look! he cries, Do we, or don't we?

He points at a lonely figure on the edge of the carriageway, holding up a card. The snow has covered it almost completely, the words obliterated into smudges of black. Anna makes to move into the inside lane, just as a lorry flashes its indicator and pulls into the hard shoulder.

Looks like he's got his lift, says Brendan, Just as well; it's one thing being charitable, but I've seen *The Hitcher*. Twice.

# Cardiff

It's a chill, grey evening, the kind that always reminds Lewis of those drab Sundays before the school week begins. In a sheltered corner of the cemetery, Manny is sitting on a bench, his body bent over; he looks like he's praying, but he's rolling a cigarette. When he finishes making one, he puts it behind his ear and starts another, blowing on his fingers to keep them moving. Lewis takes a final look at the headstone. He brought some flowers because he thought it was what people do; now he thinks they look ridiculous. Wayne never showed any interest in flowers; he should've put twenty Bensons on the plot. He can't imagine what else Wayne would want; the body in there belongs to a child, and Lewis feels too far from childhood, now, to comprehend what it was like. He ambles back to Manny, shoulders hunched against the stiffening wind.

He was just a kid, he says, sitting down.

You all were, says Manny.

He puts out the tip of his tongue and licks along the edge of the paper, twists the roll-up between his fingers, and hands it to Lewis.

I can't picture what he would look like now, says Lewis, What he'd be doing. I'm pretty sure he wouldn't have wanted flowers.

He nods in the direction of the grave, where he laid the bunch on its side. There was no vase to put it in. The cellophane wrapper sighs in and out in the wind. Manny turns an eye in his direction, holds up the lighter, and waits for Lewis to angle his head to it.

Take my Carl, he says,

I'd rather not, says Lewis, which makes both men smile.

Alright then, take Sonia, says Manny, after a beat, Now she's all grown up and la-di-dah and got herself a whatyamacallit—

Career, fills in Lewis.

Four by friggin four, says Manny, And yet, when I thinks of her, I don't ever see that. I don't see a grown-up woman. I only ever sees her as a kid, banging about in the kitchen on her roller skates.

She always was a fast one, says Lewis.

Manny thinks he's deliberately missing the point.

What I mean is, when you love someone from small, you think of them that way. They stay little. Especially if you don't see them—or they don't want to see you.

She'll come round, Lewis says, not believing it for a minute. He didn't actually meet Sonia, but he's heard enough about her now to understand that she wasn't the forgiving type. She had taken a dim view of the business, Manny said, was all set to get the police involved, until Carl persuaded her otherwise. When Manny took Lewis's side, she severed all contact with her father.

After the fight on the beach, Lewis hadn't given her another thought; he'd found what he was looking for, and had repaid Carl in a way that both men understood. For Lewis, the episode was finished; not so for Manny. He'd asked Lewis to come back to Cardiff and see him, stay for a couple of days.

I've got a son I don't want and a daughter who don't want me. I reckon that just about makes you family, he'd said.

It was Manny who'd had the van cleaned up; it was Manny's idea to visit Wayne's grave; it was Manny who, for Lewis, was just about family.

He leans closer now to Lewis, trying to get out of the bitter wind, and reaches in his pocket. He takes out Wayne's silver chain and passes it over. After a few long minutes, Lewis finds his voice.

How much did this cost you? he says, eyeing the inscription.

It was in the van, in the footwell, says Manny, jerking his head aside so the wind catches him face on, Under a pile of rubbish.

Still covering for him, says Lewis, feeling the silver grow warm in his fist, What is it you do, Man? Do you sell on? Take orders? What? I thought you weren't into drugs. Bloody scagheads, that's what you called them.

And that's what they are. You won't believe me, says Manny, But what I does is stays out of Carl's business. And if Carl had still got your bloody chain, he wouldn't *still* have it, if you get my drift. Apparently, he was a bit distracted, what with trying to stay alive and all.

Lewis holds the chain up against the light.

I was raging, he says.

Manny turns on him, his eyes fierce.

It's got to stop, he says, You can't go *on* raging, but you do, because you're stuck back then. It'll kill you, see—if it don't kill someone else first. And I'd rather you didn't murder our Carl, if you don't mind. You've caused me enough agg for one lifetime.

Lewis lets out a laugh,

Manny, let me tell you. I feel a million times better for decking *your* Carl. He's had it coming twenty years. Now it's finished.

Finished enough to make peace with your mam? asks Manny.

Aye, says Lewis, but he looks away.

I could fix it for you if you want . . . be a sort of—Manny searches his head for the phrase—Intermediate, he says, satisfied he's found it.

Can't fix it, says Lewis, with a pained grin, It's not fixable.

We'll find a way, says Manny, There'll be some way. Just tell me you're willing.

Aye, says Lewis again.

Without thinking, he puts the chain to his mouth and licks it. It tastes faintly of salt, of a salt-scent, blowing off the sea.

# THIRTY-SEVEN

At Winterton, Anna turns past the Fisherman's Return and along the back lane. The snow glitters blue under the moonlight, and lies so thick, she can't tell what's road and what might be pavement. Without warning, the car veers silently to one side and noses into a hedge, dislodging a thick drift onto the windscreen.

We've arrived, then, says Brendan, pulling on his gloves.

They walk up to where the road forks, Anna instinctively taking the left-hand side. The sky is clear and sharp; before them, the house stands alone in the darkness, the To Let sign coated with a layer of snow.

This it, then? The detour? Says Brendan.

I saw this place before, says Anna, standing back and admiring it. She voices the idea that's been developing ever since they set off.

You know what you said, Brendan, about people not settling in London?

Hmm–hmm, he says, nodding as if he knows what's coming.

You might be right.

She leans over the wall and wipes at the board with her glove, peering at the numbers on the bottom.

It's no good, I can't make it out, she says, Let's ask at the pub.

Brendan looks about him, up and down the lane, his eyes following the track to the dunes. In the wide space beyond, a thousand stars hang in the sky.

Shall we ask about rooms as well? he says, trudging behind her, 'Cos I can't see us getting to your mum's house tonight.

~ ~ ~

Vernon is on his knees in the kitchen, reaching into the back of the cupboard. He doesn't notice Rita until he catches sight of her slippered feet on the flags.

Ah, Rita, there you are, he says, burying his head again in the darkness, You gave me a start.

Cabbage, what on earth are you doing in there?

Babychams, he says, muffled, Just a tic.

They were here, Cabbage, she says, tapping a finger on the work surface, They're always here, on a tray. What have you done with them?

Trying to get his attention, she puts a hand on his shoulder and gives it a squeeze.

Found them! he cries, lifting a glass out of the cupboard and holding it up for her to take. Without looking, she puts it on the counter, offering her hand for the second glass. Vernon grips her fingers with his own.

As I'm already down here, he says, And as you're here . . . as we're both here . . .

In this kitchen, says Rita, trying to move him on.

. . . I'd like to say something.

Make it quick, Cabbage, I'm very thirsty.

My dear, lovely Rita, he says, his upturned face a deep shade of pink, Will you marry me?

She turns her head away, and for such a long time, he's beginning to think she's smothering a laugh.

I was going to, erm . . . the ring is . . . it's in the glass. I was going to . . .

When Rita turns back, her mouth is set in a tight line.

You were going to put it in a glass of champagne, she says, Just like in the film.

Just like in the film, Rita.

She peers over the counter to check, then gives him a broad, teary smile. In the hall, the answering machine cuts in. They both ignore it.

Did she say 'yes' in the film, Vernon? asks Rita.

I believe so, he says.

She puts out her other hand and helps him up, his knees cracking as he rises off the floor.

Is that your daughter's voice? he says, holding her close.

I can't hear a thing, darling, says Rita, Can you?

~ ~ ~

The van is parked on some dirt ground behind Manny's allotment. The rust on the bonnet and over the wheel arches has been obscured by the respray, but Lewis can still see the many dents in the bodywork, which haven't been knocked out, and one or two that are new to him. Both men sit in silence up front, staring out of the window. At the back of the allotments where the fields used to be there's a new estate, the houses lit up with carriage lamps and garden lights. They twinkle across the valley like Brigadoon. Beyond it is the river. Lewis can't see it from here, but like an old scar, he can feel it. The wind brings in sharp pips of snow, sticking to the windscreen like grit.

These'll be gone soon, Manny says, pointing at the regular black oblongs which mark out each allotment, More houses, see. People don't want to grow their own veg, they want to own their own home.

Lewis sucks his teeth and says nothing. He's been sitting with Manny for nearly an hour now, trying to decide. Manny has been more patient than he'd give him credit for, but he can tell his time's almost up.

And Barrett won't be there? he asks again, just to be sure.

Manny gives him a look, but doesn't deign to reply.

And she won't have some other boyfriend hiding in the pantry or something. Under the bed.

I just told her you'd pay her a visit, son. I didn't say *when*, I didn't say *today*, I just said you'd do it. Sometime.

And she said? he asks.

And she said, 'If the lad wants to come and see me, that's up to him.'

Very touching, says Lewis, turning his head and staring out of the side window. Manny blows on his hands and buries them under his armpits; he's fed up and he wants Lewis to know it.

She was never any good with words, but did she care about you—both of you. Might have struggled to show it sometimes, your mother, but she had a heart of gold.

As Manny talks, Lewis screws his eyes up; try as he might, he can't imagine what might be in her heart. And Manny's speech, about love in the doing, not the saying, only makes Lewis remember her actions at the hospital. He didn't know, then, what the look on her face meant, only that it wasn't good. He understood it wasn't loathing or anger—he could deal with that. Now he's lived long enough to recognize it for what it was: it was indifference. Lewis makes a decision: he doesn't want to risk having to see that look again.

Sorry, he says, Not today.

What about tomorrow? Manny asks, I could come with you if you like.

Tomorrow, says Lewis, biting his lip, 'Ask for me tomorrow, and you shall find me a grave man.'

I'll take that as a maybe, then, says Manny.

Lewis pulls up at the corner of the street. He gets out of the van and walks round the back to the passenger side, holding the door open while Manny levers himself out. When he sees that Lewis isn't following, Manny turns on his heel and trots back.

Come and get yourself some stuff if you're planning on leaving me. Clothes and that.

Lewis tugs at the front of the sweatshirt Manny had given him.

These'll do fine, he says, but when Manny reaches in his pocket and passes him a bundle of notes, Lewis doesn't refuse.

You'll get it back, he says.

The two men embrace briefly, under cover of darkness.

*Mañana,* says Manny.

Or the day after that, says Lewis, I'll be in touch.

Manny stands under the streetlight and watches as Lewis drives away.

# THIRTY-EIGHT

It's as cold inside the cottage as it is outside. Anna and Brendan follow the estate agent through the rooms as she talks:

The water can be put back on, but there's never been a phone connection here, you are aware of that, aren't you?

There are two rooms upstairs: a plain bedroom, which looks out onto the lane, and at the back of the house, an ancient bathroom with a sloping roof. The dormer has been left open, and on the window-sill, there's a ridge of snow. The bath and the floor are speckled with droppings and feathers. The estate agent tugs at the window-lock, which comes off in her hand.

Like I said in the office, it's not really habitable, she says, leading them back down the stairs, And we haven't been rushing to let it because of the slip.

The slip? asks Brendan.

I'll show you, she says, Please, you must be very careful.

She opens the back door on to a Siberian wind. All three stand huddled in the doorway. The garden is completely overgrown, moulded by snow into brilliant white banks and dripping trees. On one side, a flint wall bulges and curves, and disappears.

They follow her as she negotiates the long path, treading in her footprints. At the far end of the property, a red tape has been wound around a line of rusted poles sunk into the earth; beyond it is a sheer drop: they can go no further.

The rest of the garden is down there on the beach, she says, And in a few years, this house will probably go the same way. So you see, it's not really a viable let any more. It's an awful shame for the owner, but our hands are tied.

Brendan looks meaningfully at Anna, but can see he's already lost her; she's standing at the edge of the tape, staring out at the sky and sea.

We've got another property in the village if you're looking for a holiday place, says the estate agent, That one's quite safe.

No, this is perfect, says Anna, I suppose there's no harm in asking the owner, is there?

~ ~ ~

Rita is in her room, sitting sideways on the recliner. She has the mirrored box open on her lap; it doesn't play a tune any more, but still holds the dried hay scent of cigarettes. She hesitates, her hand hovering over the box, breathing in the smell of years ago. They had parties all the time, in those days; dinners for his colleagues, cocktails with the boss and his wife—what was her name? Maureen, or Margaret, or Marjorie—and then the golf club evenings and the functions . . .

Functions, she says, snapping the word out like a curse.

She liked her cigarettes, then. She liked the colours of the Sobranies; and in her fingers, how slim they were. How slim she was. Rita looks down at herself, at the mottled veins on her legs, and the slippers with the ridge of wool running around the foot. Marta had bought them for her, from the market, after the first time she fell. They were supposed to be more practical than the mules Vernon gave her for her birthday, which were covered in sequins and pink fur and had kitten heels. She eases one slipper off with her foot, then the other, and boots them under the bed. She feels better, until she sees the state of her toenails.

You know, Len, Vernon won't be doing with all this stuff in here, Rita says, looking about her, I'll have to find somewhere else for it.

She pokes about amongst the trinkets and rings, finds the tourmaline one, and threads it on her middle finger. The joint is so swollen now, she can't get it over the knuckle. The diamond Vernon gave her is, if anything, a little loose; the stone hangs sideways, resting heavy on her skin. She stares at the tourmaline ring for a long while before wrapping it in a tissue and putting it in her handbag. She removes the diamond ring and takes it to the window, where she holds it to the light. As if in danger of being observed, she glances back into the room; first she breathes on it, then she scratches the stone along the pane, three times, gratified to see a clear scoring on the glass.

It's the real thing, she says, with a little laugh, But I already knew that. You wouldn't mind, would you, Len? Not as if I haven't taken my time. Not as if I'm rushing into anything.

She stands still and vacant for a minute or two more. When she finally rouses herself, she wonders at the box open on the chair, as she'll wonder one day about the scores on the glass, as if a cat has scratched at the window.

~ ~ ~

The caravans are sprawled across a churned-up patch of wasteland; on one side is a municipal park, and on the other, a recycling centre housed in a huge metal warehouse. The greyness of the morning has drained the colour from everything. Despite the early hour, a line of traffic has come to a standstill while a man at the head of the queue leans out of his car window to argue with another man in overalls. Both of them are jabbing their fingers in the space in front of them. Lewis bypasses the argument and heads straight for the travellers' site; he has one more thing to do before he leaves Cardiff. Behind a barred gate at the opening to the field, a child is sitting on an upturned bucket, eating a piece of toast.

I'm looking for a man called Magic Sam, says Lewis, Is he here?

Without a word, the boy takes off to the far end of the field, disappearing into a purple trailer. Lewis waits, listening to the car horns blaring and a stream of expletives as the row at the entrance gathers momentum. He doesn't immediately recognize Sam: when Lewis last saw him, he had dreadlocks and a long wispy beard, but the man standing and waving from the step of the trailer is completely bald, except for a massive quiff at the front of his head. Despite the snow-cold wind, he's naked from the waist up, his dark skin riddled with tattoos. On the left breast, exactly over the heart, are the concentric circles of a shooting target, complete with lines and numbers and an exclamation mark in the centre. This, at least, Lewis remembers.

Bullseye, says Lewis, firing his finger at it. Sam puts out both hands and grips Lewis's arm, which turns into a bear-hug. Lewis breathes in the smell of sweat and hash and hair-oil.

Come in and have a sit, Sam says.

I'm here for a favour, says Lewis, stalling at the step.

I know you are. But come and sit anyway. Must be time for breakfast.

Inside, the walls are covered with mirrors, some plain broken pieces, others decorated with ornate designs. Pots of enamel paint and nail varnish litter the bench seats. Lewis stares at them, not knowing where to put himself.

They're Joanna's, says Sam, lifting aside a small table and hooking it up against the wall, She does the mirrors up and sells them at the craft market in town. Gets them free from the tip. No one likes a broken mirror.

Unlucky, says Lewis, tracing a design with his fingers.

Lucky for us, though, says Sam, She can't do enough of them.

Across the ceiling of the trailer, dangling from lengths of coloured string, a dozen or more mirror mobiles twirl in the draft, scattering sparks of light.

It's weird. Must be like living in a kaleidoscope.

Like a disco ball, I says, laughs Sam, Look at this, now.

The mirror behind the washing-up bowl has been turned to the wall. Sam lifts it over and holds it for Lewis to look at. It has a face etched into the glass, so when Lewis looks into it, he sees himself and someone else, all at the same time.

Freaks me out, it does, says Sam, I can't have it hanging there while I'm doing the pots.

Or shaving, says Lewis.

Fuck me, you'd end up butchering yourself, says Sam, laughing.

He pours an inch of liquid into a tumbler and passes it to Lewis.

Special rum, he says, Now, what can I do for you?

Lewis takes a breath.

I've got a van out there needs to go back to its owner, he says, But I've got to be somewhere else.

Sam gives him a tired smile.

Yeah, I understand. Van to go back. But what I said was, what can I do for *you*?

# THIRTY-NINE

The snow melts out of London in two days, turning to pock-marked heaps of road slush and flat grey patches of slippery ice. An overnight downpour clears away the last of it, choking the drains and causing localized flooding. There follows two weeks of threatened rain, which the grey mornings promise but never deliver. The city is bone dry, still as a picture, as if it's waiting for permission to come to life again. On the east coast, the snow takes longer to dissolve, clinging to every surface, lying untouched under the hedgerows, glittering in the sunless shade. On Anna's old tape machine, her mother's voice issues a quivery warning:

. . . Sso we'll exp-t you at lu-unch-time, don't f-gt to---cl-thes and your good ssshoes and rem-br to bring a h---H-v a ssafe jour--

Anna and Brendan do relays as they unload and re-load the car. Anna's packing is haphazard and optimistic; some of the boxes are secured with sticky tape, some with string, but mostly they are open, bulging, spilling their contents onto the yard. Brendan's possessions are minimal: a few suit-bags, two cases, and some brightly coloured cartons sealed with gaffer tape. Each one is labelled, and Anna has been given instructions to stack them in the hall. She heaps them up anyhow against the wall.

There's a word for people like you, says Brendan, taking a plastic bin liner full of clothes and squashing it into the boot of Anna's car.

And there's a word for you, she shouts, grappling with a box marked Atlases, It's—

Don't say it, he says, I am merely a neat person, that's all.

But why have you got so many of these? she says, dropping the box of atlases on the step, I mean, there's only one world, isn't there?

Brendan gives up on the bin liner and slams the boot, trapping the foot of a pair of tights in the door. He says nothing, but gives her a pitying look. When they've finished, they stand in the kitchen, drinking tea from Brendan's mugs and studying the paint squares on the wall.

I like this one, he says, pointing at a patch of dusty blue, What's it called?

Borrowed Light, she reads.

That's grand, he says, Very apposite. Maybe for your bedroom.

It's your bedroom, now, B, says Anna.

Until you wake up one morning and find yourself floating off to Holland. Then I'll expect you straight back here. Deal?

Deal, she says.

~

She takes a last look round the flat and down the path to the garden, taking in the brambles and weeds and the rooftops beyond it. There's a thrill in her blood when she thinks about the view at her new home: the sky, the sea, the sky and the sea.

Ready to brave the morning rush? Brendan asks, and mimicking her mother's voice, Have you pecked your good ssshoes?

Anna laughs.

You sound just like her, she says, You two are definitely going to get on.

~  ~  ~

In the doorway of the dining-room, Marta stands guard, a tea-towel in one hand and a silver tray in the other: if that woman so much as goes near the table again, she'll bang her on the head with it. Rita glides past, giving her a beatific smile, and surveys the arrangement. She moves the vase of flowers slightly to the left. She pauses, chin down, considers the move, and shifts the vase back to its original place.

Mrs Calder, says Marta, trying not to raise her voice, It's all perfection in here. Why not wait in the lounge and I'll bring you a drink?

Rita ignores her, picking up a knife and breathing on it, rubbing it on her sleeve, carefully placing it back on the table-cloth. She finds a wrinkle to smoothe out, a fleck of lint to brush away. Marta can't bear to watch.

Mr Savoy, she says, catching Vernon coming down the stairs, She is making me insane. I have spent hours to do all the preparing. Please, tell her to go away.

Vernon is wearing full morning dress. He pokes at the cravat stuffed into the top of his waistcoat.

How's that? he asks, standing in front of the hall mirror, That's good, Vernon, he says, through shuttered lips, That's very good.

He catches Marta's fierce stare in the glass.

We're so excited, he cries, The big day!

Seeing her face unchanged, he tries a diversion.

I do hope your Kristian will be here on time, he says, Only, he's the designated driver, you know.

Marta looks at her watch. Noting the change in her expression, Vernon happily waves her away.

Go on, go and get your glad rags on. We'll hold the fort down here.

~

In the dining-room, Rita is re-arranging the candles. The sky through the picture window is ice blue. Vernon watches as she moves from one candlestick to another, her hands trembling as she tries to line them up in a neat row.

That Marta, she says, She does her best, you know, but look—they weren't right. How's that now? she asks.

It's perfect, and you're perfect, he says, But it isn't like you to fuss. You're not worrying about Anna, are you?

Rita ducks her head, turning away so he can't read her face.

You did tell her, didn't you, Rita?

The sound of the doorbell saves her.

I'm just about to, she says, straightening up and moving slowly to the door.

~ ~ ~

Lewis is lying belly-down on the sand, his eyes fixed on the rolling waves.

You got to get deep, Sam had said, You got to get under, under that top layer. The top layer always renews itself, see, always comes back the same. You got to get deep enough to leave a trace—but too deep, and you're in trouble.

Sam wasn't talking about water in any form; not ocean, nor river, nor lake. He wasn't talking about drowning. They were in Sam's caravan, drinking his special rum, eating corn-flakes from the packet, and he was showing Lewis his latest tattoo.

Too deep, and it all goes wrong. The pain's really bad, for starters, and then the dye drifts inside you and everything on the outside comes up blurred.

Sam was lounging on the bed, his face dappled with re-fracted light from the mirrors hanging from the ceiling.

This one, look, he said, pulling back a square of dressing on his inner arm to reveal a livid circular scab, This one's a nautical star. Red and black—the red pigment's difficult, see, cos it itches and burns. You can't scratch it. You've got to understand why it hurts; only then can you leave it alone. The pain goes in the end.

Sounds like a lot of aggro just for a tattoo, said Lewis, smiling.

We've all got them, man, said Sam, Even you. Some of them are invisible, that's all. Some too deep to be read.

~ ~

Lewis has been awake since dawn, watching the night slip away behind the dunes; now, a pale sun hangs over the sea. He reaches up to feel the place where his bottom lip was opened, reaches into his mouth, where he counts his teeth, running his finger over them. The scar is almost imperceptible to the casual gaze: a straight line of lighter skin below his lip, like a ghost mouth that never opens. Lewis feels again the airless sensation of sinking. It's like a dream, the clarity of it, the water pouring in through the half-open window on Wayne's side, the slow tilt sideways of the car. Carl is screaming, slapping his hands on the driver's window, and Lewis sees himself, banging on the back window, and now he sees his hand, moving freely through the black pane, feeling the rush of cold water. A million tiny squares of glass swim around him and away. He goes after them, chasing the lights to the surface, forgetting Wayne, wanting just to feel the air on his skin. When he opens his eyes on the muddy bank, he's disappointed not to the see the giant standing over him.

Lewis appreciates now that the giant would have been his father. He doesn't know whether he has ever seen a photograph, or whether it was some buried image—a child's fantasy—of how a father might look. He feels sorry about it, but not as sorry as forgetting Wayne. You've got to understand why it hurts, Sam had said; only then can you leave it alone.

He doesn't know how he got the cut under his lip; from breaking out of the window, perhaps, or when he was being dragged onto the bank. He didn't feel any pain, just the taste of blood in his mouth, like molten iron.

He has been living on the coast now for two weeks, camped in the dunes: that's fourteen sunrises and fourteen sunsets; fourteen mornings of waking to the cries of the gulls and fourteen nights of falling asleep to screeching owls and squeaking bats. But he shouldn't count; counting is too much like control. That was another thing Sam had said, later, when it was approaching dusk. Lewis had instinctively reached over to pull on the light-switch dangling above his head.

Let the dark come in, Sam had said, What's the point in trying to stop it? You know it's out there.

Lewis smiles at the memory. He would've said, Because I'd rather let the light in, my friend, but he was happy enough to sit and listen to Sam, spinning his cracked philosophy in the gloom.

Lewis had thought then that all Sam had given him was an day of peace and some dubious alcohol. Now he realizes that, just like his famous tattoos, Sam's words—however rationally Lewis might dispute them—had got under his skin. He rises from the sand, brushing the stuck grains off his clothes, and heads up onto the dunes. Out at Scroby, he can see the turbines turning on the horizon. The sky beyond is pale pink; the sea, the colour of a pigeon's wing. Lewis sings under his breath: *It's a nice day to start again. It's a nice day for a white wedding.*

## FORTY

The bride wears apricot; she has a tiara on her head and a mink stole round her shoulders. A crowd has gathered outside the Hollywood Cinema, watching the arrival of a silver Bentley. Marta backs out of the car and holds out her hand to Rita: she's struggling with her stole, which has got away from her, but as she sees the onlookers, she forgets everything. She throws her arm up in the air and poses like a beauty queen. The groom and best man arrive in Vernon's convertible. After Kristian makes several attempts at reverse parking, the chauffeur of the Bentley intervenes and puts it on a bay across the road, earning him a round of applause from the crowd. All four wait on the pavement, squinting in the afternoon sunlight.

Where is he? says Rita, looking up and down the street.

Vernon takes her hand.

He's walking with Anna, darling. She wanted to get changed, remember? They won't be a minute.

Who's walking with Anna? she asks.

Brendan, he says, It *was* Brendan, wasn't it?

Rita gives him a crazed look.

What on earth are you talking about?

~

Brendan and Anna are marching along the golden mile, having a row. They can see the wedding party directly ahead, her mother's tiara twinkling like a beacon. Vernon has his back to her, entertaining the crowd. It can't be possible at such a distance, but Anna is convinced she can hear him laughing. Brendan is half-running, trying to keep up with her.

Just don't worry about it, he's saying, It's no big deal.

She's gone stark bollocking mad, Anna says, Why didn't she just say she was getting married? Eh? Eh?

Catching up, Brendan clutches at Anna's arm and swings her to a halt.

Because she didn't want you to put the mockers on it, he says, panting, Now be a grown-up for once. It's her day. C'mon.

He leads her towards the group, who all turn to wave at them.

Spare me the cliché, B, says Anna, It's always her day. Did you see the way she looked at me when we arrived?

Brendan runs a critical eye over her; she's wearing a creased floral dress she dug out of the bin liner in the car, and her desert boots.

No, I didn't notice, actually. I was preoccupied with other matters, he says, Anyway, you look alright now.

What was that lecture for, then? she asks, About making myself presentable. She always says that! *Presentable*. As if I'm some sort of frump who can't be expected to do any better.

She did have a point, he says, That poncho was horrible.

I was dressed for a car journey, Brendan, not a frigging wedding in a frigging . . . multiscreen.

That's right, he says, suddenly looking down at his shoes.

Kristian is the first to greet them. He bows gallantly to Brendan, and offers Anna his arm. Her mother stands still on the pavement, her eyes searching the street. When she catches sight of Anna, she hooks onto her free arm.

This is my daughter, she shouts at the onlookers, who let out an ironic cheer.

That's my girl, she says, You look quite—

Presentable, says Brendan, winking at Anna.

I was going to say beautiful, says Rita.

In the foyer, the manager directs them past the popcorn counter and through a side door in a carpeted wall.

They're putting on a special screening after the service, says Rita, Just for us. Aren't they, Vernon?

The most romantic film in history, so she tells me, he says, pawing at his cravat.

*Now, Voyager?* asks Brendan.

*Casablanca?* offers Kristian.

Rita glances from one man to the other.

*Random Harvest,* she says, You boys will just love it!

~ ~ ~

Lewis stands outside the cinema and lights a cigarette. There are four films being shown: two action movies and two children's films which look like action movies, only animated. Inside, the foyer is disappointingly modern: Lewis was hoping for stucco, for gold leaf and velvet, but there's a long marble-effect counter for processing tickets and numerous food concessions competing for space.

Just like everywhere else, he says, under his breath: and just like everywhere else, a boy in a porter's uniform comes across to tell him it's a completely non-smoking complex. The boy looks him up and down, hesitating; he can't believe that this man who looks like a savage has come to watch a matinee.

Sorry, says Lewis, clipping the lit stub in his fingers, But there's supposed to be a wedding here today.

That'll be in the private function room, says the boy, They've started, I think, but I can go and check for you?

Don't bother, says Lewis, I've come this far, another hour or two won't make any odds.

# FORTY-ONE

He takes the passageway down the side of the guest-house and finds himself in the car park at the back. His courage has sunk away with the sun. He just wanted to look at her again. He'd waited all afternoon, sitting on the steps of the memorial, for a glimpse of the returning party. Now, noticing Vernon's car parked askew in front of the garage, Lewis realizes that they must have come round the back road and through the garden. Peering over the wall, he sees the path has been strung with fairy lights and silver balloons, bobbing in the dusk. The sound of voices and laughter blow in and out on the breeze. He would just like to look at her, just once. He brushes the front of his jacket, wipes his hands over his head and down the stubble on his face, sniffs under his armpits. His fingers find a roll of weathered paper in the inside pocket. He passes his hand over it, trying to straighten it out, and creates instead a long dirty smear across the paper. Under the streetlight, Lewis unfurls Anna's seascape sketch, now creased and battered with wear.

Inside, someone is playing the piano: a rousing chorus of Here Comes the Bride, followed by I'm Getting Married in the Morning, with much halting and restarting and bursts of laughter. He pulls himself over the wall and creeps alongside the bushes, up the path, until he's at the side of the house. In the picture window, they are lit up like a stage-play. A man

with curly hair is sitting at the piano, with Kristian bending
across him, turning the sheet music over; at the head of the
table, Rita is half-sitting on Vernon's lap, so close, that if she
turned her head, she would see him staring in. She's shouting
encouragement to Kristian, yelling at him to sing up. Lewis
can see Marta beyond them, but Anna isn't in view. Just as he
cranes his neck to get a glimpse further into the room, Anna
walks across the frame. She bends into Vernon's shoulder and
whispers in his ear, making him wobble with laughter. Lewis
watches, his chest heaving, as she moves over to the piano,
putting her hand on the man's shoulder and kissing the top of
his head. Rita gets up from Vernon's lap and comes across to
look out over the garden. She looks directly into Lewis's eyes.

Rita is admiring, in her reflection, the locket at her throat.
It's a wedding present from Marta and Kristian, a vintage Danish design in pearl and amethyst. It glitters brightly back at
her, but not so brightly as Lewis's eyes, wild as a cat, as he
senses discovery. Rita lifts her handbag off the chair and directs Vernon to fetch more champagne.

I'm just going to check on the birds, she says, sliding the
door open and stepping into the garden. Lewis is almost at
the wall.

Mr Lewis, she calls, You've forgotten something.

She points to the roll of paper on the grass. He turns about
and meets her halfway.

Can't be skulking out here, she says, When there's a party
going on.

Congratulations, he says, And I'm sorry I couldn't make
it. Like I said when I rang, I only wanted to see Anna.

Rita waggles a finger in her ear, gives him a knowing look.

Unless I'm as deaf as my daughter, you *said:* you've sorted
your life out and now you're ready to say something. I believe you were quoting *me*.

Lewis smiles despite himself.

Show me your hands, she says, waiting as he splays them
out. She turns them over, then holds them.

Come inside, she says, It's not too late, you know. Come inside.

Lewis can feel nausea rising in him; he hasn't eaten for days; he's filthy; he's bone-tired and he's sick now, of everything; he's sick and he's frightened. He would like to go and lie down on the sand and let the sea wash him away.

I'm not ready, he says, telling the truth.

Neither is she, she says, with a nod to the house, But when you are—

She opens her handbag, and as she does so, Lewis puts his hand up: he thinks she's about to offer him money. She takes out a wrap of tissue paper and puts it in his palm.

For when you *are* ready, she says, closing his fingers round it.

A late afternoon in early spring; Anna is at work on the garden. She spent a whole week hacking at brambles, tugging up weeds and turning the soil, until she was barely able to stand up straight. Today, she'll put some plants in the ground. She thought she'd be systematic, lining up the pots of seedlings she's bought from the garden centre in a neat row next to the path. But by dusk, the plants are still waiting in their pots and the mess is mightier than ever. She follows the path she has made beyond the safety tape to the edge of the plot. The remains of a military bunker lie directly on the beach below, dashed into pieces by the sea: they look like massive dice, rolled by a giant hand. Her way down to the sand is easy from here; the concrete blocks act as perfect stepping stones. She won't go down tonight; it's enough, after a full day's work, just to stand and look out over the ocean. The days get longer inch by inch, and inch by inch she is reclaiming this land, as inch by inch the sea will take it away. Nothing lasts forever, Lewis had told her, but all Anna wants is to borrow a small piece of it, for a while.

A fishing boat passes on the horizon, heading towards port. Anna can see the lights in gold and rose, flecking the water, and the gulls, like shreds of silver in the sky around it. Sometimes, she sees dog walkers on the beach, or a warden from the nature reserve, patrolling the sand; but there are days when she sees no one. When she's ready, she'll have visitors. Her mother and Vernon are eager to come, as is Brendan, whose texts are full of spelling mistakes and a sudden enthusiasm to visit Norfolk.

At the back door, a tree she doesn't know the name of has burst into flower: tiny white clusters with a heady scent. Anna upturns a wooden crate and sits under the tree, nursing her beer, listening to the last birdsong. The night falls so soft that at first, she doesn't notice she has company; a shadow rising up from the cliff, as if he has walked straight from the sea. She knows this shadow as well as her own: it's Lewis, coming out of the darkness. Anna smiles; she can't see how it looks to him, the pain and hope all mixed.

It's me, he says, taking a breath, I've got something to give you. From your mother.

It's a long way to come, she says, Just to deliver a message.

Lewis opens his fist. The tourmaline ring, like a solid piece of ocean, gleams in his palm.

I think she'd want you to wear it, he says, watching as she puts the ring in her pocket.

And what do you want? she asks.

He leans against the wall and fetches out his tobacco. He looks as if he's considering his answer, but he's not. He's searching for a word.

You, he says, finding it.

Anna spends a long minute with her face turned away, staring into the night.

How are your problems, she says, Still cubed?

Maybe only squared, he says.

Anna holds her hand out flat, looks directly up at him.

Give me one of them, she says, but instead, he places a roll-up in her palm.

You can smoke inside, you know, says Lewis, almost smiling.

Yeah, we could, says Anna, But I've given up, nearly.

Me too, he says, cupping his hands over hers while she lights it.

Out at sea, the fishing boat moves closer to the shore. If anyone on board was looking, they would see a necklace of luminous stones at the water's edge, the cliffs crumbling onto the sand, and above them, a small red circle of light, burning a hole in the darkness.

# ACKNOWLEDGEMENTS

I am grateful to Dannie Abse for permission to use his poem "A Woman to a Man," included in *Jazz Poems* (Pocket Poets series, Vista Books, London).

Lewis's first encounter with his nightmarish Wandsworth flat can be found in the short story "Shorthold," featured in the anthology *Wales Half Welsh* (ed. John Williams), published by Bloomsbury.

The song that Wayne so loves and with which he drives Lewis insane is a sample from "White Wedding" by Billy Idol, although Wayne was a total Generation X fan and could have irritated his brother with any number of their hits.

For their support and assistance, I'm indebted to Derek Johns at AP Watt, to Elisabeth Schmitz and the whole team at Grove/Atlantic, Inc., and to Ursula Doyle at Picador, without whom the tights, stockings, pop socks debate may never have taken place. The jury's still out . . .

To my family and friends, and once again, to Steve, for putting up with everything, love and many thanks.